"I thought I would love Greg forever, but…"

"But what?" Daniel asked.

"But now I get angry. He knew how dangerous his mission was and he still let me go along. I shouldn't have been there."

"No, you shouldn't have."

Again Sarah was surprised she was telling Daniel this. She hadn't even told Serena. "I'm not blameless, though. I can be persuasive sometimes, and Greg had a hard time saying no to me."

"I can imagine. I get angry at him, too, for taking you into that situation. He must have been so blind in love that he ignored the dangers."

"That's just it," she said. "If he really loved me, why would he do that?"

Daniel turned from the window. "I don't have an answer for you." All Daniel knew was that he would never expose her to that kind of danger—even if it meant he'd never see her again for the rest of his life.

Dear Reader,

For those of you who have written and e-mailed me to ask about Sarah's story, this is it. Sarah was first introduced in *The Wrong Woman* (Harlequin Superromance #1125) as the identical twin of Serena.

Separated at birth, the sisters met for the first time when they were thirty-one years old. Their personalities were very different—Serena was sweet and outgoing while Sarah was quiet and reserved. It took time for me to plot Sarah's life, but once I started the story quickly took shape. Sarah struggles to overcome her turbulent past and has to adjust to having a real family and an identical sister. Finding the perfect man for her wasn't easy, but one man kept coming back into her life—Daniel Garrett. But there was one problem—Sarah didn't like Daniel. So the tug of emotions began and Sarah's story became more emotional than I'd planned.

I've never wanted two characters to find happiness as much as Sarah and Daniel. As you read their story I hope you will feel the same.

Warmly,

Linda Warren

You can contact me at www.lindawarren.net, www.superauthors.com, lw1508@aol.com, or you can write me at P.O. Box 5182, Bryan, TX 77805. Your letters will always be answered.

The Right Woman
Linda Warren

HARLEQUIN®

TORONTO • NEW YORK • LONDON
AMSTERDAM • PARIS • SYDNEY • HAMBURG
STOCKHOLM • ATHENS • TOKYO • MILAN • MADRID
PRAGUE • WARSAW • BUDAPEST • AUCKLAND

ISBN 0-373-71221-9

THE RIGHT WOMAN

Copyright © 2004 by Linda Warren.

This edition published by arrangement with Harlequin Books S.A.

® and TM are trademarks of the publisher. Trademarks indicated with ® are registered in the United States Patent and Trademark Office, the Canadian Trade Marks Office and in other countries.

www.eHarlequin.com

Printed in U.S.A.

In this book there is a little girl who lights up the world.
I dedicate this book to the little girls who brighten my life
with their special personalities (the great ones):
Jaci Siegert, Emily Robertson, Reagan Phillips,
Cassidy Siegert, Jamie Siegert, Taylor Tharp,
Hunter Phillips, Megan Rychlik and Charity Patranella.

And to the new additions to our family,
Jessica Reagan and Nikki Herring.

Acknowledgments

I'd like to acknowledge the following people for sharing
their expert knowledge so graciously: Kristen Tubbs, LPC-I,
Laurie SoRell, M.A., and Laurie and Lee Fay
for answering my endless questions about Dallas.

Books by Linda Warren

HARLEQUIN SUPERROMANCE
 893—THE TRUTH ABOUT JANE DOE
 935—DEEP IN THE HEART OF TEXAS
 991—STRAIGHT FROM THE HEART
1016—EMILY'S DAUGHTER
1049—ON THE TEXAS BORDER
1075—COWBOY AT THE CROSSROADS
1125—THE WRONG WOMAN
1167—A BABY BY CHRISTMAS

Don't miss any of our special offers. Write to us at the
following address for information on our newest releases.

Harlequin Reader Service
U.S.: 3010 Walden Ave., P.O. Box 1325, Buffalo, NY 14269
Canadian: P.O. Box 609, Fort Erie, Ont. L2A 5X3

CHAPTER ONE

NOT AGAIN.

Sarah Welch rushed through the emergency room doors, her heart slamming against her ribs so hard that she had to stop to catch her breath.

Another rape.

As a licensed professional counselor in private practice with Dr. Karen Mason, psychologist, she should be used to this. It was her *job* to provide the hospital with assistance for the victims of violent crimes. But some things were impossible to get used to.

It would have to happen while Karen was away, Sarah thought as she tried to locate a nurse. There was no one at the desk so she hurried down the hall. She loved her work, but at times she felt so inadequate, especially when she came face-to-face with the person—the victim. In truth, though, this was her specialty. She'd once been a victim and knew the crippling fear that overtook the body, mind and soul.

"May I help you?"

Sarah turned toward the voice. "Yes. I'm Sarah Welch with Dr. Mason's office. Dr. Daley called about a rape victim."

"Oh, yes." The nurse shifted the charts in her arms. "The doctor is waiting for you. Come this way."

The nurse opened a door and Sarah followed her into the sectioned-off emergency area. She stiffened when out of the corner of her eye she noticed Daniel Garrett and a couple of police officers standing to one side. She didn't spare them a glance.

What is Daniel doing here?

Every time she saw him something in her unwillingly froze. He was a reminder of the past—a past she wanted to forget. She quickly wiped him from her mind as she walked up to Dr. Daley.

"Hi, Sarah," Jim Daley said, scribbling in a chart. "Karen out of town?"

"Yes. She'll be back on Monday."

"That's too late." Dr. Daley gave her the chart. "I need someone to talk to this girl now. She's been severely traumatized. Physically she'll be fine, but I'm concerned about her mental state. She's not responding to anyone and she refuses to see her parents."

"How is she otherwise?"

"The rapist almost killed her and would have if someone hadn't interrupted him. He banged her up pretty bad. Her neck is black and blue from attempted strangulation and her voice is hoarse from the injury." He took a breath. "Her name is Brooke Wallace and she's eighteen."

"Oh, no." There it was. That familiar chill running up her spine.

"The rape kit has been done and the police are waiting," Dr. Daley added, glancing toward the policemen. "This is the third rape in two months in the same area. Brooke is the first victim to survive. The other two girls died at the scene so the police are eager to talk to this one."

"I see," Sarah murmured, trying to control an attack of nerves.

That still didn't explain what Daniel was doing here.

He worked narcotics. What did he have to do with this case?

Opening the chart, she began to read. Now she understood why Daniel had been called in. The rapist had given the girl an injection of heroin, a fact not mentioned in news coverage of the other rapes, and Daniel was an expert on drugs and drug dealers in Dallas. He knew every small-time pusher and the big drug lords like...

"We have her in one of the rooms." Jim's voice penetrated her thoughts. "Earlier she was thrashing around, almost violent. We're not sure how much heroin he gave her—waiting on the toxicology report— so I was hesitant about giving her anything. We're flushing out her system and she's calmer now, lying in a fetal position, unresponsive. Just see if you can get her to talk to you."

"I'll try."

"Her parents are in the waiting room, frantic, but when I mentioned they were here, she became even more hysterical. Try to get her to see them."

Sarah nodded and walked into the small room. The girl was just as Jim had said, curled into herself and staring off into space. An IV was in her arm. Memories dark and deep stirred, a reminder of a time when she, too, needed to shut out the world and everyone in it. Still, there were sleepless nights and days that tortured her...

She pushed away those debilitating emotions and moved to the side of the bed.

DANIEL WATCHED SARAH until she disappeared into the room. She wore a dark business suit with a blouse buttoned to the top, her red hair coiled neatly at her nape. Every time he'd seen her in the past five years, she'd looked the same—nunlike. But no matter how hard she tried, she couldn't disguise her beauty; copper-red hair, porcelain skin, gorgeous blue eyes and a body that women envied and men fantasized about.

He shifted uncomfortably. Thoughts of Sarah Welch filled a lot of his sleepless nights. He never quite understood why—but then again, he did. It was good old-fashioned guilt and it gnawed away at him, especially when she ignored him as she had a few minutes ago.

She disliked him intensely, that was all too obvious. She held him responsible for her fiancé's death. Greg Larson, a member of his narcotics squad, had been killed while doing undercover work. Sarah had witnessed the murder and been kidnapped by the drug lord, Rudy Boyd, and forced to strip in one of his clubs. After being rescued, it had taken her a while to recover from the traumatic events.

The sad part was that Sarah should never have been put in that situation. Greg had broken the rules by exposing Sarah to danger, and that's what bothered Daniel. He had failed in his role as leader. He had failed Greg and Sarah by not making Greg understand how dangerous the mission was and how breaking the rules, no matter how tempting, was out of the question. That was a burden he was never going to lose. The guilt of losing one of his own because he hadn't known Greg's secret activities—that he was in love and foolish enough to involve his girlfriend in his job.

"Goddammit, can you believe this?" Homicide Detective Russ Devers interrupted his reverie.

Daniel straightened from leaning against the wall. "What are you talking about?"

"Sarah Welch went into the girl's room."

"I know. I saw her."

"Any chance of us getting to question the girl tonight just got blown to hell."

"Don't be so damn eager, Russ," Daniel said. "The girl's been through a horrendous ordeal and she needs some private time with someone that understands."

Russ's eyes darkened. "Whose side are you on?"

"Justice," Daniel told him. "I'm always on the side of justice."

"Yeah, fat chance of that happening with the victim's number one advocate on the case."

"Sarah's been there, Russ. She's knows what it's like to be a victim, to be abused, so cut her some slack."

Russ started to pace. "Why the hell can't Ms. Welch understand that the faster we catch this creep, the less victims there'll be? The first few hours after the attack are crucial. The memory is still fresh in her mind and she could give us important information. We have two girls dead and not one damn clue as to who's doing this. We need something, Daniel, and we need it fast."

"I'm aware of that. That's why I'm here in the middle of the night."

Russ stopped pacing to stare at Daniel. "The needle in the girl's arm throws me. You can't think of any MO that matches?"

Daniel shook his head. "The rapist gives the girl a dose of heroin and leaves the needle in her arm. We've never had anything like that before. Rudy Boyd was the big heroin dealer in Dallas and now he's on death row. My team is investigating the other known heroin dealers and I've checked out the small-time hoods that followed Boyd, but they're all clean.'' Daniel shoved his hands into his jeans' pockets. "We just have to wait. We'll get to talk to the girl.''

"Yeah, even Ms. Colder Than Ice can't stall us forever.''

Daniel grimaced at the nickname the cops had given Sarah. It was well known that Sarah Welch fought fiercely for a victim's protection from further trauma. This kept the police from getting vital information when they needed it, but somehow Daniel couldn't fault her motives. He understood her reasons and he understood her. Oh, God, he had to stop thinking about Sarah Welch.

SARAH PULLED A CHAIR UP to the bed and sat facing Brooke. She was blond, blue-eyed and pretty. And so very young.

Go by the book. Go by all the techniques you've learned on how to handle victims like this. Sarah kept repeating the words, but she recognized this was not a textbook case. This girl needed someone who could empathize. Sarah had been there and now she'd have to share a part of herself that she hadn't shared with anyone except her twin sister, Serena. That was the only way to help Brooke Wallace.

"Hi, Brooke,'' she said. "I'm Sarah Welch, a counselor.''

No response. Not even a blink.

"I know you don't want to talk, but I'm here if you want to.''

Nothing.

Suddenly, Brooke's bottom lip trembled and tears rolled from her eyes. Sarah waited, trying not to stare at the bruises on Brooke's body. Her neck was purple and blue and the skin had been broken in several places from blunt pressure. There were dark spots on her face and arms, too. Sarah realized how lucky Brooke was to be alive, but she was very aware the girl wasn't ready to hear that.

"I wish I had some magic words to make you feel better. All I can say with certainty is that the pain will lessen as each day passes."

Still no response.

"You might wonder how I can say that." She swallowed, dredging up the courage to keep talking, to keep pushing, gently. "I don't share this with many people, but I was once abused by a man and I know what you're feeling right now. You want to die. You wish you were dead. You even pray that you will die. Death is preferable to what you're feeling."

Brooke's eyes focused on Sarah. "You were raped?" Her voice was raspy.

This is what Sarah wanted—a response. Now she had to follow through. "I was kidnapped by a drug dealer who murdered my fiancé in front of me. He didn't rape me physically, but he raped my mind and my soul." Her breath was trapped in her chest and she had to take a moment. "He…he forced me to strip in one of his clubs and he made me strip in front of him and he…he touched me in ways a woman fears, dreads—against her will."

"Did you feel dirty?"

"Yes."

"I do, too. I want to take a bath to wash his smell from my body, to wash everything away. But it will still be there, won't it?"

"Only if you let it."

"How do I stop it?"

"By letting people, your family, help you."

"No." She shook her head. "I can't see my parents."

"Why?"

"Because this is my fault. They said I couldn't go to the party, so I lied and said I was spending the night at my friend's house, then my friend and I went to the party."

"Right now your parents are more worried than angry with you. They need to see that you're okay." Sarah didn't know Brooke's parents. She was going on how most parents would react.

Brooke didn't say anything, just plucked at the sheet with her fingers.

"This is how you start to get better—by facing life again. Your parents love you, don't shut them out."

"Mom said I could always talk to her about anything, but I don't think I can talk about…about…"

"You don't have to," Sarah assured her. "They only need to see you."

Dr. Daley stuck his head in the door and motioned Sarah outside. Sarah stood. "I'll be right back."

An anxious expression came over Brooke's face. "You won't leave, will you?"

"No. I'm just going to speak with the doctor."

Brooke was responding, asking questions. That was good, very good.

Sarah met Jim outside the door. "The police are getting antsy and want to question Brooke. I told the detective it's up to you, so you might want to speak with them."

"Fine," Sarah replied and walked to where Daniel, another detective and Russ Devers stood. She'd dealt with Russ before. He was a macho, take-no-prisoners type of cop who never quite understood how his brusqueness affected a traumatized person. She didn't like him. The other man, she didn't know. Daniel, she knew—too well.

"When can we see her?" Russ asked point-blank before she even reached them.

"I'm not sure. I—"

"Listen, Ms. Welch," Russ interrupted in a scathing tone. "This girl is the only person alive who can tell us anything about the rapist. That sicko is on the loose and we need information and we need it now. Do you understand me?"

"Yes, I understand you, Detective Devers, but if you go barging in there and bombard her with questions, she'll shut down completely and you won't get a thing. She won't talk to her parents and she's barely talking to me. I need more time."

"Goddammit." Russ swung away in anger.

"Calm down, Russ." Daniel looked at Sarah.

She felt her insides tighten. She'd seen that compassionate gaze before and she didn't need Daniel's concern, nor did she want it.

"Sarah, it's crucial that we speak with her," Daniel said. "Two girls are dead and she's the only link the detectives have to the rapist. We need your help here."

Sarah knew how the cops felt about her and it didn't bother her. What bothered her was their disregard of the victim's feelings. What they didn't realize was that she wanted the creep off the streets as much as they did. They just disagreed on how to go about doing it. In this case, though, she was aware that time was of the essence.

"I'll see what I can do." With that, she went back to Brooke.

BROOKE WAS IN THE SAME POSITION, but this time she turned when Sarah entered. Before Sarah could say a word, Brooke said, "They want me to talk, don't they?"

"Yes, the police are waiting."

"I can't," Brooke cried. "Please don't make me."

Sarah resumed her seat and reached through the bed rail for the girl's trembling hand. "I'm not going to make you do anything you don't want to do."

Brooke took a deep breath and Sarah tried to think of a way to reassure her yet convey how imperative it was for her to talk. "Have you read anything about the other rapes in the paper?"

"Yes. He killed them."

"That's right, and he will continue with his crimes until he's caught."

"You mean, he'll rape another girl?"

"He's what's known as a serial rapist and he won't stop until he's put behind bars."

The silence dragged as Brooke thought about the situation. "They want my help, but I don't know anything."

"You might and not realize it."

"Did you have to tell your story?"

"Yes," Sarah said. It had taken all the courage she had.

"I—I…" Brooke stopped and started again. "I don't think I can, but I don't want this to happen to another girl and…"

"And what?"

"Will you stay with me while I talk to them?"

A sigh of relief escaped Sarah. "Yes, I'll be right here."

"Okay," Brooke said. "I want the police to catch him."

Sarah patted her hand. "I'll get them."

Outside the room, she addressed all three detectives. "She'll see you, but please take it slow and don't push her."

"Ah, Ms. Welch, I wouldn't think of doing that," Russ replied with his usual sarcastic wit.

Sarah didn't respond as they entered the room, but she went to the girl and held her hand. "Brooke, this is Detective Devers and Detective Garrett. I'm sorry—" she glanced at the other cop "—I didn't catch your name."

"Joel Sims, ma'am."

"They're going to ask you some questions."

"Okay," Brooke replied.

Daniel decided to take the lead and stepped in front of Russ. "Can you tell us what happened, Miss Wallace?"

Russ glared at him, but he didn't care. Russ had no tact, no propriety. After seeing the shattered innocence in the girl's eyes, Daniel broke the rules for the first time in his career. He knew this wasn't his case—it was Russ's job to do the questioning. But the sight of this traumatized girl made him protective, gentle.

Brooke's hand gripped Sarah's. "I—I went to this party and there were older college students there doing drugs, drinking and having…and having sex. The party wasn't like I thought it would be and I was uncomfortable and left. As I was walking to my car someone grabbed me and pulled me in the bushes and…"

Daniel waited a minute, then said, "I know this is difficult, but we need to hear what happened next."

Sarah squeezed her hand and Brooke continued. "I screamed and he hit me a couple of times and told me to shut up. I kept screaming, but no one heard me because the music was so loud. Then he…" Brooke visibly swallowed. "He ripped my clothes off and something stung my arm then he…he pushed my legs apart…and…he hurt me. He hurt me." Brooke wept silently and her body trembled.

Silence filled the room.

"It's okay, Brooke," Sarah said, comforting her, rubbing her arm. "Can you continue?"

Brooke nodded and brushed away tears. "When… when he was through, I felt something around my neck and it grew tighter and tighter and I couldn't breathe. I was choking and he was laughing…then someone began talking by the parked cars and he let go and ran off. I tried to scream, but my throat was too sore. I managed to get up and I was dizzy and felt weird. I stumbled over to a couple talking by their car and they called 9-1-1."

"Did you recognize the man?" Daniel asked.

"No. It was dark and I was scared."

"Besides telling you to shut up, did he say anything else?"

"He, uh, kept asking how I liked it. Did I like it now? It…it was awful and I was sick to my stomach with revulsion. Please, I can't talk about it anymore."

"It's okay," Daniel told her. He glanced at Russ and received a cold stare in return. Russ wasn't pleased with Daniel's intervention and Daniel didn't care—sometimes he had to do what he felt was right.

Russ moved to the bed. "Then let's back up to the party. Was there anyone there you knew?"

"Yes. My friend, Whitney, and I went together, but she left with some guy."

"Any other people?"

"Yes, several students from the university."

"Did you speak with them?" Russ was doing his usual—firing questions. The girl seemed to be holding up, though.

"Yes."

"What about?"

"Mostly about drugs. Everyone was doing them and they wanted me to do them, too, but I told them I didn't do drugs."

"Who are they?"

"A guy named Neal, and Brian Colley who gave the party." Russ and Joel scribbled names on a pad.

"Anyone else?"

"An older guy who brought the drugs, but I don't know his name. Neal pointed him out to me and said he was going to be offended if I didn't participate. I refused again and left."

"Now think, Miss Wallace," Russ instructed. "You heard the voices at the party. Can you identify any of those voices as the rapist's?"

Brooke shook her head. "No. I was so scared. I don't know who he was."

"Are you sure?" Russ kept pushing.

Brooke nodded.

"Now, Miss Wallace, that's hard to believe, you spoke to several guys at the party. Surely you can remember something."

"I can't."

"Did you drink anything at the party?"

"A glass of wine."

"Did you make out with anyone?"

Brooke's face crumbled. "No."

"You did nothing but watch. You didn't participate in—"

"The questions are over," Sarah broke in. "She's told you all she knows."

"Ms. Welch…"

"The questions are over, Detective Devers," she repeated firmly.

Russ's eyes narrowed.

"Thank you for your cooperation, Miss Wallace." Daniel intervened before Russ could do any damage.

"Please catch him."

"We'll do our best."

The trio left the room. In the hall, Russ turned on Daniel. "Don't you ever do that to me again. I'm the lead detective on this case and you were way out of line taking over the questioning. You're only here for your expert knowledge, that's it."

Daniel held up both hands. "I realize that, but you have as much tact as a telemarketer."

"Don't start with me, Daniel, or I'll report you."

"Go ahead. I've had about all I can stomach of this job."

Joel stepped between them. "Let's put the person-alities aside and concentrate on what we've just learned."

"Yeah." Russ jammed his notebook into his pocket. "Now we locate Brian Colley and get a list of everyone at the party. Our rapist was there and I have a feeling Miss Wallace knows him. If Ms. Colder Than Ice hadn't stuck her two cents in, I'd have gotten it out of her."

Daniel was stunned at Russ's insensitivity, but he didn't say anything. Words would be wasted on Russ.

Russ and Joel started toward the door. Russ turned back. "Daniel, we're through with your expert knowledge. I'll inform your lieutenant that we don't need your help anymore."

"Fine," Daniel replied. The two men stared at each other in stony silence. Russ was the first to look away and he hurried toward Joel.

DANIEL LET OUT a long sigh of frustration, trying to get Brooke Wallace's story out of his head, trying not to see the look in Sarah's eyes. He was tired. Tired of crime. Tired of dealing with cops like Russ. Tired of the bad guys always winning. He was just tired in general and he knew he was at a point in his career where he had to make a decision.

He raised his head and saw Sarah talking to a couple, obviously Brooke's parents. When they went inside the room, Sarah sank into one of the chairs in the hall and buried her face in her hands. Daniel's chest expanded at the defeated picture. He remembered the day he'd pulled her, barely breathing, pale and terrified, out of Rudy Boyd's closet. He hadn't known if she'd ever make it back to the real world after what Boyd had done to her. But she'd been a fighter, just as he sensed Brooke Wallace was, and she had rebounded with strength and determination.

Sarah had been the star witness for the prosecution in Boyd's trial and she had held up beautifully, as she had in the appeal, making sure Boyd paid for Greg's death. Mentally, though, he wondered how strong she was. Looking at her now, he feared she hadn't fully recovered.

Unable to stop himself, he headed toward her. He knew he shouldn't. He was the last person she wanted to speak to and although he didn't understand why, *now* he had to talk to her. He'd always thought it best to leave her alone, but tonight he didn't heed his instincts.

Since Sarah had been a witness at Boyd's trial, they'd been thrown together numerous times and he'd encountered her on several occasions in the years that had followed. On each encounter she treated him the same, with disguised disdain. They had to talk. He recognized this wasn't the time or the place, but he was tired of putting it off, just like he was tired of so many things in his life. Tonight Sarah Welch was going to tell him to his face why she hated him.

Then he could forget he'd ever known her.

CHAPTER TWO

SARAH BRACED HERSELF as Daniel sat beside her. What did he want? Why couldn't he just leave? It had been a horrific night and she didn't want to talk. If she looked at him, she'd see that expression he always wore when he was around her.

"Are you okay?" Daniel asked softly.

There it was—that worried tone. She restrained herself from gritting her teeth. "Yes, I'm fine. Why wouldn't I be?" She raised her head, but didn't look at him. She just wanted him to go away and to leave her with her thoughts.

"Well, a young girl's life has been altered forever and I can see it has affected you."

This time Sarah gritted her teeth; she couldn't help herself. Then she calmly answered, "I'm human and what Brooke Wallace has just endured would affect anyone."

"But for you it's different."

She clenched her jaw so tight that it hurt. *Go away, Daniel. Please go away.*

Daniel could sense that she wanted him to leave and normally he would, but not tonight. Tonight they were going to talk even if those frosty blue eyes chilled him to the bone.

He took a deep breath and clasped his hands between his knees. "Why do you hate me so much?"

"I don't hate you."

"You're stiff as a board and you won't look at me. That's not a positive, happy-to-see-you reaction."

A tangible pause followed.

"Okay, Daniel." Those cool eyes looked directly at him. "You make me uncomfortable, but it has nothing to do with you personally. You remind me of the past and when I see you, I relive that awful time. I just want to forget it. But you're always there with your worried glances, asking how I am. I don't need you to be concerned about me. I'm fine, and I think it would be best if we stayed away from each other."

He'd asked and he'd gotten his answer. It was the reaction he'd been expecting so he didn't understand why he couldn't leave it alone—leave her alone. But he couldn't wait any longer. Everything had to be brought out into the open then maybe he could let go of whatever the hell was bothering him.

"There's another reason, isn't there?"

"Like what?" Her eyes never wavered from his.

"Greg."

She looked away.

"You blame me for his death." He said the one thing that had stood between them for the past five years.

She bit her lip. "You were his boss, his leader. Why wasn't someone there to help him? Why wasn't someone there to save his life?"

"Greg volunteered to go undercover in the strip clubs to nail Rudy Boyd. A personal bodyguard doesn't come with undercover work. It's dangerous. We all know the risks and we gladly take them to get scum like Boyd off the streets." He took a long breath. "You're right about one thing, though. Greg's death is my fault. I should have been on top of his activities, but I didn't have a clue you were with him. That's something I'll never be able to forget.''

When she didn't say anything, he stood. ''So we'll agree to stay out of each other's lives. That shouldn't be too hard because I'm quitting the force.''

Her head jerked up. ''You're quitting the force?''

Daniel hadn't made his final decision until this very moment. Talking to Sarah, hearing the pain still evident in her voice, he made his choice—one he'd been wrestling with for months.

''Yeah.''

''Why?''

He shoved his hands into his pockets. ''I'm burned out and I've had my fill of seeing victims like Brooke Wallace. The good guys are losing and there's nothing I can do about it. I just have to get away.''

''I hope it's not because of something I said.''

''Don't worry, Sarah. I have a very thick skin.'' He glanced toward Brooke's door. ''I hope you're able to help her.''

Sarah followed his gaze. ''Me, too.''

His eyes caught hers. ''But who's going to help you?''

She glanced down at her hands. ''You're doing it again.''

''Yeah,'' he sighed. ''I'm sorry. It's just part of my nature, but I can see you haven't dealt with the past.''

''That doesn't concern you.'' She gripped her hands together.

''You're right about that, too. Just remember that Rudy Boyd isn't worth the pain you're putting yourself through.''

''I...''

"Goodbye, Sarah. Have a good life." He turned and headed for the emergency room doors.

Outside, he sucked the frigid January air into his lungs, letting it cool the heated emotions inside him. For the first time in ages he felt good about himself. He wasn't exactly clear about the future. He might take a cruise or go fishing on the Texas coast. He just wanted to get away from the darker side of life and to find some sunshine. He wanted to laugh, to feel happiness again. All that was out there—he just had to find what was right for him.

Zipping his bomber jacket, he headed for his car thinking that, at forty, a man shouldn't have to find himself. He should already know who he was. But all Daniel felt was a discontentment he couldn't shake. And Sarah Welch had been a big part of that.

Now he planned to put her out of his mind, out of his future.

SARAH WATCHED DANIEL leave with mixed feelings. She didn't want to run into him all the time, but she didn't want him to quit his job, either. He was a good cop—even *she* knew that. An uneasiness settled in her stomach as she hoped she'd had nothing to do with his decision. But she felt she had.

She picked up her purse and slipped the strap over her shoulder. She'd had this strange relationship with Daniel since her involvement with Greg and Boyd.

Relationship? She wasn't sure what else to call it. All of a sudden, he was in her life. He was kind, understanding and supportive of the trauma she'd been through—and that's what irritated her. She obviously blamed him for Greg's death. That had become clearer as the years had passed. She knew, though, that it hadn't been Daniel's fault. She and Greg had lied to him. Daniel had no idea she'd been living in the apartment with Greg, who had gone to great lengths to ensure Daniel wouldn't find out. Daniel would never have allowed her to be in that situation. She'd wondered several times over the past years why Greg had. Love. They'd been so in love that nothing else had mattered—not even their safety.

He'd been her fiancé, yet she couldn't even conjure up Greg's face anymore. It was a blur, just the way she wanted the past to be. She'd made so many mistakes.

At thirty-one she should have been wiser, should have been more attuned to the danger Greg had put her in. But sometimes emotions were hard to control. Like now, at thirty-six, she was beginning to acknowledge that she'd made another mistake in blaming Daniel for Greg's death. She'd been more responsible than Daniel. She'd been the one to persuade Greg to let her tag along. And Rudy Boyd... Nauseating feelings welled in her stomach at the mere thought of him. Sometimes when she closed her eyes, she could feel his disgusting hands on her body. She fought the image—as she always did.

She swallowed, admitting something else to herself: Daniel's kindness irritated her because he shouldn't be kind to her at all. He should be upset with her for her involvement. Yet he'd never said a word. That was Daniel, though. He was as gentle and caring with Brooke as he'd been with Sarah. If Daniel left, there'd be too many cops like Russ Devers in charge.

Now what did she do? She didn't want to talk to him yet she didn't want him to quit his job, either. That left only one option.

Daniel Garrett, why can't you stay out of my life?

Mr. and Mrs. Wallace came out of the room and Sarah turned her attention to them. Bob Wallace walked off down the hall, a shattered expression on his face, and Lois came up to her.

"I want to stay with my daughter, but she said for me to go home. I'm not sure what to do."

"If she wants you to go home, then that's probably best," Sarah told the woman whose eyes were filled with tears.

"I don't want her to be alone." Lois twisted her hands in agitation.

"I'll stay until she falls asleep," Sarah offered.

"Thank you. That makes me feel better." Lois glanced toward her husband. "Bob's having a difficult time. She's his little girl, his tomboy. She does everything with her father—fishing, riding four-wheelers and the yard work." Lois wiped at her eyes. "I'm not sure how to help him. I don't even know how to handle the rage inside myself."

"It will take time, Mrs. Wallace. Just be there for each other and for Brooke. Listen and be supportive without being critical."

"I'll try. I don't understand why this happened to my daughter. She's a good kid. She's never given us any problems and now…" Her words trailed away.

Sarah put a comforting arm around her, realizing for the first time that this was probably how Celia and Gran felt after her rescue from Boyd. They'd wanted her to talk, but she would only talk to Serena. She hoped they'd be as patient with Brooke as her family had been with her.

"We have two more daughters at home. What do I tell them?"

"Just be honest and reassuring."

Lois wiped her eyes again. "Please help my daughter."

Sarah patted her shoulder. "I'll do my best."

Lois nodded, walked to where her husband stood, and they left the emergency area.

Dr. Daley motioned to Sarah. "I got the toxicology report back—a very small trace of heroin. Evidently she must have been fighting so hard he couldn't get a full dose into her arm. I just gave her a sedative so she should be asleep soon."

"Thanks, Jim. I'll check on her."

She took a deep breath and entered the room. Brooke was back in a fetal position staring at the wall. Sarah sat in the chair by the bed.

"Did they leave?" Brooke asked.

"Yes. Your parents have gone home."

"My father…he…he couldn't even look at me."

"He's just upset at what's been done to you and your life. You're still his little girl."

"No, I'm not." Brooke pleated the sheet with her bruised fingers. "I'm not a girl anymore. That's been taken from me. I'm different now. Daddy knows it and I know it."

"I'm not going to lie and sugarcoat what's happened to you. Life will be different and it's up to you how different it will be. I can see you have enormous inner strength, that's why you fought so hard to live, and that strength will see you through. You have two parents who love you, which will be a tremendous help in the days ahead."

"Did your parents help you?"

"No. My parents were dead. They died the day I was born."

"Oh. What happened?"

"It's a long, complicated story, Brooke."

"Tell me, please," Brooke begged. "Just keep talking. You have a nice voice and if you're talking, I can't think."

Serena was the only one who knew her full story. Talking to people, sharing her feelings, had never been easy for Sarah and she knew it was because she and Celia, her adoptive grandmother, had moved around so much while she was growing up. She'd never had a chance to form lasting friendships. It had always been her and Celia against the world.

"I have an identical twin sister," she found herself saying.

"That had to have been fun when you were growing up."

"We didn't grow up together. I met her for the first time five years ago."

"Oh," Brooke murmured. She was falling asleep, so Sarah kept talking.

"When our mother, Jasmine, was eighteen, she fell in love with an older man, John Welch. He'd dated Jasmine's mother, Aurora, in high school. Since Jasmine and Aurora had a tumultuous relationship, her dating John only added to the discord in the family. Finally, Jasmine ran away to be with John, who separated from his wife Celia. Then Jasmine got pregnant."

She paused, thinking Brooke was asleep, but the girl opened her eyes. "What happened next?" she asked.

"Jasmine lived with John above his mechanic's shop, but as the babies started to grow inside her, she became miserable and wanted to go home. John always talked her out of it. In her ninth month, she called Henry Farrell, her father, to tell him she was coming home. But she never made it. When she'd told John, they'd argued and he managed to get into the car with her. They crashed not far from their apartment.''

''And they died?''

''Not right away. Jasmine lived long enough to deliver my sister and me. John was able to talk to his wife, Celia, and ask her to raise his daughters. Jasmine agreed, signing papers to that effect before she died.''

''Why did they want Celia instead of Jasmine's parents to have you?''

''As I said, the relationship was not good between Jasmine and Aurora, and Jasmine felt that her mother couldn't truly love her daughters since John was the father. John felt the same way.''

''Did it happen that way?''

''Partly. Henry, Jasmine's father, couldn't live with that decision so he went to talk to Celia and they made a deal. Henry and Aurora would raise one twin and Celia would raise the other.''

''Who raised you?''

''Celia. Aurora and Henry raised Serena.''

''You never saw each other after that?''

''No. Celia and I never stayed in one place long because she feared Henry and Aurora would hire an attorney to try to take me, too, since they were the biological grandparents. And the Farrells worried that Celia might change her mind and want Serena back since she actually had custody. For over thirty years they avoided each other and Serena and I never knew of the other's existence until...''

Brooke was breathing heavily—she was finally asleep. Sarah started to get up, but the story kept running in her head. *Until Ethan Ramsey saw me stripping in one of Boyd's clubs.* That one night had saved Sarah's life.

Ethan, a private investigator, was now Serena's husband. That night he'd come to Dallas to try to persuade his brother, Travis, to come home for a visit. Travis played in a band and liked the nightlife. Ethan hated that lifestyle, but went out to a strip club hoping to persuade Travis to come home.

Two months earlier Sarah had fallen madly in love with Greg Larson, a narcotics cop, while she'd been working on her Masters in psychology. She'd worked as a waitress when she wasn't in school. She'd met Greg at the restaurant and the attraction was instantaneous. At the time she'd been deep into her thesis on the lives of strippers, what made them do it and why. She'd felt it was bland and needed more—she'd wanted up-close-and-personal experiences. When Greg had told her about the undercover mission he was about to undertake, she'd thought it a great opportunity for her research. He'd resisted at first, but had eventually agreed because they hadn't wanted to be apart.

She'd gotten a job as a waitress in the strip club without a problem, but she'd been unprepared for the seedier side of life. The job was degrading and disgusting and nothing like working in a restaurant, as she'd thought it would be. But as long as Greg was there, she'd felt safe. Then Rudy Boyd, the owner of the club, had taken an interest in her. When she'd rebuffed him, it had made him angry.

She and Greg had decided it was time for her to leave, to go home to Celia. The night she was packing, Boyd and two of his men had shown up at the apart-

ment. Boyd had somehow found out that Greg was a
cop out to get him. He'd shot him without a second
thought, right in front of her. She'd never been so
scared or horrified in her life. Holding Greg's limp
body, she'd waited for the sound of a bullet to end her
life, too, but Boyd had had other plans.

He'd also learned of her thesis work and had taken
the disks from her computer, telling her she was about
to get a real first-hand look at a stripper's life. She'd
said she would never strip. He'd laughed, and put a
knife to her throat, and said she had a choice—death
or stripping.

She'd kept thinking that if she could stay alive, she
might manage to get away and go to the police to tell
them what had happened to Greg. As days turned into
weeks, she hadn't known how much longer she'd be
able to continue to do something so humiliating, so
repulsive. It had taken all her strength to go on, but
that strength eventually waned. Then a miracle happened.

Ethan Ramsey had come to the club. Seeing how
nervous she was on stage, he'd sensed something was
wrong, though he hadn't thought much about it at the
time. The very next day he'd met Serena in Fort
Worth. Looking suave, polished and beautiful, he
couldn't help but recall the familiar, distraught face of
the woman of the night before. He'd given Serena his
card, telling her that if she needed help, to just call
him.

Serena had thought it a come-on line. But Ethan's
story about the stripper that looked just like her, had
haunted Serena's mind. She'd eventually hired Ethan
to find the stripper—and he had. Serena and Sarah had

found each other, too, learning they'd been deceived by the people who'd raised them.

In the end it had all worked out. Sarah now lived with her grandmother, Aurora Farrell, forming a relationship they should have had years ago. Sarah finished her degree and Rudy Boyd had been convicted of capital murder. The best part was that Serena and Ethan had fallen in love, gotten married and now had a three-year-old daughter, Jassy, named after Jasmine, their mother.

The connection between her and Serena was unlike anything Sarah had ever experienced. They were identical—looking at Serena was like looking in a mirror. It was as though they were the same person, yet different. At times, they could read each other's minds, which was scary to Sarah, who had always been a private person. It was also wonderful to have someone who knew her so well. There wasn't anything she couldn't tell Serena and vice versa.

Sarah stood and brushed Brooke's hair back from her face. The medication had finally taken effect and Brooke would be out for a while. It was what she needed—lots of rest. Sarah picked up her purse and the chart, and made her way from the room.

She couldn't have made it through that terrible time in her life if it hadn't been for Serena. *Daniel had been there, too.* She brushed that thought away as she wrote in Brooke's chart. Handing the chart to the nurse, she walked to the doors and out into the night. .

The cold wind blew against her and she shivered. She'd been in such a hurry to get to the hospital that she'd forgotten her coat. She ran to her car and quickly started the engine, hoping it would warm up quickly.

It was late so there wasn't much traffic. Stopping

for a light, she thought back to the day Ethan and Daniel had pulled her out of Boyd's closet, where she'd been hiding from her captor. She had passed out, but had come to as Daniel checked to see if she was still breathing. All she'd had on was a robe and a pair of bikini panties… His head was on her chest… Her robe was open, her breasts exposed. Every time she'd seen Daniel after that day, she'd remember his face against her naked skin and it filled her with shame and embarrassment.

She'd taken off her clothes in front of men. It was hard for her to believe that now, but she had done what she'd had to do to stay alive. It was a debilitating memory forever etched in her mind. The reality of what had happened to her was still hard to understand. And Daniel was part of that reality. He'd seen her at her worst. She didn't like being reminded of that.

Her hand went to the silk blouse buttoned at her neck. She never let anyone see her body anymore. After all this time, she still didn't want a man to see her, to touch her. Maybe that part of her life was over.

The thought upset her. She didn't want to be this repressed for the rest of her life. As a professional, Sarah recognized that her behavior wasn't healthy.

She had the urge to talk to Serena, but it was too late to call so she would wait until the morning. She also had to tell Serena and Ethan about Daniel—that he was quitting. Then maybe she'd lose these guilty feelings.

Again, she knew that wasn't going to happen until she faced whatever was between her and Daniel; guilt, blame, irritation or something deeper. There was an undeniable tension between them and until it was resolved, she'd have no peace.

CHAPTER THREE

THE NEXT MORNING Daniel rolled out of bed feeling good and he knew he'd made the right decision. He put on a pot of coffee and after his shower, wrapped a towel around his waist, grabbed a cup and went back to the bathroom to shave.

He rubbed shaving cream over his rough stubble then looked at himself closely in the mirror. There were lines around his eyes that he hadn't noticed before. Worry lines—that's what they were called. Well, he had plenty of worry in his type of work so he wasn't surprised, nor did it bother him.

He wondered how Brooke Wallace was this morning. It was only five, so he hoped she was sleeping, getting some rest, because she had a rough road ahead of her. As he scraped the stubble away, he found himself unable to stop thinking about Sarah. She could help Brooke—Daniel knew that she would. But would it bring back painful memories for her? He threw his towel on the bathroom vanity. No, he wasn't going to do this. He wasn't worrying about Sarah Welch anymore. Her life was none of his business.

In the bedroom, he saw that his answering machine light was blinking. He listened to several messages before his mother's voice came on. "Daniel, we're still in Paris and having a great time. Your father is enjoying seeing his old friend, Jon Paul. His daughter,

Yvette, is asking about you. She remembers you from her visit to America. She likes you a lot and she's so beautiful. Wish you were here. Please think about your father's offer. You work too hard and your job is so dangerous. Not sure when we'll return. Don't forget to check on Drew. Goodbye.''

Turning off the machine, he sat for a moment and stared into space. His father had been trying for years to place him at the helm of Garrett Enterprises. His grandfather had started a construction company then expanded the business to erecting shopping malls in Texas, eventually venturing in to other states and to Europe. Recently the company had scaled back on construction projects, but his father still managed extensive interests all over the country.

Daniel had always felt he wasn't cut out to be a businessman. Ever since he was small, when people would ask what he wanted to be when he grew up, he'd always say, ''A policeman.'' His parents thought he'd outgrow this particular ambition, but he hadn't. After getting a degree in criminal justice, he'd entered the police academy, much to his parent's dismay. Then something happened that had changed his life forever.

Growing up, Daniel had spent a lot of time watching out for his brother, Drew, who was five years younger. But in college Drew got in with a bad crowd and started to do drugs. For a long time, Drew hid this from Daniel and their parents. One night at a party, Drew overdosed on heroin and almost died. He'd been in a coma for days. When he'd finally come out of it, his brain had been affected and he'd ended up with the mental capacity of a ten-year-old. He still had a problem putting words together and he stuttered until he could form the thought in his head. Those first years had been difficult as Drew had struggled to find a way to express himself. They'd all been very patient and grateful he was alive.

That had been fifteen years ago and not much had changed. Drew would be a child for the rest of his life. For Daniel, a lot of things had changed. He'd gone into narcotics and spent the past fifteen years trying to take down the big drug dealers. Every time one was put in prison, though, another popped up. It was a losing battle, but Daniel had fought tirelessly—until now. Was he giving up? No, he needed a break from that world.

And Sarah didn't want him around.

For a moment he let himself feel just how much that hurt. How much it had influenced his decision. How much he'd been hoping that, last night, she'd reach out to him. But he knew he was the last person she'd turn to for anything.

He ran his hands over his face as thoughts of her did their usual number on his control. The day they'd rescued her, Daniel's only thought was to make sure she was alive. He'd laid his ear against her chest—not even aware her robe was open. Now, sometimes, late at night, when he was tired and drained, he could actually feel her satiny skin and the softness of her breasts. And he knew Sarah had made a profound effect on him. Serena had, too, but not in the same way.

Serena was soft-spoken and had a sweetness that went all the way to her soul. They were identical in looks, both beauties, but not in personality. Sarah had a coolness, a reserve about her that was intriguing, mystifying and sometimes intimidating. He knew it was only a facade she'd acquired over the years to protect herself from life and its disappointments.

That facade was firmly in place, though, and no man was getting behind it. Greg had, but he'd been killed. Now, Sarah didn't want to feel any more pain.

He had to stop thinking about her. The only way to do that was to start seeing other women—women who actually liked him.

His mother had said that Yvette was asking about him. She was blond and blue-eyed and had an incredibly sexy voice. Muriel had been distressed for years about his single status and he'd avoided her matchmaking efforts at all costs. Her taste in women wasn't the same as his. Yvette just might be what he needed, though. Maybe he'd buy a plane ticket, pick up Drew, and surprise their parents.

The more he thought about it, the more he liked the plan. He'd talk to the lieutenant about his decision on Monday. Since this was Saturday, Daniel didn't want to bother him. He'd type his letter of resignation tonight and have it ready. Then he'd fly away to France and Yvette.

First, he had to attend to a couple of things.

SARAH TRUDGED TO the kitchen for coffee. It was 5:00 a.m. and she'd only slept a couple of hours. She wanted to get to the hospital before Brooke woke up, though. Putting the coffee on, she turned as her grandmother came into the kitchen.

Aurora Farrell wore a long, beige-silk robe and gown. Her white hair hung down her back and her posture and features were elegant, almost regal. It was hard to believe she was in her seventies.

"Morning, Gran," Sarah said, kissing her cheek and grabbing the teakettle. Gran preferred tea while Sarah favored coffee in the mornings.

"Morning, darling." Aurora took a seat at the kitchen table. "What are you doing up so early? It's Saturday. Surely you're not starting to clean the house at this hour of the morning."

"Partly. I've stripped my bed and have a load of laundry going, but I have to run to the hospital for a bit. I have a patient to see."

Saturday was her cleaning day. It was the only time she had to do housework and she couldn't afford a cleaning lady. The house was so big and Sarah was finding it difficult to maintain the house on her salary and with her busy schedule. This had been Gran's home since she'd married Henry Farrell and Sarah wanted her to stay here as long as she could. Sarah wanted to be here, too. It's where she should have been raised as a child with Serena. Staying here wasn't going to bring her childhood back, though. Serena wanted her to sell the house, but how would she tell Gran? Over the past five years they'd formed a good relationship and Sarah couldn't see changing any part of their lives.

At times, she felt as if she'd stepped into Serena's place—worrying about Gran, taking care of her. When she and her sister had met, Serena had been at her wit's end trying to pay the note and bills on the house. Before his death, her grandfather had borrowed a lot of money he couldn't pay back and, unfortunately, Gran was used to a certain lifestyle. She was a compulsive shopper and spender. The situation had come to a head with the bank threatening to foreclose on their home.

Then Sarah found out that Greg had left half his life insurance to her. At first she hadn't wanted to accept it, then she and Serena had a long talk. Greg wanted her to have the money, to have a better life, and Serena'd thought Sarah should spend the windfall on herself. Sarah had other plans. She took the money and paid off the note on the house and all the bills, with Serena protesting the whole time. It had felt good to be able to help Gran and Serena, but she was still struggling to stay afloat with the upkeep of such a large house. In the summer, it was worse with the pool and yard to maintain.

"I'll strip my bed and finish the laundry while you're gone," Gran said.

Sarah placed a cup of tea in front of her. "Thanks, Gran. That would help a great deal."

"As you know, I'm not fond of housework, but I'll help all I can." Aurora stirred honey and lemon into her cup.

Sarah knew that. Gran had lived a life of privilege and it was difficult for her to adjust to a different lifestyle. But these days she stuck to a budget that Sarah planned for them. It was the only way they could manage, so Sarah was grateful for Gran's cooperation.

"Just don't tell any of my friends."

"I promise." Sarah smiled. "You're up early. Do you have plans?"

"No." Aurora took a sip. "The older I get, the less I sleep." Gran wasn't known to be an early riser. Sarah wasn't, either, but she rarely got to sleep in. Her life demanded early hours and long days but she wouldn't have it any other way.

"Well, I'd better run," Sarah said as she noticed it was almost five-thirty. "I'll drink my coffee while I dress."

"Sarah?"

"Yes?" She stopped in the doorway.

"Have you heard from Serena?"

"Not for a couple of days."

"It's been three days since I've heard from her. I hope nothing's wrong."

"I'm sure there isn't," Sarah assured her. "But I'll call her tonight and we'll have a long chat and find out all Jassy's latest antics." At Gran's somber expression, she added, "That phoning thing—it works both ways."

"I know," Gran replied. "I called last night and I even called this morning, trying to catch them, and there wasn't an answer. I just can't imagine where they'd be at this hour. Ethan's father didn't even answer."

So that's why Gran was up early. She was worried about Serena. Now Sarah was, too. "I'll call as soon as I get back," Sarah promised and rushed back to kiss Aurora. "Stop thinking bad things. They're fine."

Aurora hugged Sarah. "I'm so lucky to have you."

"We're both lucky. Now I have to go."

THIRTY MINUTES LATER Sarah was on the way to the hospital. She didn't worry too much about Serena because she didn't have a sense that something was wrong. Even though they hadn't been raised together, they still had that connection, that special bond that existed between twins. It was one of the perks that delighted Sarah about being a twin. It was almost surreal at times—like when Jassy was born.

Sarah had woken up in the middle of the night and sensed that Serena needed her. The baby wasn't due for two weeks, but Sarah had immediately called the airport and booked a flight for her and Gran to San Antonio. Serena had gone into labor at the same time that Sarah had woken up in Dallas. They'd arrived there in time to watch Jassy make her appearance into the world.

They'd laughed about it afterward. Ethan had said he hadn't needed to call because Sarah and Serena had a physic connection. And they did.

So she wasn't really worried now. She felt that Serena and Ethan had probably taken a weekend away together and left Jassy with Molly, Ethan's sister. Molly had a little girl six months older than Jassy and they loved to play together. But Serena always called when they were going away and that was what was niggling at her. Still, she didn't let herself get paranoid. She had to put her personal life aside and concentrate on Brooke.

BROOKE WAS NOW IN A room upstairs and Sarah went to the nurses' station to get her chart. Reading through the contents, she asked the nurse on duty, "What kind of night has she had?"

"They brought her up about 4:00 a.m. and she never woke up, and I haven't heard a peep out of her."

"Are her parents here?"

"No, but Detective Garrett went in to see her a few minutes ago."

"What! The police are not allowed to question her without supervision." She was trying to control her anger.

The nurse held up a hand. "Hold on, Ms. Welch. I didn't say anything about someone questioning her."

"Why else would he be here?"

The nurse frowned. "You don't know Daniel very well, do you?"

"What?"

"I've worked for over thirty years in this hospital and I know Daniel Garrett. He often comes by to check on a patient—overdoses, victims of shootings and the like. That's the type of person he is. I can assure you he's not questioning Brooke Wallace."

Sarah took the chart and walked toward Brooke's room feeling duly chastised. The nurse was right—Daniel was always there for the victim. He'd been there for her during Boyd's arrest, his trial and the appeal. Through it all Daniel had been unfailing in his support, as he was with everyone. She'd admitted as much to herself yesterday, so why had she felt a flash of anger when the nurse had mentioned his name?

What was really bothering her? Did she want to be more than a woman in an endless line of victims to Daniel? Of course not. She just didn't want him to see her as a helpless female—that's all. She didn't want anything else from a man ever again—including Daniel.

She was lying.

She groaned inwardly at the war going on inside her. Her emotions were like a tennis ball being constantly batted back and forth until she was exhausted from the struggle. She had to decide what she wanted from Daniel, what she expected from him. Because, like it or not, he was in her life. Their jobs threw them together and she had no right to tell him to stay away from her. She had to apologize. Of that she was very certain.

Just as she reached the door, Daniel came out. He stopped short when he saw her then walked on without a word.

She hurried after him. "Daniel."

He halted and slowly turned around. "I'm sorry. I

didn't think you'd be here this early. I only stopped by to see how Brooke was doing. She's awake and I didn't ask her any questions about the rape. I only reassured her that we'd catch this guy.''

"You won't, though.''

He blinked. "What?''

"You're quitting the force. If you do that, you won't catch him.''

He was watching her closely. "Russ has a good team and they'll find him.''

"Russ is a macho idiot,'' she blurted before she could stop herself.

"He's also a good cop.''

"No, he isn't, but you are.'' It came out almost as a whisper.

His dark eyes narrowed. "What is this, Sarah? Last night you told me to stay away from you in a voice that could cut glass and this morning you're saying I'm a good cop in a voice I don't recognize. To say I'm confused is putting it mildly.''

"Could we talk for a minute?''

Daniel held up both hands. "I don't think so. We said all we had to say last night. You're right, I've worried about you too much and it's time for me to back away. Time for me to do a lot of things and some of them have nothing to do with you.'' He took a deep breath. "With Serena and Ethan being so far away, I wanted to be there if you needed someone. But you've made it plain on more than one occasion that you're fine and don't need anyone. You see—'' he glanced down the hall "—I have this flaw—I want to help everyone. I've finally recognized that that's not always possible.''

"Daniel—''

He cut her off. "If you have a problem with Russ, just call Lieutenant Bauer and he'll take care of him."

"Daniel…"

"Goodbye, Sarah. After today you won't see me again. I'll be flying to Paris on Monday and I'm not sure when I'll be back." He turned and strolled toward the elevators.

She watched until he disappeared behind the closing doors. She let out a long breath, not even realizing that she hadn't been breathing. For a moment she didn't know what to do. All she could think was that she hadn't had a chance to apologize. Daniel hadn't wanted to hear anything she'd had to say. She deserved that. She had been cruel last night, hurting him when he'd been nothing but kind to her.

At Boyd's trial, Serena had sat on one side of her and Daniel on the other, encouraging her and letting her know she had the strength to face Boyd and to describe in open court what he'd done to Greg and to her. She wondered now if she could have done it without him.

She moved toward Brooke's room. He'd said he was going to Paris. Did he have family there? Or was he taking a special woman? She suddenly realized that she didn't know anything about Daniel or his life. Did he have a family? He wasn't married, she knew, because Serena had mentioned it. Who *was* Daniel Garrett?

She shook her head as she entered the room. It really didn't matter. She had just severed all ties to the man and she felt an emptiness in her stomach at her thoughtless actions.

BROOKE WAS LYING on her side, staring at the wall. The IV was still in her arm.

"Good morning," Sarah said as she took a seat.

"Morning, Ms. Welch," Brooke responded.

"How are you feeling?"

"Sore, and my neck and throat hurts."

"That will heal with time."

"And the nightmare, the shame and horror—does it go away, too?"

No. It will be with you the rest of your life.

She should have been able to say yes with confidence, but she couldn't. The truth of that hit her like a slap in the face, the sting creeping into tiny crevices in her mind that she had boarded up against the pain. She hadn't dealt with what had happened to her. She could see that now. Daniel had seen it, but she hadn't.

She gathered her thoughts, her knowledge. "It will be hard." She spoke the truth and more truths followed. "You have to make a concentrated effort to move on with your life. You have to talk to people, especially when you're hurting, and don't shut people out." *Like I did.* "People want to help you." *Daniel did.* "It will take a lot of love and support, but eventually you will be able to put it behind you." *Like I have to do now.*

"I don't like talking about it."

"A good counselor or therapist will help you with that and you don't have to talk until you're ready."

"I like talking to you."

Sarah reached into her purse and pulled out a card. She wrote a number on the back. "This is my cell phone. You can reach me today or tomorrow, any time you want to talk. On Monday make an appointment at the office. Dr. Mason usually handles these cases for the hospital. She's very good and you'll like her.''

"Can I talk to you?''

"Sure.'' Somehow Sarah was hoping she'd say that. For so long she'd refused to open those doors that were so painful, but by helping Brooke she could also help herself.

"I remember you talking about your family last night," Brooke said. "Are you close to your twin now?''

"Yes, we are.''

"I have two sisters younger than me and I don't know what to say to them.''

"I think you'll find that you won't have to say much. They'll just want to comfort you.''

"Yeah. People have been real nice. Detective Garrett was here earlier and he's so nice and good-looking. I just thought that cops in the movies were that handsome.''

Was Daniel handsome? Of course he was. He was tall, lean, with dark eyes and hair. At times his hair curled into his collar. His features were strong and chiseled, his nose straight and his lips… Oh, my. She touched her warm cheek. She'd noticed Daniel more than she'd ever thought. Denial—she'd been firmly in denial. But not anymore.

She was going to take her own advice and make an effort to move on with her life. She couldn't remember the last time she had actually laughed, felt silly or giddy. It was time for a change.

Brooke's parents entered and Sarah stood. Lois ran to her daughter and hugged her. Her father did the same.

"The doctor said you can go home soon." Bob Wallace wiped away an errant tear.

"I don't know."

Brooke seemed afraid and before Sarah could say anything Bob added, "Don't worry. No one's ever gonna hurt you again. Not as long as I'm around."

Brooke's fears eased and Sarah knew she was going to be okay with the love and support of her family.

"I'll go," she said. "If you need anything, just call."

"Thank you, Ms. Welch," Brooke replied. "Will the police still be questioning me?"

"Yes." Sarah glanced at Bob. "Call if you need me, but I feel your father can handle them."

"Yeah." Brooke nodded confidently and Sarah slipped out of the room.

WHEN SARAH GOT IN her car, she grabbed her cell phone. She had to talk to Serena. *Serena, please, please, be home.* The phone rang and rang then the answering machine came on. She clicked off, wondering where Serena could be. This wasn't like her. But Sarah still wasn't worried.

She drove toward Fort Worth and home, and realized it was almost noon. She had the house to clean and laundry to do yet. But the emotional tennis ball in her head kept bouncing back and forth with a ferocity she couldn't ignore, couldn't deny any longer. She had to sort through what she was feeling, about Daniel, about her life, and the only way to do that was to talk, as she'd told Brooke. She could talk to Karen—she had many times—but she didn't open up to her colleague the way she did with Serena. She had to talk to her sister. *Where are you, Serena?*

She drove into the garage and smiled. Ethan's truck was parked to the side. Serena was home. Sarah jumped out and ran to the house. The door burst open and Jassy flew toward her, her red hair in a ponytail, bouncing.

"Sari, Sari, Sari, it's me," she shouted.

Sarah dropped her purse and caught Jassy, swinging her around and into her arms, then she just held her tight.

"Look at me, look at me." Jassy wriggled and leaned away from Sarah. "Look how big I get. Daddy says I grow like a weed. Daddy says he's gonna put a rock on my head. Daddy says I getting too big for my britches."

Sarah kissed her cheek. "Daddy says a lot."

"Yeah. Daddy knows everything."

Jasmine Marie was the light in her father's eyes and she worshiped him. Serena taught school and Ethan kept Jassy while Serena was at work. Ethan had retired from the FBI and he occasionally did P.I. work, but since Jassy's birth he only took care of his daughter. He'd been married before and had lost a son, so he tended to be overprotective. That's why Serena made him go away for the odd weekend. She wanted Jassy to be around other people.

"Where's Daddy Says?" She teased her little niece, using the name that Sarah called Ethan because every other word out of Jassy's mouth was "Daddy says."

"In the house with Mommy and Gran. Mommy said I could watch for you and I saw you first."

The door opened again and Serena came toward them.

"I gonna go tell Daddy you're here." She slipped

from Sarah's arms, ran around her mother and back into the house.

The sisters embraced. Two identical young women—same red hair, same blue eyes, same height and body shape and weight, except Serena's hair was now shorter and hung in a natural style past her shoulders. Sarah's was still long and wound into a knot at her nape.

Sarah clung to her sister, then she did something out of character. She burst into tears.

Serena just held her.

Finally, Sarah pulled away and brushed away tears. "I'm sorry. I guess I'm a little emotional or I'm just really glad to see you."

Serena looked into her eyes. "Sarah, what is it?"

Sarah blinked and admitted something that she hadn't been able to before. "I need to talk. I need help."

CHAPTER FOUR

SARAH QUICKLY GOT HERSELF under control. "I don't want Jassy to see me crying. We'll talk later."

"Are you sure?" Serena asked with a worried frown. "Ethan's an expert at taking care of our daughter."

"Yes. Right now I just want to enjoy my family."

Arm-in-arm they walked into the house. Ethan immediately got up and hugged Sarah. Tall and lanky, with dark good looks, Ethan was one of a kind. He'd been shot in the hip while working for the FBI and now walked with a slight limp, but since he was in such good shape it was hardly noticeable. If she had to use a word to describe Ethan, it would be honorable.

Daniel was a lot like that. Where did that thought come from?

"See, Daddy," Jassy said, crawling into Ethan's lap. "I told you Sari was here. I saw her first."

Ethan pulled her ponytail. "Yes, you did."

"Were you surprised to see me, Sari?" Jassy asked. "Yes."

"Mommy said we were going to surprise you."

"You certainly did that. Gran and I were concerned. We both tried calling and got no answer."

"I called last night and before six this morning," Gran told them.

Ethan looked lovingly at Serena. "Serena was feeling a little down yesterday so I took her out to dinner last night. That didn't help a whole lot and I knew it was time for a visit. We were on the road at three this morning.''

"Isn't he wonderful?'' Serena asked of no one in particular, her eyes on her husband.

"Daddy Says gets my vote for wonderful,'' Sarah teased.

"We love Daddy,'' Jassy chirped in. "Daddy says he put me in the truck, but I don't 'member. Daddy says I was sleeping like a log.''

"I'm just so glad you're here. I was feeling a little down, too, and I needed this. But I haven't had a chance to do the housework or anything.''

"It's all done.'' Serena smiled.

"What?''

"Gran was doing laundry when we got here so I helped her finish, then I made the beds and put linens in our room. I dusted, mopped and vacuumed. Ethan took out the trash and swept outside.''

"You didn't have to do that.''

"I wanted us to have a chance to visit and now we do.'' Serena linked an arm through Sarah's.

Almost on cue, Ethan stood. "I'll take Jassy and see if I can track down Daniel. I haven't talked to him in a while.''

Sarah's heart skipped a beat. Should she tell Ethan that Daniel was quitting his job? No. She'd let Daniel do that.

"What about lunch?''

Jassy clapped her hands. "I'm gonna get a Happy Meal. Mommy said I could.''

Ethan grimaced. "Daddy's really looking forward to this.''

Jassy heard the displeasure in Ethan's voice. Her bottom lip dropped. "Mommy said I could."

Serena quickly took her out of Ethan's arms and kissed her. "Yes, my baby. Since you did so well in your gymnastics class I said you could have a treat."

"I jump real high, don't I, Mommy?"

"Higher than anyone else."

"And I can turn a flip, too." She looked at Sarah. "Wanna see?"

Serena held her tighter to keep her from getting down. "You can put your shorts on tonight and show Sari and Gran everything you can do. I think Daddy's ready to go." Serena kissed her again. "Have a good time."

Ethan took Jassy from Serena, giving his wife a lingering kiss in the process. "See you later," he whispered to Serena, then walked out the door with Jassy talking non-stop.

Sarah opened the refrigerator. "I made chicken salad last night so I wouldn't have to cook today. I'll cut up some fruit and we'll have lunch."

"I'll make the tea," Serena offered.

For the next thirty minutes they were busy preparing and eating the meal. Gran sat back and smiled.

"It's so good to have my girls together, but now I'm going to take a nap. I haven't worked this hard in ages."

After Gran left, they cleaned the kitchen. Sarah poured more tea into their cups. "Let's go into the den."

Serena curled up in a comfortable chair and Sarah sat on the sofa. She kicked off her shoes and drew up her knees.

Serena sipped her tea and waited.

"How are things in Junction Flat?" Sarah asked, unable to say the words she wanted to, had to, say.

"Great. I love the peace and quiet and I love teaching."

"I don't have to ask how you and Ethan are doing. You're still so in love."

"Yes." Serena grinned. "That will never change, but no marriage is perfect. We have problems, too."

"Ethan's overprotectiveness with Jassy?"

Serena brushed back her hair. "It was such a battle to let her take gymnastics and it all stems from his fear of losing her like he lost Ryan. His son was about Jassy's age when he fell off those boxes and died from the injuries to his head."

"It has to be devastating to lose a child."

"Yes, and Ethan knows he goes overboard. He's just so afraid, but I've told him that we can't keep her locked up away from the world. We have to let her grow."

"What did he say?"

"He understands, but it's difficult for him to do. I explained the running and jumping would be good for her. She'd learn how to fall."

"Did he agree?"

"Not for an instant and he was so nervous watching her I thought I'd have to tie him to his seat."

"He just loves her," Sarah said.

"Yes. Ethan loves very deeply. That's one of the things I love most about him."

"You're very lucky."

"Hmm." Serena's eyes grew dreamy. "And I have a solution to our problem."

"What?"

"Another baby."

Sarah raised an eyebrow. "Does Ethan agree?" Ethan had gone through such pain over losing his son that he'd never wanted to have another child. It had taken Serena a year before she was convinced that he was ready.

"Let's just say I'm working on him. He spends all day with Jassy and when she starts school, he's going to be lost without her. Another child would definitely divide his attention and worry."

As Sarah listened, she wished her life was that simple, her problems so easy to solve. Serena and Ethan loved each other and they would work out their differences, but Sarah feared her pain was too deep to ever assuage. She had to try, though. She couldn't stay in denial forever.

Serena watched her for a moment. "My life's not what you wanted to talk about. What's wrong, Sarah?"

Sarah rested her chin on her knees and stared down at her toes. She used to paint her nails, but she hadn't done that in years.

"Sarah—" Serena prompted.

She took a long breath. "I've told you so many times that I'm fine. I realized today that I'm not."

"What happened?"

Sarah told her about Brooke Wallace.

"How awful."

"It is," Sarah agreed. "When she asked me if the shame and horror would ever go away, I should have been able to say yes. But I couldn't honestly say that, and it shook me."

"What did you say?"

"I told her that in time with a concentrated effort she could put it behind her and that she had to talk to people.'' She shook her head. ''I haven't done any of that. I pushed what happened to me to the back of my mind and I've never really faced it or conquered all those bad feelings. Instead I've burrowed further and further inside myself until...'' She stopped. ''Do you know what the cops call me?''

''No.''

''Colder Than Ice. And it's true. I'm frozen inside and I can't feel anymore. I won't allow myself to feel. I can't...I...''

''Oh, Sarah.'' Serena jumped up and went to her, holding her tight. ''I think you've done remarkably well considering all you've been through.''

''No. I just did what I had to—going through the motions of living.''

Serena leaned back. ''You saw your fiancé killed then you were brutalized by a drug lord and forced to strip in a disgusting club. After that you found out you had an identical twin sister and a grandmother you knew nothing about—and Celia, the woman who raised you, who you thought was your grandmother, was really your father's wife. That's a tremendous amount of trauma for anyone to deal with.''

When Sarah didn't speak, Serena added, ''I'm so proud of you and I'm sure listening to that young girl's terrifying story brought back a lot of painful memories.''

''It didn't bring them back—that's what I'm trying to tell you. I've never let go of them. I haven't dealt with my past. I help other people, but I can't help myself. Even Daniel knows that.''

''Daniel?''

''I see him occasionally when I'm working and when I do, he looks at me with such concern and em-

pathy. That irritates me. He always asks how I am.
That irritates me more. I've tried to understand why
that is, but I've never found an answer. Last night he
was at the hospital and after everyone had left he
asked why I resented him so much. Words spilled out
before I could stop them and I said some hurtful
things."

"Like what?"

"Like I blame him for Greg's death and I don't
appreciate him always looking over my shoulder to
make sure I'm okay. I don't need his help or concern
and I told him to stay away from me."

"Oh, Sarah."

"I know. He's been nothing but kind and helpful.
He saw something, though, that I couldn't—that I'm
falling apart. I lashed out because…"

"Because what?"

Sarah swallowed hard. "Because it goes much
deeper. I realized that today, too." She stared off past
Serena's shoulder. "Remember that day Ethan and
Daniel rescued us from Boyd's apartment?"

"I'm not likely to ever forget it."

"I was so afraid Boyd was going to kill you and
Ethan like he killed Greg. I passed out and when I
came to, I was lying on the floor and Daniel had his
ear against my breasts. At first I didn't know what was
going on, then I realized my robe was open and I
didn't have anything on but a pair of bikini panties. I
knew he was a policeman and I was so embarrassed."

Serena rubbed her arm. "You shouldn't be. We
were all very worried about you. Daniel was just trying to see if you were still breathing. I don't think he
even noticed you were almost naked."

"But I noticed." She blinked back a tear. "Sometimes I dream I'm on that stage, taking off my clothes, and I hear the men hollering and whistling. I didn't want Daniel to see me like that.''

"Are you saying you have feelings for Daniel?"

"No, but I don't want him to see me that way."

"What way?"

"Like a slut."

Serena caught Sarah's face and turned it so she could look into her eyes. "Listen to me. You're not a slut. No one, including Daniel, sees you that way. You're a beautiful, talented, courageous young woman. And you're strong—stronger than I ever could be. I love you and I'm so glad you're my sister."

Sarah wrapped her arms around Serena and rested her head on her shoulder. "Help me, Serena. I don't want to feel like this anymore. I want the pain and nightmares to stop. I know all the textbook stuff, but it's hard to apply that to myself."

"Okay, then, let's do something different."

Sarah pulled back. "Like what?"

Serena became thoughtful. "Well, you say you're cold, so let's warm you up."

"Do you have something in mind?"

"Yes, and of course this is a lay person's point of view—to make a woman feel better about herself, it helps to make her look great on the outside. Once you gain some confidence in your femininity again, I think the rest will follow. As a counselor you'll have to sort through all the debris that's making you feel this way and I'll be here to help you any way I can."

"Thank you," Sarah replied, gaining confidence from her sister. "True healing comes from here—" she placed a hand over her heart "—and here." She pointed to her head. "But in my case, working on the exterior couldn't hurt and I know exactly where to start.'' Excitement bubbled inside her. She had to change herself outwardly before her emotions ever had a chance to heal. She unbuttoned the top two buttons on her blouse, then thought, What the hell? and undid another.

Serena jumped up. ''And the hair. We need to do something with the hair.'' Her eyes grew bright. ''Let's do a complete makeover. We have the whole afternoon to create a lot of warmth.''

Sarah got to her feet. ''What about Ethan, Jassy and Gran?''

''I'll call Ethan on his cell phone. He's been wanting to visit a ranching supply place here and Jassy's happy as long as she's with her daddy. I'll leave Gran a note. After the busy morning, she'll be glad for a break.''

''Then let's do it,'' Sarah said with gusto.

''Okay.'' Serena studied Sarah. ''I'm thinking shorter hair. What are you thinking?''

Sarah smiled. ''I'm thinking I'm so glad you're home.''

DANIEL WALKED INTO the police station and found Russ Devers slipping on his jacket, ready to go out. Russ was, as Sarah had said, a macho cop. Daniel and Russ had clashed many times, mainly about correct police procedure, which Russ tended to ignore. He broke the rules constantly and his lieutenant had a list of complaints about the methods he used to get the job done. There were complaints about his appearance, too. His hair was pulled back into a ponytail and his clothes looked as if he'd gotten them out of the hamper. He chewed constantly on a toothpick, fighting a smoking habit. But Russ was good at solving crimes, so the grievances were filed away.

"What's the matter, Daniel?" Russ spouted off. "Didn't you get the message last night? I don't require your help anymore."

Daniel clenched his jaw at Russ's attempt to assert his authority. But he'd come here for a reason.

"I didn't come to argue with you, Russ. I came to apologize."

Russ stopped stuffing papers into his pocket and looked up. "Well, I'll be damned. You're actually admitting you were wrong."

"Yes. I stepped over the line last night and I apologize for that."

Russ shrugged. "What am I supposed to say? That I won't report you?"

"Do whatever you feel you have to. Just go easy on the girl. She's just a kid."

"Don't tell me how to do my job," Russ spat, biting down on the toothpick. "That girl knows something and I'll get it out of her as long as Ms. Welch stays out of my way."

Daniel sighed heavily. "If she knows something, which I doubt, you'll never get it out of her by using heavy-handed tactics."

"You really piss me off with that 'good cop' attitude."

"Well, Russ, you catch this guy and I'll stay the hell out of your way forever."

Russ was ready to say more, but Joel walked up. "Ready, Russ?"

"Yeah." Russ picked up his cell phone and attached it to his belt. "We're meeting with the kid who threw the party to get the names of everyone who was there. Then we'll have the name of the rapist and Miss Wallace will help to finger him.''

"I hope you catch him," was all Daniel said.

Russ brushed past him. "I will, and I don't need your help."

Daniel didn't respond. He didn't feel he had to.

Russ stopped and turned back. "Thanks for the apology."

Daniel nodded and watched in silence as Russ and Joel walked away. He hadn't mentioned that he was quitting the force. It wasn't any of Russ's business. *He was quitting.* For the first time, the word played in his mind. He'd never quit anything in his life and the words suddenly stuck in his throat. *He was quitting.*

His phone buzzed and he wiped the thought away.

"Daniel, it's Ethan."

"Hey, Ethan, how the hell are you?" He'd never felt so glad to hear his old friend's voice.

"Fine. I was hoping you had time for lunch."

"Sure. I'm free."

"You might change your mind when I tell you where I'm at."

"Try me."

"McDonald's."

Daniel laughed. "You have Jassy with you."

"Yeah."

"Tell me which one and I'll be there as fast as I can."

Within ten minutes he was pulling up at a McDonald's. He found Ethan in the kid's area watching Jassy on a slide.

He shook Ethan's hand. "It's good to see you. Let me get some coffee and I'll be right back."

He returned with a steaming cup in his hand. Sitting,

he pulled his coat tighter around him. "It's cold out here."

"Try telling that to my daughter."

Daniel watched Jassy as she played with another little girl. "Man, she looks just like Serena." *And Sarah. Don't think about her.*

"Yeah. Isn't she beautiful?"

Daniel shook his head in amusement. "You still have that lovesick quality in your voice just talking about Serena."

"Life's been pretty wonderful lately," Ethan admitted.

Daniel took a sip of the hot coffee. "So how's the rest of the family?"

"Fine. Molly's happy being a wife and mother again. Travis is in Nashville and it looks like he's finally going to get a record deal."

"Last time I saw him he was singing with this woman who had an awesome voice. They were getting a lot of attention here in Dallas."

"It was like a domino effect. Someone saw them and told this guy from a record company, then he came down and invited them to Nashville. They've been there about six months."

"Hope it works out for him."

"Me, too. He's been dreaming about this since he was fifteen."

"And Walt? How's he?"

Ethan leaned back. "Now that's a whole other story. My father has been seeing Mrs. Alma Ferguson about five years now. The other night I caught him sneaking in at five in the morning. I told him I didn't understand why he didn't just spend the whole night. He's in his seventies and as long as he practices safe sex I was okay with it. He did not appreciate my sense of humor and he had a few choice words to say about respecting my elders. So I'm just letting Pop do his thing. He's happy. Mrs. Alma's happy. And I'm staying out of it."

Daniel twisted his cup. "I hope when I'm that age, I'll still be thinking about women."

"Anyone in particular?"

Suddenly Daniel saw blue eyes and red hair.

"Daniel?"

"What?"

Ethan raised an eyebrow. "You seem a bit out of it today."

Daniel ran both hands through his hair. "I'm quitting the force."

"What!"

"I'm tired, Ethan. Tired of crime. Tired of the bad guys always getting the best of us. I lock a bastard up for selling drugs to kids and he's back on the street within a week doing the same thing. The revolving door never stops and I've had it."

"I hate to hear that. You're one of the best cops I've ever worked with."

"Your sister-in-law has a different opinion." He shouldn't have said that, but it seemed to slip out. *Stop thinking about her.*

"Sarah?"

"I guess it all comes back to Rudy Boyd and all the lives he's destroyed."

"But you got him, Daniel. He's on death row waiting for an execution date."

"That won't change things for Sarah or Greg."

"You can't blame yourself."

"I do, though. I should have been aware of what Greg was doing."

"You trusted him—like I've trusted men under me. Greg broke that trust, not you."

"Yes, but that doesn't help me to sleep better at night."

"Daniel…"

"Daddy, Daddy." Jassy crawled into Ethan's lap. "Did you watch me, Daddy?"

"I'm always watching you." He wrapped his arms around her. "Do you remember Daniel?"

Jassy nodded and said, "Hi."

"You have the most beautiful blue eyes," Daniel said, mesmerized by their brightness.

"I got my mommy's eyes," she told him.

"Sarah has them, too." He didn't even realize he'd spoken the words out loud until he saw Ethan's face.

"Mommy and Sari are just alike, but Daddy and me can tell them apart. We know Mommy, don't we, Daddy?"

"You bet we know Mommy."

Daniel stood. "I'd better go."

"Why don't you come back to the house with us? Serena would love to see you."

Daniel shook his head. "Thanks, but I've been working on a case and I have some loose ends to tie up. After I see the lieutenant on Monday, I'm flying to France to see my parents."

"Sarah will be there," Ethan added with a sheepish grin as if he knew exactly what was on Daniel's mind—a woman he couldn't get out of his head.

"Ah, Ethan, I think you're reading me like a book."

"I recognize the signs." Ethan got to his feet with Jassy in his arms. "Take some time. Don't give up a career you love out of guilt, and stop blaming yourself for things you have no control over. Most important, talk to Sarah.''

Daniel didn't tell Ethan he already had. He didn't want his friend caught in the middle. He'd deal with the situation in his own way.

''I'll think about it,'' he said, reaching over to kiss Jassy's cheek. ''Kiss your mom for me.''

''No.'' Jassy frowned. ''You can't kiss my mommy. Only Daddy kisses Mommy.''

''Jasmine Marie,'' Ethan scolded gently. ''That's not nice.''

''I'm sorry.'' Jassy hung her head.

Daniel touched her soft cheek. ''It's okay and I promise to never kiss your mommy.''

''Okay.'' Jassy glanced up at him, her eyes bright again. ''I kiss Sari for you. Sari needs lots of kisses.''

Daniel's stomach tightened at the innocent words, but he felt the simple truth in them, too. How nice it would be to kiss Sarah Welch. He shook Ethan's hand and strolled away, a slight curve to his mouth.

Only in my dreams, Jassy. Only in my dreams.

CHAPTER FIVE

SARAH HAD A GREAT TIME. She relaxed and enjoyed her afternoon with her twin. They talked, shopped, laughed and made fun of each other with sisterly love. In the mall, they ordered a decadent chocolate-fudge sundae then spent two hours in a beauty salon getting a pedicure and a manicure. Sarah also had her long hair cut into a casual style that hung around her shoulders.

They ignored the many stares and glances they received, but they were secretly amused. Two identical redheads were an eye-catcher.

Since she was on call, she had to take a couple of phone calls, but other than that they had the afternoon to themselves. Later, she went by the hospital to check on Brooke. Her family was there, so Sarah knew she was okay.

They picked up food to cook on the grill for dinner and Ethan played chef, then Jassy put on a show with her jumping and flipping. Sarah and Serena talked until after midnight and Sarah felt herself opening up, confiding and exposing the destructive emotions inside her. All this time and she'd thought she was fine. It took Daniel's words and Brooke's question to make her realize she was far from a full recovery.

She'd made a start with her sister's help and she intended to go forward now. Sarah felt as if she'd been living in a darkened room and someone had suddenly opened a door, letting in the fresh air and sunshine. She could feel its warmth slowly seeping into the coldest part of her. The feeling was liberating. She realized it was only a small step and she had a long way to go, but she was ready to face life again with Serena and her family behind her.

All too soon, they were saying goodbye and Sarah experienced a moment of sadness for all the years she and Serena had missed. But they had each other now and that's what counted.

She held Jassy close, not wanting to let her go.

"Oh, I forget," Jassy said, planting a big kiss on Sarah's cheek. "That's from Daniel."

Sarah felt the blood draining from her face. It was one of those unexpected moments that left her vulnerable and speechless. Ethan hadn't said anything about his visit with Daniel. Evidently she'd been mentioned.

"He wanted me to give Mommy a kiss, but I said no, that only Daddy kisses Mommy. I tell him I kiss you."

"Oh, I see," Sarah murmured in a low voice. Daniel really wanted to kiss Serena. Who wouldn't?

Ethan took Jassy out of her arms. "Come here, munchkin, before you get yourself in a lot of trouble." Ethan hugged Sarah. "Call Daniel," he whispered, and took Jassy to the truck.

Serena was talking to Gran and Sarah was only vaguely aware of their voices. *Call Daniel.* What had Daniel told Ethan?

"I enjoyed this surprise visit," Gran was saying.

Serena kissed Gran. "Remember you and Sarah are coming to spend the week during spring break."

"I'm looking forward to it."

Serena hugged Sarah and they held on tight. "I'm a phone call away," Serena said.

"I know, and thanks."

Serena leaned back. "You're going to be fine and you look marvelous."

Sarah curtsied. "Thank you. I look like my sister."

They laughed and it felt so good to have that happy feeling again. Serena ran to the truck and Jassy waved frantically.

Sarah waved until they were out of sight. Linking her arm with Gran's, they went back into the house.

"I thought I'd go to Hazel's," Gran said. "They're playing bridge at her house." Gran was an avid bridge player and she tried to never miss a game.

"Sure, Gran," Sarah replied. "Go ahead. I've got a lot of work to catch up on."

"Are you sure? I don't want you to be lonely."

"I'm fine, Gran."

"I do love your new hairstyle."

"Thanks. Now go have fun and—" Her phone rang, cutting her off. "See, I'll be busy."

"'Bye, darling."

"'Bye, Gran," Sarah called after her, and clicked on her cell phone.

It was Brooke and she was upset because the police were waiting to question her again and she wanted Sarah there. Sarah grabbed her purse and jacket and headed for the hospital.

She hurried down the corridor to Brooke's room, hoping Daniel would be there. Ethan was right. She had to talk to him. She didn't blame him for Greg's death and she had to tell him that.

She turned a corner and saw Russ and the other

detective, Joel, standing outside Brooke's door. Daniel wasn't here. Her heart sank.

Russ had his back to her, but Joel saw her. He nudged Russ. "Ms. Welch is here."

Russ swung around, ready to unload on her, but his jaw dropped and no words came out. His narrowed eyes slid over her, taking in the cobweb of glistening copper hair that hung around her face and shoulders. She had on a white V-necked sweater, tan slacks and a dark suede jacket. Russ's eyes seemed glued to her cleavage.

She felt a moment of panic, but only for a moment. Up until now Russ had only seen her in blouses buttoned to her throat. His stare didn't make her angry and she didn't feel herself shriveling up inside because a man was looking at her. She knew that was a good sign. Finally she was letting herself mend.

Russ recovered quickly. "We've been waiting for almost an hour. It's good of you to show up."

"I got the call less than thirty minutes ago and I came immediately."

"Then let's see her because I don't have any more time to waste."

Sarah and the detectives walked into the room and Brooke's parents quietly slipped out. Brooke was sitting up in bed and Sarah went to her side.

"Are you ready?" Sarah asked.

"Yes. Now that you're here."

Sarah nodded to Russ and he laid some papers in Brooke's lap. "Those are names of everyone at the party. Take a good look, Miss Wallace, and tell me if you recognize any of them."

For the next thirty minutes Russ questioned Brooke

about every male on the paper, but she didn't have any answers, or at least not the ones Russ wanted.

Brooke held up well and Sarah admired her strength. Russ didn't pressure her or use his usual macho tactics and Sarah was grateful for that. Afterward Sarah sat with Brooke until her parents returned. She left the hospital wondering where Daniel was. She didn't think he'd quit in the middle of an investigation—that wouldn't be like him at all. But what did she know about Daniel? That he was reliable, compassionate, loyal, supportive, kind and the list went on. She knew nothing about his personal life or his family and she'd never heard Ethan say anything about them, either.

That's probably the way it should stay, she decided as she pulled into her garage. Still she didn't want to be part of the reason he'd quit his job. She'd rectify that the next time she saw him. She just didn't know exactly when that would be.

THE NEXT MORNING Sarah was in the office early. Karen was back and they had several cases to discuss.

"My, don't you look great," Karen commented when Sarah walked into her office.

Karen was in her forties, slim with dark hair and eyes. She'd been a very good friend over the past four years, taking Sarah on as a counselor even though she was just out of school, because she believed she could do the job. As a psychologist, Sarah thought Karen was the best. She had a warm personality that invited confidences and Sarah had confided in her many times. But she could only share that deep inner pain with Serena and she knew it had to do with their special bond.

Sarah sat down. "Serena came home for the weekend and we had a girl's day out."

Karen glanced at the scooped neckline of Sarah's beige blouse. "I'd say it was a lot more than that."

"Yes." Sarah smiled. "I'm finally letting go of some of the pain."

"What brought this about?"

Sarah crossed her legs. "Something someone said to me and I realized I've been suppressing a lot of emotions."

Karen watched her. "I've never pushed you because I realized you needed time. Some people are like that, but I'm seeing some wonderful changes in you." Karen paused. "Do you want to talk?"

Sarah smiled. "Maybe later. Right now I'm feeling pretty wonderful and I've got a client waiting."

"I do, too, but we'll have to take an evening and celebrate." Karen glanced at her date book. "Seems as if we're both going to be very busy for the next few days."

"I hope you got some rest while you were away."

"Oh, yes, even though it was a psychology conference, Harmon and I made time for each other." Karen's husband was also a psychologist, but they didn't practice together. They felt that would be too much togetherness.

They went over the weekend cases and Sarah explained in detail about Brooke. Karen left for the hospital to visit with Brooke and an elderly woman who'd been beaten during a robbery.

Sarah was booked for the day and she spent the next few hours listening to people's problems. She realized that's what she did best—listen. Her first patient was a woman, Mrs. Carter, who was in her sixties and wanted to leave her husband of forty years. She said she wasn't happy and didn't love him anymore, but the more Mrs. Carter talked, Sarah could hear that she did. The couple had stopped talking to each other so Sarah asked her to invite her husband to a session.

She had a young mother of two whose husband had left her for another woman. Her parents were paying for the sessions and all the woman needed was for someone to listen to her. Soon she'd have confidence in herself again because she had great family support.

Sarah wasn't so sure about the sixteen-year-old boy she saw. He had so much anger in him and at times he refused to talk. Dwayne had told a friend in school that he'd dreamed of killing his father and that boy had relayed the information to a teacher who had reported it to the principal. The principal had called Dwayne's mother, who'd insisted he get counseling before the boy did anything foolish. When Dwayne wouldn't talk, Sarah'd get out the cards and they'd play. It was the only way she could get him to relax and to open up. After a few sessions Sarah discovered Dwayne was not a bad kid. He was just incredibly hurt by a father who had remarried and had another son. Dwayne didn't feel as if his father loved him anymore. Sarah was very pleased when Dwayne's father agreed to attend some sessions. That helped tremendously.

And her day went on…

DANIEL STOPPED BY Drew's apartment on the way to work. Even though his brother functioned at the level of a child, he insisted on having his own place. His parents in turn agreed only if Drew had a caretaker. Claude was a real find and he lived with Drew and drove him wherever he wanted to go. He'd been a nurse and he enjoyed the freedom of working in a home atmosphere. Drew was well taken care of and he felt independent.

In the past Drew had had problems getting along with his caretakers and in anger he'd run away and disappeared for a couple of days. He hadn't done that since his parents had hired Claude. It was a good arrangement—Daniel's parents didn't worry and neither did Daniel.

He rang the doorbell several times before Claude opened it in a bathrobe, yawning. It was clear that Daniel had woken him up.

Claude's hair was sheared close to his head. In his fifties, he was heavy-set with muscles. He worked out all the time and took Drew with him to the gym. As of yet, Claude hadn't talked Drew into exercising.

"Sorry, didn't mean to wake you."

"It's okay," Claude said, scratching his head. "We watched movies until two this morning."

"I just wanted to check on Drew."

Drew came out of his bedroom in baggy pajamas, his dark hair tousled. His eyes were glazed and Daniel knew it was from the medication he took for seizures—a result of brain damage. As long as Drew stayed on the medicine, he would be fine.

"Dan-iel, Dan-iel," he said in surprise and ran to him.

Daniel embraced him. "How you doing, buddy?"

"'kay. W-w-we w-watched movies."

"Yeah. I heard," Daniel replied. "I got a call from Mom and she wanted me to see if you were okay."

Drew frowned. "You t-t-treat me like a baby."

Daniel put his arm around Drew's shoulder, noticing how thin he was. Drew never ate much but the doctor had said that Drew was fine so Daniel had tried not to let his anxieties get the best of him. "We worry—that's all."

"Yeah." Drew yawned.

"I'll let you two get back to sleep and I'll talk to you later."

"You c-c-catching any bad guys?"

"I'm trying."

Drew suddenly hugged him. "I—I—I love you."

Daniel's breath burned in his throat. It was so hard to see Drew like this and for a moment he wanted to rant and rave at what life and drugs had done to his brother. Instead he hugged Drew firmly. "Love you, too, buddy."

Outside he had to take a couple of deep breaths. He didn't tell Drew about his plans to fly to France to be with their parents. He'd tell him when it was time to leave. That way he wouldn't be sitting around waiting. Now he had to talk to the lieutenant.

DANIEL WALKED INTO Bill Tolin's office and laid a letter on his desk. Bill didn't even raise his head. He kept writing in a file.

"What is it, Daniel?"

Daniel cleared his throat. "I'm resigning from my job, sir."

Bill still didn't look up. He was a cop who'd been around the block and was only a few years away from retirement. It was known around the department that Lieutenant Tolin was a hard but fair man. He was also known for his sharp tongue.

"Get your ass out of my office, Daniel. I don't have time for this today."

Daniel took a breath. "Sorry, sir. I'm serious about this."

Bill closed the folder and leaned back in his chair. "Why?" His blue eyes demanded a straight answer.

"I've had a lot of discontentment lately and the other night I stepped over the line. When I start doing stupid things, it's time to back away."

"I see," Bill said, crossing his arms over his chest. "Did you kill someone?"

"No, sir."

"Did you break the law?"

"No, sir."

"Then get your ass back to work."

"I have to do what's best for me, sir."

"I don't give a rat's ass for what's best for you. I run the narcotics squads and I do what's best for everyone. Right now we have a rapist on the loose and somehow he's tied to narcotics. You're the best man I've got and until this creep is off the streets, you're not going anywhere."

"Are you refusing my resignation?"

"You got it."

"Well, sir, that's going to be difficult when Russ is..."

Bill waved a hand. "I'm aware of what happened the other night and I've spoken with Lieutenant Bauer from homicide and we're in agreement. It's kind of hard not to step on Russ's ego, so apologize, forget it and get on with this case. Understand?"

"Yes, sir."

Daniel moved toward the door.

"Daniel?"

He looked back.

Bill had the resignation in his hand. "Take this and I don't want to see it again. At least not until I retire."

Daniel took the letter.

"You know, Daniel, it's been my experience that when a man your age is experiencing discontentment, it has something to do with a woman. So get her out of your system before I really lose my temper."

Daniel saluted with the letter and Bill nodded.

He sank down at his desk and took out the airline tickets that had been faxed to him. *What am I thinking?* Spend time with his parents? His mother would start her matchmaking schemes and his father would constantly bombard him with reasons he needed to be at Garrett Enterprises. That sounded like his own private hell. The thought of Yvette wasn't even appealing anymore. That sexy voice had a whine to it—like a cat clawing at a screen door. Now he was glad he hadn't mentioned anything to Drew. He didn't want to disappoint him.

Leaving in the middle of a case. *What was he thinking?* Once he'd gotten to France, he'd have been back here in a flash. No way was he going to leave a rapist on the street—not as long as he could help.

Thanks, Bill. Thanks for the wake-up call.

And he was right. Sarah Welch was in his system like a virus and he wasn't sure how to alleviate the problem. A round of antibodies wouldn't help. He had to do this cold-turkey.

He'd told Sarah he'd stay away from her. Maybe that wasn't going to be possible—yet. But he'd keep their contact to a minimum. He wouldn't ask how she was. He wouldn't care how she was. He would do his job and keep Sarah at a distance.

That's the way she wanted it. That's the way he needed their relationship to be.

He was lying to himself.

TOM HUDSON, a narcotics cop on Daniel's squad, walked in.

"Anything?" Daniel asked.

"Not a damn thing." Tom removed his jacket. "Jack and I tried to locate Freddie Frye, but he's hiding somewhere. He's got to come out sometime and we'll get him."

"Keep looking," Daniel said. "He supplies a lot of college parties and we need to talk to him. Where's Jack?"

"Talking to his wife. Marital problems again."

Daniel sighed as Jack Meades walked in. Before Daniel could speak, he said, "I know, Daniel, keep my personal life at home."

Daniel raised an eyebrow. "That would be nice. Now get back out there and find Freddie."

Jack frowned. "We've been searching for four damn hours. I need a break."

Daniel nodded. "Take a break, but remember that Brooke Wallace would like a break, too."

Jack said a foul word and swung away.

Tom grabbed his jacket. "I'll talk to him. He's just having a hard time at home. Some days this job stinks."

"Find Freddie," Daniel shouted after him.

Russ flopped into a chair across from Daniel's desk. "Cracking the whip?"

"Trying to keep everyone focused."

Russ clasped his hands behind his head. "Looks like you're still on the case."

"Yes. I was told."

"Lieutenant Bauer informed me, too, so don't give me orders and don't interfere in my investigation."

Daniel bit back a retort. "That goes both ways."

Russ nodded.

"I'm willing to work together to catch this bastard," Daniel added.

"Me, too," Russ replied, and got down to business. "I went to see Miss Wallace yesterday and I believe you're right. She doesn't know the rapist. I gave her a list of the men who were at the party and I watched her face closely. There wasn't a flicker of recognition or revulsion as she read the names."

Russ threw out the olive branch by admitting that Daniel was right and Daniel realized it took a lot for him to do that. Now they could focus on the case.

Daniel pulled his chair forward. "There's something I'm missing with this heroin needle left in the arm. It reeks of Rudy Boyd so I'm going back to do more checking on the pimps and dealers associated with him. And hopefully Jack and Tom can locate Freddie. If he didn't supply that party, he knows who did."

Russ propped his feet on Daniel's desk. "Speaking of Boyd, Sarah Welch was at the hospital while we spoke to Miss Wallace. It took a moment for me to recognize her."

"Why?"

"Ever since I've known her she's worn these business suits with blouses buttoned to the neck and her hair pulled back so tight it gave her a pained look. Yesterday her hair was hanging loose around her shoulders and she had on a sweater that was low-cut. Hell, she has breasts—nice breasts. She's actually beautiful. Never thought that before. I've been divorced a year now and I just might ask her out.''

Daniel's pulse hummed louder and louder with each word out of Russ's mouth. He'd been upset with Russ a lot of times over the years because of his attitude, and now was no exception. He wanted to reach across the desk and hit him hard for daring to talk about Sarah in that tone of voice. Realizing he'd reached the point where he was no longer objective about Sarah, he swallowed back emotions he wasn't ready to acknowledge and tried to act as blasé as Russ.

"You want to date Colder Than Ice?"

"Yeah. I'd like to warm her up."

I'd like to drive my fist into your face.

With that thought, blasé went right out the window.

Daniel stood. "Sarah's been through a great deal, so if you are even slightly familiar with the word tact, I'd suggest you use it when dealing with her."

"Hey." Russ removed his feet from the desk. "Am I stepping on toes here? I notice you're always talking to her."

"No. She's hates my guts." Daniel felt a stab in his stomach. It was the truth. "But I got to know her pretty well during Boyd's trial and she's very vulnerable. Now, I've got work to do and so do you. I'll call you later."

Daniel walked away thinking Russ could date whomever he wanted—even Sarah.

He was lying to himself—again.

SARAH LEFT WORK a little after five and was ready for a relaxing hot bath. She wanted quiet, absolute quiet. She planned to soak for about an hour and to use the scented, soothing bath oil Serena had given her for

Christmas. Gran was at one of her bridge games and wouldn't be home until later, so she'd have the house to herself.

She picked up her cell phone and called Celia. She hadn't talked to her in a couple of days. Even though Sarah had a hard time understanding how Celia could have lied to her for so many years, she still cared about her. It had been the two of them for so long and Celia had taken care of her the best she could.

Celia had truly loved John Welch. That's the only explanation for her agreeing to raise his child from an affair with another woman, Jasmine, Sarah and Serena's mother. Sarah didn't remember Celia ever dating. Celia worked as a waitress and she flirted with the men, but none ever came to the house or stayed over. If she saw anyone, she did it discreetly. As an adult, Sarah realized how lucky she was to have had someone to raise her with those kinds of morals.

"Hi, Celia, it's me." In the background Sarah could hear parakeets chirping. Growing up, that was the first sound she heard in the mornings and the last she heard at night. Celia loved parakeets and had raised and sold them for as long as Sarah could remember, spending many weekends traveling to shows or fairs selling the birds. She smiled as she thought of Aurora's obsession with bridge and Celia's with parakeets.

"Hey, honey, it's good to hear from you. I just got back from a fair and I did really well."

"That's great. You doing okay?"

"You know me, honey. I just keep going. When are you coming over?"

This was a big problem—dividing her off time between Aurora and Celia. "Tonight I'm exhausted, but

Gran has another bridge game on Wednesday. I'll come over then.''

''Why does Aurora have to be out for you to come here?'' Sarah could hear the resentment.

Before Sarah could respond, Celia added, ''That sounded bitchy. Aurora is your grandmother and I'm just someone who raised you. But I did what John and Jasmine wanted me to do—take care of their children. I wasn't financially able to take both of you and I was glad when Henry offered to take Serena. At the time I did what I thought was best.''

''I know, Celia.'' Sarah would never fully understand what happened back then and she had a lot of feelings about her parents, grandparents and Celia to work through. ''How about if I come over tomorrow after work and you can fix your spaghetti and meatballs?''

''Oh, honey, I would love that.''

''Good. I'll see you then.''

Sometimes, Sarah felt like a wishbone, with Aurora pulling from one side and Celia from the other. She had to get her life in order before she completely snapped.

Walking through the back door, she wondered what it was about this house that made her feel she needed to be here. She should have been raised here with Serena, she told herself so many times. But it was more than that—it had to do with her mother. Jasmine had grown up here and Sarah wanted to feel some connection to the woman who had given her life. So far she hadn't found anything in common with the rebellious Jasmine who'd run away to live with a man old enough to be her father.

In that instant she realized that her getting involved

with a cop on an undercover mission was just as impetuous and dangerous. Though the thought was frightening, she was uplifted by it. A lot of things became clear in that moment. She was searching for her roots, roots that gave her security, an identity of who she really was.

No. She knew who she was, but the day she found out she had a twin and a grandmother had changed all that. Now she was striving to be accepted. By whom? She didn't honestly have an answer—it was just the way she felt.

She groaned and went into her study, removing her jacket and kicking off her shoes. When she'd paid off the note on the house with Greg's insurance money, she'd done it because she'd wanted Gran to be able to stay in her home. But was there more to it? Had she done it so Gran would love her, maybe as much as Serena? There it was, out in the open. Now she had to face it, deal with it and move on.

She sat on the sofa. Was she struggling to make ends meet, to keep this house up so Gran would love her? Yes, that was it—she couldn't lie. She desperately needed her grandmother's love.

Sarah was sure Serena loved her, knew what that kind of sisterly love was like. It reached empty, hollow places in her, but she was never sure about Gran. Sometimes she felt like a substitute Serena.

Again, she thought, she might be like her mother. Jasmine never felt loved by Aurora. Why was she thinking these things? Why was she making herself miserable? Sarah and Gran had a good relationship.

She got to her feet and picked up the mail from her desk, where Gran had left it. She wasn't analyzing herself anymore tonight. Now she was going to look at the positive side, the good feeling of having a family.

"Bills, bills, bills," she mumbled, going through the mail. "What's this?" She placed the bills on the desk and looked at the business-size envelope with her name scrawled across the front. She reached for the letter opener and sliced through the top and pulled out a letter. Her heart jackknifed into her throat as she stared at the frightening words.

Counsel the little girl real good, Sarah baby. 'Cause you're next.

CHAPTER SIX

SARAH COULDN'T BREATHE. She couldn't move. All she could do was stare at the horrifying message, suspended somewhere between hell and the memory of Rudy Boyd. Her hand trembled and the letter fluttered to the floor.

That's what he'd called her—Sarah baby—and she knew the letter was tied to him in some way. From the deepest recesses of her mind, a place she kept locked, his voice surfaced. *Sarah baby, take your clothes off. Sarah baby, show me all the moves you'll make tonight. Sarah baby, I'll never let you go. Sarah baby. Sarah baby.*

Oh God! Oh God! Oh God! All the terror, the revulsion of that time engulfed her and her body began to tremble violently. Then just as swiftly, her newfound strength kicked in and she methodically began to gain control. *No. No. No.* Rudy Boyd was not getting to her again.

She grabbed the phone. She wasn't even aware of what number she'd dialed until she heard a voice say, ''Dallas police station—narcotics.''

Narcotics. She'd called narcotics in Dallas and she knew why.

''Dan—Daniel Garrett, please.''

''I'm sorry. He's out. Can I take a message?''

"Yes. Yes. Tell him to come to Sarah Welch's house immediately. It's urgent."

"Can I help?"

"No. Please send Daniel." She hung up the phone and stared at the paper on the floor. Where did it come from? Who would do this to her? Rudy Boyd was in prison, but could he have mailed the letter? Daniel would find out. Daniel would take care of this.

"Stay calm. Stay calm," she kept repeating to herself.

DANIEL'S CELL PHONE buzzed and he picked it up.

"Sarah Welch is looking for you. She called the station a few minuets ago. Said to come to her house. It's urgent."

"Did she say what it was about?"

"No. I asked if I could help her, but she said no. She wanted you."

"Thanks, Kevin."

Daniel clicked off wondering what the hell that was about. They'd agreed to stay away from each other and now she was calling his work asking to see him— at her house. That didn't make sense. Something had to be wrong. He roared onto the freeway and headed for Fort Worth.

He'd been to her home many times before during the trial and the appeal, so he found it without a problem. He rang the doorbell and waited. When she opened the door, he noticed the transformation Russ had mentioned, but he zeroed in on the fear in her eyes. It was almost like the first time he'd seen her— the day he and Ethan had rescued her from Boyd.

He stepped inside. "What's wrong?"

She turned and walked through the living room into

a study. He followed. She pointed to a paper lying on the floor. He knelt to see what it was and he now understood her fear.

"Where did this come from?"

"It was in…in my mail. Here's the…"

"Don't touch anything." He stopped her, got to his feet and pulled out his cell phone.

Sarah heard him talking to someone at the police station and knew officers would be all over the place in a matter of minutes. Her legs felt wobbly so she walked into the living room and sat on the sofa. She'd been feeling so good and now she could feel herself freezing up, the coldness returning.

No. No. No. She wouldn't allow herself to sink back into that deep freeze of emotion. She could handle this. Daniel was here. She could get through this.

Daniel came in and sat beside her. "Are you okay?"

No. I'm not. But she couldn't get the words out.

"Stupid question, huh?"

She stared into the dark warmth of his eyes and saw the concern she used to loathe. But today she welcomed it, needed it. She'd been so unfair to him.

"I'm sorry, Daniel. I said some hateful things to you and I—"

"You don't have to explain anything," he interrupted her.

She didn't. That's the type of man he was—forgiving, loyal and incredibly kind.

"The letter was in with your other mail?" he asked.

"Yes. I guess Gran got it out of the box this morning." She looked down at her hands. "That name is what he used to call me. I know he's in prison, but I can't shake the feeling that Rudy Boyd is behind this.

Is he allowed to mail letters?'' She tried to calm the nausea in her stomach.

He took a deep breath. ''It doesn't have a post-mark.''

Her eyes flew to his. ''What? You mean someone hand delivered it?''

''Looks that way.''

The nausea became a rolling tide and she jumped up and ran into the bathroom in her study.

Daniel ran after her, but he stopped at the door feeling a little sick himself. He looked down at the letter on the floor and the sickness turned to anger. He'd get the bastard if it was the last thing he did on this earth.

The doorbell rang and Daniel went to let the officers in. Russ burst through the door like a cannonball.

''Where's Ms. Welch?''

''She's in the bathroom and she's not feeling well, so go slow and go easy.''

''Okay, Daniel. You're starting to get in my face again.''

''I'm gonna do a lot more than get in your face if you do anything to upset her.''

The two men measured each other then Russ said, ''Okay. This is a big break and we have to make the most of it. Where's the letter? The forensic team is here to dust for prints.''

Daniel and Russ went into the study and Russ read the letter and glanced at the envelope. ''Warning his next victim. The other rapes and murders were in Dallas. This is Fort Worth. This doesn't add up.'' He glanced at Daniel. ''What do you think?''

''I think something stinks and Rudy Boyd is connected to the smell. 'Sarah baby' is what Boyd used to call her.''

The technicians entered the room and Russ gave them explicit orders on what he wanted done. Daniel motioned for Russ to come into the living room.

"He knows where she lives," Daniel said. "We have to put her in protective custody."

Russ scratched his head. "I'm not exactly sure who *he* is—the rapist or one of Boyd's soldiers."

"That's crossed my mind," Daniel admitted. "Boyd had a group of young men who would do anything for him. Remember how many of them were in the courtroom when he was sentenced to die? I'll get the name of every one of those hoods who were there that day. But if it's the rapist, then that means he's watching Miss Wallace's room. Get a guard on her immediately. Maybe the rapist thinks she can identify him—who knows? Either way we have to guard both women until we find this bastard."

"I agree. I'll call for a guard on Miss Wallace and since we're out of our jurisdiction here, the lieutenant will have to let the Fort Worth police know what's going on. Then I'd like to talk to Ms. Welch."

"No," Daniel said sharper than he'd intended. "She doesn't know anything. She just came home and the letter was in her mail."

Russ frowned. "I'm lead detective and if I want to question her, I will."

"No, you won't." Daniel clenched his jaw, then added, "If you have a problem with that, call the lieutenant. Sarah's been through enough and you're not badgering her as long as I'm on this case. I'll question her and you can be present, but that's it."

Russ eyed him strangely. "You said there's nothing between you and Ms. Welch. I think you lied."

"I saw what she went through with Boyd and right

now she just needs a little understanding and compassion.''

''And you're more than willing to provide that, huh?''

''Stuff it, Russ.'' Daniel brushed past him and went back to the study to see if Sarah was out of the bathroom.

SARAH WIPED HER FACE with a wet washcloth and stared at herself in the mirror. She hardly recognized the frightened woman looking back at her. *Not again. Not again.* Fear was not doing this to her again. She was stronger now and she wasn't letting that emotion take control and debilitate her—like before. She was fighting back and she welcomed the anger charging through her. No way was she going to be a willing victim.

She took a long breath and opened the door. Several police lab technicians were dusting for prints. The letter and envelope were now in a plastic bag. The techs nodded at her and she walked around them to the door, looking for Daniel. She saw him standing in the doorway.

Daniel came toward her. ''Better?''

She bit her lip. ''Yes.''

He glanced at the people in the room. ''Let's go to the kitchen where we can talk.'' Taking her arm, he guided her through the living area. He stopped at the built-in bar and poured something in a glass, then they continued to the kitchen. She saw Russ out of the corner of her eye, talking on the phone. The last thing she wanted was to have to talk to him.

She sank into a chair at the table. Daniel placed the glass in her hand.

"Drink it. It'll help to calm you."

She sipped the dark liquid. It was some of Gran's best brandy, only served on special occasions. She supposed this qualified.

Daniel pulled up a chair. "We have to discuss some things."

"Okay." She took a big swallow.

"It's not safe for you to be here now, so we have to put you in protective custody until we catch this guy."

"Like before?"

"Yes," he answered quietly.

"But I have commitments, clients to see. I can't just run away and hide."

"I'm sure Dr. Mason will take care of your clients until this is over."

Sarah fidgeted with her glass, remembering the seclusion and isolation of the hotel room as she'd waited to testify at Boyd's trial. He'd threatened to kill her so she'd had to be kept safe. Even though she was being guarded, Boyd had tried to get to her. In the end his guys shot several officers and Ethan. She *hadn't* been safe.

She raised her eyes and, as if Daniel could read her mind, he said, "I know the last time ended badly, but this time no one's getting near you. Trust me."

"You can't make that promise because you don't know *who's* doing this."

Daniel looked away. "You're right. I don't and we've never found the snitch in our department." She could see how heavily that weighed upon him. His gaze swung back to her. "I can only promise to do my best. If you can't trust me…"

"I trust you," she said in a rush, and his eyes

caught hers. In that instant, five years of tension and resentment came to an end. They both knew it.

"Thank you," he replied. "I'll handle this personally. Very few people will know where you are." He paused. "Now you have to call Serena and make arrangements for your grandmother. It's not safe for her to stay here, either."

Sarah swallowed. "I don't understand why this is happening."

"I don't, either, but we'll get through it."

She liked the way he said *we*. The last time she'd been under guard, she'd had Serena with her because they looked so much alike the police were afraid that Boyd's goons would mistake her for Sarah. This time she would be alone. She'd relied upon Serena's strength, but now she'd have to rely upon herself…and Daniel.

She took another big swallow, the brandy burning as it went down. But it also bolstered her.

Daniel handed her a phone. "Call Serena. I'll be in the other room making arrangements."

"Thank you," she said, gripping the phone.

DANIEL WALKED INTO the living room and Russ poked a phone at him. "Lieutenant Tolin wants to talk to you."

"Yes, sir," Daniel said into the mouthpiece.

"I've talked with the Fort Worth P.D. and they'll help us any way they can. I've also posted a guard at the hospital so bring Ms. Welch in and I'll call Rob, who handles protective custody."

"No, sir. I'll guard Ms. Welch personally."

"Excuse me?"

"The last time this happened to her several officers

and Ethan Ramsey were shot because there was a leak in the department. I want to make sure that doesn't happen again. The only way to accomplish that is to do it myself."

"Lieutenant Bauer and I need you on this case instead of baby-sitting. We have qualified people to do that."

"But she doesn't trust them. She trusts me and I think the police department owes her that. Besides, we still don't know who leaked the location of her hiding place before Boyd's trial."

"Daniel…"

"We can't put her through that again and we can't guarantee her safety by putting her in the system. Bill, please let me do this."

For a long moment, Daniel heard nothing but silence.

"This goes against all the rules and I don't know why in the hell I'm even considering this. It isn't protocol—we could both lose our jobs."

"Because it could save her life."

There was silence again, then, "Okay, Daniel, but I need you to help Russ during the day. Pick someone you trust to guard her during that time. And, of course, I'll have to clear this with the chief."

"Thank you, sir." His chest expanded with relief.

"But, Daniel, I don't want any screwups like before. No one, even myself, is to know where she's being kept. This is a little unorthodox, but in this case I don't see any other way. I'm trusting you implicitly. Just try not to get too emotionally involved with Ms. Welch."

Too late.

"Yes, sir," he answered instead.

"Do you have an officer in mind that you feel is beyond reproach—someone you can trust?"

Daniel thought for a minute and knew he didn't want anyone on his squad or on the homicide squad. It had to be someone fresh without any connections to the first case. "Yes. Chad Thomas."

"He's a patrol cop." Surprise sharpened Bill's words.

"Yes, sir, but I've known him since he was a kid. I helped him get into the academy. He's smart, reliable and one of the best cops I've seen in a while."

"Okay. You got him."

"Thanks. Could you send him to Sarah's house?" Daniel gave the address. "And have him come in plain clothes, but bring a uniform with him. Cap, too."

"Sure."

"And can you make arrangements for me to see Rudy Boyd?"

"What the hell for?" the lieutenant barked.

"I have reason to believe that this note is a message from Boyd. The answer to everything that's happening lies with him. I'm certain of it. He likes to brag and seeing me face-to-face will be an opportunity he can't resist. He might let something slip—something that will help us solve these rapes."

Daniel heard a long sigh. "Dammit. I think Boyd is somehow connected, too. I'll make the arrangements, but wrap this up as fast as you can. We're getting a lot of flack on this thing."

"I will."

"Keep me posted and try your best to get along with Russ."

"Yes, sir."

"What did he say?" Russ asked as soon as Daniel clicked off.

"I'm taking her to a safe place with one guard."

"Where?"

"The location won't be available to anyone."

"Why the hell not?" Russ objected.

"Because of what happened the last time, I'm not taking any chances."

"Are you saying I can't be trusted, Daniel?"

Daniel sighed. "Put your ego away. It's getting in the way of this investigation. If you have a problem with the way things are being done, call Lieutenant Bauer."

"You really piss me off."

"Yes. We're both aware of that. Now let's get back to work."

"Well, Daniel, since I'm not allowed to speak with Ms. Welch, there's not much else I can do here. Joel and I are going to apply some pressure to Brian Colley and see what comes up."

"In the morning I'm making a trip to Livingston to see Rudy Boyd," Daniel told him.

"Because of the wording in the note?"

"Yes. By talking to him, I think I can get a feel for how he's involved in this thing."

"You're probably right," Russ conceded. "In the meantime, I'll cover all the bases here."

"Good. Maybe by tomorrow night we'll have some answers."

"Would you like for us to leave a guard at the door?" Joel asked.

"No. It's best if everyone left." Daniel was hoping everyone would be gone by the time Chad arrived.

"You're taking a helluva risk," Russ snapped.

"Yes, Russ. I'm aware of that."

Fifteen minutes later, the techs and officers were gone from the house. Daniel walked into the kitchen and saw that Sarah was still on the phone.

"No, Serena," Sarah was saying. "You can't come here. It's too dangerous."

Sarah turned to look at him. "Daniel's here. Why don't you talk to him?" She gave him the phone, obviously having no luck convincing her twin.

"Hi, Serena."

"Daniel, please convince her to come with Gran. She can't go through this alone."

"She's not alone. I'm here."

"Daniel." He could hear the frustration in her voice.

Ethan came on the line. "Sorry, Daniel. Serena's not taking this well."

"I can tell, but assure her that it's not safe for Sarah to be in Junction Flat with your family. It could endanger everyone."

"I'll try to get that point across to Serena."

"Good. I'll have Mrs. Farrell on the next flight out of Dallas. I'll call back and give you an arrival time."

"Thanks, Daniel, and don't let anything happen to Sarah."

"I'll guard her with my life."

"I know you will."

Daniel hung up. "Serena's a little upset."

Sarah tugged both hands through her hair. "Sometimes it's hard to believe that someone loves me that much."

"Why?" he asked with a puzzled frown.

Before she could answer, the door opened and Aurora walked in. She laid her purse on the table and smiled at Daniel.

He smiled slightly, noting Mrs. Farrell's elegance. Her white hair was coiled neatly at her nape. Her clothes were impeccable, as were her manners. Sarah would someday be the same, Daniel thought. She already possessed a grace unlike any woman he'd ever seen, except maybe Serena.

"There were a lot of police cars at the intersection," Aurora said. "Is something going on?"

Sarah put an arm around her shoulders. "Let's go into the living room. I have something to tell you."

Daniel stood behind the sofa as Sarah told her grandmother what had happened.

Aurora threw her arms around Sarah. "Oh, no, darling. This can't be happening to you again."

"I'll be all right, Gran, but I have to go into protective custody for a while."

"You mean, stay in a hotel or something?"

"Yes."

"Then I'm going with you. I don't want you to be alone."

Sarah was shocked. She never expected Aurora to make that offer. "You can't, Gran. It's too dangerous."

"I don't care. You need me and I'm going to be there for you."

"Oh, Gran." Tears sprang from Sarah's eyes and she couldn't stop them from rolling down her face. Earlier she'd questioned her motives for trying to keep this house, for trying to keep Gran comfortable, wondering if, in Gran's eyes, she was a substitute Serena. Now she knew she wasn't. Her grandmother loved her and any resentment that lingered from the past was completely gone. Because she knew for sure, the tears flowed faster.

Aurora held her. "Darling, please don't cry."

Sarah pulled back and wiped away tears with the backs of her hands. "I'm sorry."

"Now what do you have to be sorry for?" Aurora got to her feet. "Come on, let's go pack our things and this nice man will take us somewhere safe."

Daniel stepped in then and his voice sounded hoarse. "Mrs. Farrell, that's not possible. Arrangements have been made for you to visit Serena."

"Serena? She lives in a small country town. What will I do there?"

"Visit with your granddaughter, Ethan and Jassy," Daniel replied.

"Yes, I would enjoy that. But no one plays bridge in Junction Flat."

Sarah chuckled through her tears. "Gran, I love you."

"I love you, too, Sarah."

For the first time Sarah believed that, really believed it. Through the turmoil, it made clear all the confusion inside of her. She wanted to be loved and she was. Now she could face this nightmare.

"Mrs. Ferguson plays bridge," Sarah reminded her.

"Yes, she does, doesn't she?"

"See? It won't be so bad in Junction Flat and Jassy will keep you entertained."

"But I don't see why I can't go with you. You don't need to be alone at a time like this."

Sarah raised an eyebrow. "You can't play bridge if you're with me."

Aurora waved her hand, her diamond rings catching

the light. "That doesn't matter. As long as you're safe, I'd give up bridge for the rest of my life."

Sarah bit her lip, unable to speak. Daniel stepped in again.

"Then, for Sarah, pack your bags and say goodbye. Someone will take you to the airport soon."

Aurora looked at Sarah. "Is this what you want?"

"Yes, Gran. Thanks for offering. It means more than you'll ever know, but I want you somewhere safe."

"I want you safe, too," Aurora cried, and the two women clung together. Sarah quickly gathered herself and took Gran's hand.

"I'll help you pack."

While Gran called her friends to let them know she'd be gone for a few days, Sarah called Karen on her cell phone to apprise her of the situation. She was shocked, understandably so, but offered Sarah all the time she needed and promised to take care of Sarah's clients, especially Brooke Wallace. Sarah told Karen she would be calling Brooke, though. She wouldn't desert Brooke without a word. Sarah then called Celia, who became very upset, ranting and raving about the Dallas police and their incompetence.

"Celia, it's not their fault," Sarah told her. "They're doing everything they can to keep me safe."

"Honey, I'm just so worried. I may not be your real grandmother, but I do love you."

Sarah closed her eyes suddenly feeling so much love that she had trouble breathing. "I know, Celia. I love you, too. I'll call you as soon as I can."

"Okay, honey, you be careful."

Sarah clicked off, staring at the phone. Aurora and Celia loved her, but in different ways. That difference didn't lessen the strength—it only made these two women very special to her.

Thirty minutes later, Aurora and Sarah were clinging to each other at the front door where two officers were waiting to take Aurora to the airport.

Aurora turned to Daniel. "Take good care of my granddaughter, Detective Garrett, because if anything happens to her, you'll have to answer to me."

"Yes, ma'am, I'll remember that."

As Sarah closed the door she turned to stare at the man standing behind her. She would now put her life in Daniel's hands, a man she'd resented for so long. It surprised her that it was so easy, but she trusted him—of that there was no doubt. After tonight, her life would never be the same again and neither would her feelings for Daniel.

CHAPTER SEVEN

AFTER GRAN LEFT things happened so fast that Sarah didn't have time to think. She had just finished packing a small overnight bag when a young officer arrived. Daniel introduced him as Chad Thomas. Tall, blue-eyed Chad didn't look old enough to be a policeman, but after a few minutes Sarah could see he was all business.

Daniel gave her a policeman's uniform to put on. If someone was watching the house, he didn't want them to see her leave. The uniform was big, but she made do, belting the pants tightly at the waist and tucking her hair beneath the cap. The three walked from the house to the garage where Daniel had parked his car. He got into the driver's seat with Chad at his side and she took the back seat. They'd left some lights on in the house to make it look as if she was still at home. Daniel backed out and headed into the night.

He drove to the Dallas police station where they changed cars. Daniel drove and drove, getting on and off the freeway several times. On Daniel's instructions, Sarah removed the uniform to reveal her regular clothes underneath as he drove up to a large motel. Chad went in to get a room.

Sarah had seen the motel many times on her drive from Fort Worth into Dallas each day to work. But she'd never been here.

"Are you okay back there?" Daniel asked.

"Yes."

Daniel could see her through the rearview mirror. "It would be best to remove the cap, too. Don't want you looking suspicious."

"Or ridiculous." She shook her hair loose. "I just forgot about it."

Daniel smiled. At least she was maintaining a sense of humor. She was going to need it in the days ahead.

Chad came back and they went into the room. It was a large suite, a bedroom and a sitting area with a microwave and a small refrigerator. Sarah went into the bedroom with her carryall.

Daniel was talking to Chad, then Chad left.

"Where'd he go?" Sarah asked.

"Home to get some rest. I'll stay during the night and he'll stay during the day."

"Oh."

He reached into the inside pocket of his jacket and pulled out a small gun. Holding it in the palm of his hand, he said, "Take it."

She stared at the gun, then at him. "I don't know anything about guns."

"It's just a precaution. If someone gets past Chad or me, you'll need to defend yourself."

She'd occasionally moved Greg's gun from the table, the counter, the bath vanity—places where he'd leave it in her way. But she'd never fired one and her blood ran cold at the thought.

Tentatively she took the weapon and felt its weight in her hand.

"It's small and lightweight, but it will do the job." He pointed to a spot on the gun. "Just release the safety and pull the trigger."

She swallowed her revulsion. "Okay."

"Put it on your nightstand, then we need to go over some things."

She walked into the bedroom and carefully laid the gun down, hoping with everything in her that she would never have to use it. She then joined Daniel on the sofa.

"Now that you're here, you won't leave until this is over," he told her.

"I know."

"Never open the door to anyone. You shouldn't have to since Chad or myself will always be with you. No one knows about this location but the three of us."

"And you trust Chad?"

"Yes."

"Then, I'll trust him, too."

"Good. Why don't you take a shower and try to get some rest?"

Daniel watched her go into the bedroom. He shrugged out of his jacket, rolled up his white shirt-sleeves and leaned back to rest his head on the sofa as this awful day played through his mind. It had started out with plans of flying to France to get away...from Sarah. He could admit that now. For years he'd been hoping for a break in her demeanor, something to show that she'd forgiven him for Greg's death. That's what he needed from her—forgiveness. While he'd been waiting he'd slowly and reverently given her his heart. And she didn't want it.

He glanced around the room. This was like a page in his fantasy book—he was in a motel with Sarah Welch. But he never wanted it to be like this. Once again he found himself being her protector, and when it was over they'd go their separate ways, to separate lives. This time, though, he wouldn't fail her—there'd be no bloodshed unless it was his own. That was a vow he made to himself.

He reached for his cell phone and called Lieutenant Tolin to see if he'd arranged a meeting with Boyd tomorrow in Livingston, where death row inmates were housed, then he checked on Drew. There was no answer. He and Claude must be out, he thought. They went a lot of places. He didn't try Drew's cell phone because he didn't want to interrupt his evening.

Sarah came out of the bedroom wearing a big T-shirt and all thought left him. She curled up on the end of the sofa with her feet beneath her. She smelled faintly of lilacs and her skin glowed. An old familiar need kicked to life in his lower abdomen, a need that he'd been suppressing for too long.

"Are you going to sleep here on the sofa?" she asked.

"What?" Her question went right through his mind.

She patted the sofa. "Are you sleeping here?"

"I probably won't do much sleeping, but it folds out into a bed if I need it."

"I won't sleep, either," she said in a low voice, smoothing the T-shirt over her thigh.

He grabbed the small cooler he'd brought in. "How about something to eat? I had Chad pick up some stuff. I'm not sure what's in here."

He peered inside. "Soft drinks, distilled water, pretzels, candy bars, beef jerky and a couple of honey buns. Good God, the man's diet is atrocious."

"Doesn't matter. I'm not hungry."

He opened the pretzels as if she hadn't spoken and held the bag out to her. She took one and munched on it.

"Can we talk?"

"Sure," he answered, taking a pretzel.

"When I got the note, I called you without even thinking. I did it automatically because I knew you'd know what to do and you'd find out who had written it. I realize that's incongruous with what I told you the other night. You must think I have a lot of nerve calling you after the things I've said to you."

"No, not really. I was becoming too concerned about you and I had no right to be. When an officer does that, it's time to back off. That's why I decided to quit my job."

Her eyes found his. "But you didn't."

"I tried, but my lieutenant wouldn't let me walk away from this investigation."

"I'm glad. I don't think I could have dealt with Russ without your help."

Her words warmed him through and through. "Thank you."

She studied the hem of her T-shirt. "I need to tell you why I feel about you the way that I do."

"You don't have to." *He didn't want to hear it, not now, not ever.*

He busied himself getting bottled water.

"Please listen."

At the plea in her voice, he settled back on the sofa, staring at the pretzel and water bottle in his hands. "Okay, but if it's about Greg's death, I think we've covered all that."

"No we haven't. I blamed you for so long because someone wasn't there to help him, but you can't help someone who's lying to you. And Greg and I lied to you. It's taken me a while to admit that. I should never have been with Greg during that assignment and he shouldn't have allowed me to go. It was like this adventure we were going on together—it was exciting, delving into the unknown. But it turned into a nightmare that continues to haunt me.''

He didn't know what to say so he said nothing.

''It was easier to blame you than to take the blame myself. Lately I've been trying to analyze my feelings, to get through the bad stuff instead of suppressing it. Serena and I talked about it over the weekend and I'd like to tell you what I told her.''

''Okay,'' he said, hardly breathing.

''That day I passed out in Boyd's apartment, I came to with your head on my breasts. My robe was open and I wanted to pull it together, but I couldn't move my arms. I didn't know who you were—all I knew was that you were a policeman and I didn't want you to see me like that. I didn't want you to think of me in that way, either.''

''What way?''

She swallowed. ''Like a slut.''

He gasped at the shock of her words.

''Every time I saw you, even during the trial and the appeal, and you looked at me with those concerned eyes, I felt as if I was on that floor, naked, exposed and vulnerable. I hated it. Since then I've covered my body as much as I could.''

''Sarah…'' He placed the pretzels and bottle on the coffee table.

She held up a hand. ''It's not your fault I felt that way. You weren't the reason I was on that floor—I was. I'm to blame for everything that's happened in my life.''

''I'm sorry I made you feel that way.'' He rubbed his hands together. ''And don't be too hard on yourself. You're not to blame for anything that went wrong with the investigation. And for the record, the only way I've *ever* seen you is as the strongest woman I've ever known.''

"Thank you,'' she murmured, feeling almost vindicated by his words.

He glanced at her. ''You've changed your appearance. Does that mean you're feeling better about yourself?''

"Yes. That night at the hospital when you said I hadn't dealt with what had happened to me, it made me angry. Then Brooke asked me if she would ever lose the bad feelings she was experiencing. I should have been able to say yes without a pause, but I couldn't. I realized then that you were right and I had to do something. I decided I wasn't going to be a victim anymore.''

His eyes held hers. ''Your strength continues to amaze me. I noticed that from the start. Most women would be falling apart right about now.''

The pretzel she'd been playing with crumbled in her hand and she brushed its remnants onto the coffee table. ''I—I want to, but I have all these people who love me. I realized that for the first time tonight and that love empowers me. When I was small, it was just Celia and me and we moved a lot. It was difficult to make friends so I hardened myself to deal with the disappointments and the loneliness. I never let anyone get too close to me.''

She paused and Daniel let her talk. It was obvious she needed to do that, to avoid thinking about what had happened.

''We didn't have a lot of money, but I was determined to get an education. I went to college during the day and worked as a waitress at night. Working my way through college took me longer than most people to get my degree. I met Greg at the restaurant where I worked and it was love at first sight. With Greg I was able to open up and to let myself love and it was wonderful. But...but...when Boyd touched me, all that ended. I couldn't feel anymore. I was frozen inside. Once again I hardened myself against the harsh realities of life. I hated it when a man would look at me and if one accidentally touched me I felt as if I was coming apart at the seams. I'm a counselor and I know how unhealthy that is, but I was powerless to change it—until this weekend. And now..."

"Sarah..."

"I took a tiny step forward, but I'm spiraling back to where I was. I'm trying to fight it, but I don't want to. It's easier to be Colder Than Ice."

Daniel inhaled a hard breath. "You know what they call you?"

"Yes, and it's true. I wanted it that way. I didn't want any of the officers to look at me as a desirable woman. I couldn't handle it. The thought of being touched in that way is repulsive to me."

He moved closer, wanting to hold her, but he was careful not to touch her.

She ran her hands up her arms. "I'm not going back into that deep freeze of emotions. I will not do that to myself or my family."

He could see she was fighting the destructive feelings with everything in her and he admired her resilience and spirit. She was a remarkable woman. "Think about Serena and Jassy," he suggested.

"Yeah." She rested her head against the sofa, her

eyes closing. "Jassy gave me your kiss, but I knew it was for Serena."

In my dreams it's always for you. He wanted to say the words, but she was drifting off to sleep and he let her. It was where she needed to be, away from the nightmare.

He sat for a long time just watching her sleep, enchanted with the freckles sprinkled across her nose. He'd never dreamed she was so starved for love. Maybe that's what pulled him toward her—that need for love, a feeling he knew very well. Growing up in a wealthy family, he'd never had that feeling of being loved. He and Drew had spent their youth in private schools away from home. In the summers, they'd attended summer camps. The holidays were the worst. They were in the Caribbean, France or wherever their parents planned to be with friends. Christmases were never at home. Daniel didn't know what it was like to be a part of a big, loving family. Sarah didn't, either.

He knew that kind of pain—that's why he was so protective of Drew. He wanted Drew to know he had a brother who cared. The good thing that had come out of Drew's drug addiction was that it had pulled them together as a family, for a short amount of time. Muriel, their mother, had tried to take care of Drew, but soon the nurses, therapists and caretakers were brought in and Muriel was off with Dan, their father, on his many business trips.

Daniel thought that Sarah would sleep better in the bed and he was unsure of what to do. He didn't want to wake her up and he didn't know how she'd react if he touched her. Finally he scooped her in his arms and carried her to the bedroom. She nestled against him and he held her longer than he probably should have.

He laid her gently on the bed and pulled the sheet and blanket over her, resisting the urge to kiss her.

She stirred. ''Daniel,'' she whispered.

''I'm right here. Go back to sleep.'' *I'll never leave you.* He meant it.

He returned to the other room, removed his shoulder holster and gun and placed them on the coffee table, within easy reach. Sitting, he took off his shoes and stretched out on the sofa.

He was tired. Every part of him was drained and exhausted, but Daniel knew he wouldn't sleep tonight, wouldn't fully rest until the bastard threatening Sarah was caught. He turned onto his side and stared at the door and window. There was only one way in and one way out. That was good. It made guarding Sarah that much easier.

Tomorrow he'd see Boyd and hopefully find a connection that would solve this case. He had to solve it and soon. For Sarah.

AT FIVE-THIRTY in the morning, he got up and put his shoes and gun back on, then checked on Sarah. She was still sleeping so he didn't wake her. He had a honey bun and water for breakfast. He wouldn't have time to eat later.

A little before six there was a tap on the door. ''It's Chad,'' he heard and quickly opened the door.

Chad came in with a bag. ''I brought breakfast tacos and some other stuff.''

''I hope it's something she likes.''

Chad shrugged. ''I don't know what women like.''

''Fruit and green stuff I think.''

Chad smiled. ''I got apples and bananas.''

Daniel slipped into his jacket. "Good. Is there anything I have to go over with you?"

"No, sir," Chad replied. "I won't let anyone in the room under any circumstances, not even if the building's on fire."

Daniel nodded. "Just let her sleep. It's what she needs."

"I'll guard her with my life, Daniel, and I appreciate you giving me this opportunity. I won't let you down."

"I'll check in several times during the day, but if anything suspicious happens, call me immediately."

"Yes, sir."

Daniel left and called Russ. "Do you have anything?"

"I leaned heavy on Brian Colley and he finally admitted there was an older guy at the party selling heroin. He said he'd seen him at other parties, but doesn't know his name."

"That's crap."

"Yeah. That's why I have his ass down at the station. I'm leaning on him until I get a name or Mr. Colley will be spending some time in jail."

"He'll crack eventually," Daniel said. "I'm on my way to the airfield. Lieutenant Tolin has arranged for a helicopter to take me to the prison. I'll call when I get back."

An hour later he crawled out of the helicopter at the Terrell Unit at Livingston. He noticed heavily armed guards in the towers, guards at the entrance and guards on horseback trailed by bloodhounds. The place had an eerie quiet that Daniel tried to shake off as a guard walked up to him and escorted him to the warden. He shook hands with Ted Reson and took in the drab, stark office.

"What can you tell me about Rudy Boyd?" Daniel asked, taking a seat in a vinyl chair.

Ted placed a large folder in front of him. "That's filled with complaints filed by his lawyer."

Daniel flipped through the letters. There were complaints about his cell, his uniform, the roaches, the food, the water and the list went on.

"Evidently, Boyd thought this was going to be a four-star hotel."

"His gall is unbelievable." Daniel shook his head.

"Somehow Mr. Boyd feels he's going to be set free. He's an arrogant son of a bitch, as is his attorney, Arnie Bishop."

"How often does he see Bishop?" Daniel was well-acquainted with Arnie. He was a crooked defense attorney—willing to do anything for money.

"He comes quite often. He was here on Saturday."

"Does Boyd see anyone else?"

"No."

Daniel stood. "I'd like to speak with Mr. Boyd."

"The guard will take you, but you have to leave your gun here."

Daniel removed his holster and laid it on the desk.

"Good luck," the warden said as Daniel followed the guard.

They went down long corridors with hollow, echoing sounds. Turning a corner, they walked down a short hall. The guard stopped at a door and spoke into his two-way radio. The door opened electronically.

"They'll bring him through the other door," the guard said. "I'll let you out when you're through."

"Thanks," Daniel said, taking a seat in one of the

two metal chairs at a metal table, the only three items in the room. Everything here was steel, solid and secure, housing the dregs of society. Boyd was the lowest. He'd shot Greg in cold blood because he was a police officer. He would have eventually killed Sarah when he was through with her. The man didn't have a conscience or a heart.

Daniel braced himself for a meeting with the devil.

CHAPTER EIGHT

THE DOOR CLANGED open and a guard ushered Rudy Boyd into the room. He wore prison white and his arms and feet were shackled, but basically he was the same—same black hair, cold dark eyes and a mocking leer as if he knew something the rest of the world didn't. He hobbled to the empty metal chair and flopped down.

"Well, if it ain't Detective Daniel Garrett," Boyd snickered. "Aren't you a little out of your jurisdiction?"

"Your crimes are in my jurisdiction," Daniel replied with as much calm as he could muster.

Boyd leaned back and stretched his shackled feet as far out as he could. "Crimes? Now that's where you and I disagree. I was just giving people what they wanted, something to make them feel better, something to make them forget their problems."

"Heroin."

"Yeah. The good stuff. I only sell the best."

"And you shot Greg Larson because he was getting too close to nailing you."

Boyd's eyes darkened. "No one puts the screws to me. No one, not even you, Detective Garrett."

"Well, Boyd, I'd say you're pretty well screwed sitting here on death row."

The leer altered for a split second, long enough for Daniel to notice it. He'd hit a nerve.

"How's the lovely Sarah?" Boyd taunted, the leer firmly in place. "You seemed very attached to her during my trial and appeal."

Daniel's heart rate quickened, but he kept his expression blank. "Why are you asking about Sarah Welch?"

"She's a beautiful woman, hard to forget. Long legs, tiny waist, breasts made for a man to caress, porcelain skin and all that red hair. Mmm, mmm, what a picture. She's like fire and ice. You have to chip through the ice to get to the fire, but it's worth the effort."

"But you never got to the fire," Daniel reminded him, trying not to react, trying to play it cool.

The dark eyes blackened to fever pitch. "Because of you, Garrett, and you will pay for that in ways you can never imagine."

"Really?"

"Yes. You and your Keystone Cops."

"We got you and you're waiting for them to stick a needle in your arm."

Boyd leaned forward. "That will never happen. Never."

There was such confidence in his voice that Daniel had to go further. "Do you know something that I don't?"

"A pissant knows more than you, Garrett."

Daniel stood. "I know you're the lowest form of life and I know you have something to do with the young girls being raped and murdered in Dallas."

Boyd didn't deny it, just kept watching Daniel. Then he shook his head. "So sad—those beautiful young girls, their lives gone just like that." There wasn't an ounce of remorse in his voice or on his face.

"The heroin in the arm—that's your calling card."

"That is a bit suspicious, now isn't it?"

The needle in the arm hadn't been released to the press so there was no way Boyd could have known about it unless he'd had firsthand information.

Boyd lumbered to his feet, the chains rattling. "Have the D.A. put something on the table and I might help you."

The bastard—he was after a deal to save his rotten life. Daniel's stomach churned.

"No deals, Boyd."

"That's a pity, a real pity. Because if I die, a lot of young women in Dallas will, too." He shuffled toward the door. "Guard," he shouted. Then he looked back at Daniel. "Look after Sarah baby, won't you?"

Daniel restrained himself from jumping across the table and strangling the life out of him. That would come soon enough.

The door banged behind Boyd and Daniel called to the other guard and quickly left the prison. On the flight back to Dallas, his mind was buzzing. Boyd *was* behind the whole thing—that was very clear. All to save his sorry life. That wasn't going to happen, not on his time. He had to put the pieces together, and fast.

The only person seeing Boyd was Arnie Bishop, so he had to be the one carrying information to the outside. But to whom?

The helicopter landed and Daniel jumped in his car and headed straight for Bill's office. He would want to know what Boyd had said, as would the D.A. Daniel felt sure they wouldn't deal with Boyd. It would take a lot to overturn a death sentence.

He picked up his phone and called Chad. "How is she?"

"She's still sleeping."

"What? It's after twelve."

"I know, but you said to let her sleep."

Sarah was exhausted physically and mentally, but he worried that she was sleeping so long. "Have you checked on her?"

"Yes, sir. She was on her back, but now she's on her side."

For an insane second, Daniel was jealous that Chad was watching her. He quickly curbed such a ridiculous thought, and told himself he just didn't want Sarah to be uncomfortable. "You might pull the door closed a bit so she can have some privacy."

"Sure."

"Anything suspicious happen?"

"No. Everything's quiet."

"You did tell the people at the desk to leave the towels and linens at the door?"

"Yes, sir. I told them I didn't want to be disturbed for anything. The towels and linens are in a bag outside the door now."

"Okay. Look outside and make sure no one's around, then get the bag while I'm on the phone."

Daniel waited.

"It's done, sir."

"Good. I'll call later."

Daniel spent the next hour with Bill going over what Boyd had said.

"He's behind these murders and rapes," Daniel

said. "He's set it all up to gain his freedom. I feel that in my gut."

"He might be yanking your chain."

Daniel shook his head. "No. He knew about the needle in the arm and he's very smug and arrogant. He's confident that he won't be executed."

Bill tapped a pencil on his desk. "This is sick. I'll have to get with the chief and the D.A., but I can tell you right now that no one's going to deal with Boyd. We just have to keep this out of the press and find who's raping and killing these women for Boyd."

Daniel got up and paced back and forth. "I feel it all goes back to five years ago. We had a leak in our department and never found who that person was."

"Internal Affairs checked that out thoroughly and everyone was clean."

"They missed someone."

"Daniel…"

"Boyd knew our every move five years ago and he knows our every move now. He knows we're busting our asses to catch this killer rapist, but we still don't have a clue. He called us Keystone Cops."

"I don't like this." Bill grimaced.

Daniel knew he had to drive his point home to get Bill's approval. "We never found out how Boyd knew Greg was a cop. Sarah didn't know how he got the information. That means the snitch that was sneaking Boyd tips also ratted out Greg."

"Goddammit." Bill leaned back and tapped the pencil on the arm of his chair, watching it as if mesmerized. Suddenly he glanced up. "What's your plan?"

Daniel felt a moment of relief. "First, we need to put a tail on Arnie Bishop and do a background check on him to see if he's just Boyd's attorney or if he's something more. Then I'd like to go through the personnel records and do a background check of the officers that were here five years ago and are still here today, and that includes homicide.''

''Personnel records are confidential. What makes you think you can find something when Internal Affairs couldn't?''

''I don't know that I can, but I'm closer to the situation and if I look at each officer's background and his immediate family something might jump out at me—there has to be a connection to Boyd.''

''This isn't going to sit well with the officers.''

''It doesn't sit too well with me that there are two women dead, another in the hospital and yet another in hiding.''

Bill threw the pencil on the desk. ''I'll have to get this okayed by the chief.''

''Thanks, Lieutenant. I just need some time to put all this together.''

''How much time?''

''Four days.''

''Okay. You have four days. But you'll have to clue Russ in.''

Daniel ran both hands through his hair.

''You do trust Russ, don't you?''

''Right now I don't trust anyone, but I'll have to give Russ the benefit of a doubt.''

''Do this very carefully and try not to step on too many toes.''

''Yes, sir.'' Daniel turned toward the door as it opened and Russ walked in.

''I've been waiting for you to surface,'' he said to Daniel. ''How did it go with Boyd?''

Daniel glanced at Bill and he nodded. He went through the whole thing again.

Russ frowned. "I worked Greg's case, so will you be poking into my life, too?"

"Yes."

"And who will be checking you out?"

"I know I'm not the informant."

"I don't," Russ shot back. "So maybe I'll look into your affairs."

"Enough," Bill shouted. "You two will work together and solve this case as Lieutenant Bauer and I have decided. Understand? There's a lot to be done and we don't have time for this bickering. And to answer your question, Russ, I'll be looking into Daniel's affairs. Everyone is under scrutiny and I mean everyone. Now get out of my office. I need a damn antacid."

Outside in the squad room, Russ said, "That Boyd just keeps on pulling an ace out of his sleeve."

"Not this time. We're going to solve this and we have to do it together."

Russ scratched his head. "That's hard to do when you don't trust me."

Daniel faced him, knowing he and Russ had to resolve the tension between them. They'd clashed many times over Russ's attitude and methods, but Daniel felt Russ was a good cop. "Give me a reason to trust you."

Russ stepped back and seemed about to give one of his smart answers, then he did a one-hundred-and-eighty-degree turn. "I'm a cop through and through—just like you. I put my life on the line for people I don't even know and I never get a thank-you. My wife divorced me and took my kid and I only get to see her every other weekend. That is if I continue to pay the child support. My wages are crappy, the hours are lousy and I'm broke. If Rudy Boyd offered me money to put food in my kid's mouth, I'd turn it down and arrest his ass for trying to bribe a cop. That's just the way I am. I'm a little offensive sometimes, but I get the job done and no amount of money would ever make me tarnish the badge.''

Daniel knew that. Russ's personality needed an adjustment, but he was a diehard cop. He had to be sure, though.

"Then let's get to work," Daniel said as he walked to his desk. "Did you get anything out of Colley?"

"Not much. He said the older guy went by the nickname of Bear and he just showed up at the party. He likes the college crowd, especially the girls. I don't think the kid really knows who the man is, but I have him and several others looking at mug shots."

"Damn. A name would have been a great help."

"After he gets through looking, I'll have to let him go."

"Yeah. There's not much we can hold him on." Daniel took a deep breath. "So do you want to take Boyd's lawyer or do you want me to?"

Russ grinned. "Oh, I'll take Bishop. Been wanting to nail him for years."

"Okay, then," Daniel said. "I'll see if I can find a leak in this department."

"That sure goes against the grain."

"Yes. It kind of rubs me the wrong way, too, but I'll still do my job."

"Especially since Sarah's life depends on it."

Daniel glared at him. "Saying things like that makes me want to punch you in the mouth."

Russ raised an eyebrow. "Is it a lie?"

Instead of answering, he mumbled, "Get to work. I've got things to do."

Russ walked off with a snicker.

Daniel pulled out his cell phone and called the motel.

SARAH WOKE UP feeling rested and relaxed, then everything came flooding back and she trembled with mind-numbing reality. Yesterday she'd been feeling so great about herself and now... She sat up and pushed the hair away from her face, not letting the fear get to her. She noticed the door was ajar and she wondered if Daniel was out there. No. She remembered he'd said that Chad would be here during the day. Last night she'd poured her heart out to Daniel. She'd never shared that part of herself with anyone but Serena, yet she wasn't feeling embarrassed or uncomfortable. Talking was good for the soul. She told people that every day, but she'd never practiced her own advice...until last night.

Daniel had listened with such compassion. She didn't remember coming to bed—had she fallen asleep on the sofa? Daniel must have carried her here. That didn't embarrass her, either. She trusted Daniel. She trusted him with her life.

She swung her feet to the floor, hoping he'd be back soon, and went into the bathroom. A few minutes later she came out in jeans and a T-shirt and made her way into the other room. Chad was talking on the phone.

"Yeah. She's here now. Okay." He handed the phone to Sarah. "It's Daniel."

She quickly grabbed the phone, her heart beating a little faster. "Hi."

"Hi. How are you?" His voice, his concern, was soothing.

"I feel much better this morning."

"It's almost two o'clock."

"What!"

"I was getting a little worried you were sleeping so long, but it's what you needed."

"I suppose," she mumbled, hardly able to believe she'd been sleeping most of the day.

"I'll be back later."

"Okay. I have my cell phone and I was planning on calling Brooke."

"Are you asking or telling me?"

"A little of both."

"Go ahead." She heard laughter in his voice. "I know you're worried about her."

"Have you found out anything?" she asked, not wanting to let him go.

"We'll talk tonight."

"Okay."

She gave Chad the phone.

"I brought you a breakfast taco, but it's not much good now," Chad was saying.

"I'm not very hungry."

"I have fruit, too." He held up a banana.

"Thanks." She smiled slightly. "I'd like that."

She sat on the sofa and ate the banana and drank bottled water wondering how long she'd have to stay in this room. How long would she have to put her life on hold?

"Do you like to play cards?"

She glanced up. "Yes. My Gran is an obsessed bridge player."

"I don't know much about bridge. How about

poker? And not strip poker. Daniel wouldn't like that.'' Instantly he realized his faux pas and apologized. "I'm sorry. That was crass of me.''

"It's okay." He'd said it so innocently that it didn't bother her.

"Damn. Daniel's gonna kick my ass.''

"Don't worry. I won't tell him.''

"But I will. I don't keep anything from Daniel, even the stupid things I say or do.''

Sarah was taken aback for a second, but then realized why Daniel had picked Chad. He was honest and straightforward and totally dedicated to his job.

"Where are those cards? I'll see if I can kick your ass." She laughed and Chad seemed to relax.

They played and talked as if they'd known each other for years, but Sarah was acutely aware of his shoulder holster and gun. On the table was another gun and there was a bag on the floor that she knew contained more weapons and ammunition. She shivered and tried to focus on the cards.

Even as they played she could see that Chad's concentration was not on the game, either. He was attuned to every noise, every sound outside the door and she had no problem beating him.

She called Brooke and talked for a while. Brooke was glad to hear her voice and it helped Sarah, too, to talk.

The day dragged on and Sarah waited for Daniel.

DANIEL CALLED SERENA and Ethan to make sure Mrs. Farrell had arrived safely and to tell them Sarah was fine. He then drove to the hospital to check on Brooke, who said she'd had a long talk with Sarah and she felt better. He was impressed with Sarah's unwavering support of Brooke even though she herself was in trouble. But Sarah was so strong that he knew nothing was going to deter her now. She was a survivor in every sense of the word.

After stopping at his apartment to take a shower and change clothes, he went to see Drew because he didn't feel he'd be able to come back for a few days and he wanted to let Claude know that.

Drew and Claude were playing pool in the game room, a gift from their parents. When Drew saw him he ran and threw his arms around his waist.

"D-D-Danny, D-D-Danny," he said, his voice high.

"How are you, buddy?"

Drew looked at him. "I—I—I beat Claude."

"Way to go." Daniel gave a thumbs-up sign.

Claude walked over and Daniel saw that his upper arm was bandaged.

"What happened?"

"C-c-cat got him," Drew answered in an excited voice.

"I was helping a neighbor," Claude explained. "Her cat got stuck up a tree and I offered to get it down, then the damn thing scratched me. I won't be offering my help again."

"Maybe you should get it looked at," Daniel said. Beside the risk to Claude's health, Daniel wanted to make sure someone was here for Drew while he was tied up with this case.

"Don't worry. I've already been to the emergency room and got a tetanus shot—everything is fine. The cat's well taken care of, had all its shots, no worry of rabies so that's not a problem."

"Good."

"I—I—I go, too," Drew put in. "W-w-wanna play pool?"

"No, but thanks, buddy. I gotta go." He glanced at Claude. "Could I talk to you for a second?"

"'B-b-bye, D-D-Danny," Drew called, already back at the table.

"I'll phone you later," Daniel called back.

In the foyer, Daniel turned to Claude. "I just wanted to let you know that I won't be around for the next few days. You can always reach me on my cell phone if there's an emergency. Otherwise I'll be very busy."

"Does this have something to do with the rapes and murders I've been reading about in the papers?"

"Pretty much."

Claude shook his head. "So sad. I don't understand how someone can do that."

"Me, neither. So please take care of my brother and make sure he takes his medication."

"Drew always gets his medication. You don't have to worry about that."

"Thanks, Claude. We were real lucky to find someone like you. Not everyone enjoys the task of caring for a ten-year-old in a thirty-five-year-old body."

"He's just an overgrown kid is the way I look at it."

"Thanks, Claude," Daniel said again as he walked out.

"You just catch that creep," Claude shouted after him.

WHEN DANIEL WALKED INTO the squad room, the chilly atmosphere had nothing to do with the weather outside. The news had gotten around that he was checking them out. The men didn't like it. He sat at his desk and could feel their stares sear through him.

Daniel had worked with all these people for a lot of years, but he'd never been the bad guy, the one they didn't trust.

He glanced around at his team—Tom Hudson, Kevin Cates, Jack Meades, Will Nobles, Lee Olson and Hugh Dawson, who'd taken Greg's place.

Daniel stood. "Okay, listen up," he said, his voice ringing through the room. "We have a leak in this department. Right now I'm not feeling too good about that. Rudy Boyd seems to know every move that homicide and narcotics make. If anyone knows the reason for that I'd like to hear it. Otherwise your lives and mine will be thoroughly investigated and scrutinized until we find an answer. If you have nothing to hide, then you don't have a problem. If you do, then you'd better talk to me now."

"I'm not sure I can continue to work with someone who doesn't trust me," Kevin spoke up.

Daniel sat on the edge of his desk. "Glad you brought that up, Kevin, because I don't like to work with anyone I can't trust, either. But the truth is staring me in the face and I can't ignore it. I visited with Boyd this morning and he knows what's happening in our department. He's well aware of the rapes and murders and our inability to solve the case. He even knows about the needle left in the arm." He paused, glancing at each of the men, men who'd covered his back many a time. "Have any of you ever considered how Boyd found out about Greg? The snitch gave him that piece of information and as a result Greg was shot and Sarah Welch brutalized."

Will jumped to his feet. "I'm with you one hundred

percent, Daniel. Greg was my partner and I want to get the bastard who did this. My life's an open book and you can read about it all you want.''

"Thanks, Will.''

Lee got to his feet. "I'm with Will. My credit cards are maxed out but it's no secret around here how my wife spends.''

Someone chuckled.

One by one they got to their feet and Daniel felt a moment of pride that they were behind him instead of against him.

"Okay, then, let's get back to work. Will and Hugh, give Tom and Jack a hand with finding Freddie. It's crucial we find out who supplied drugs to that party.''

"You got it,'' Will said and slipped into his jacket.

Daniel saw Russ motioning to him from the doorway and he walked over. "What's up?''

"Got the lab work back,'' Russ said. "Nothing. No one's prints in Ms. Welch's house or on the letter that shouldn't be there.''

"Damn.''

"Got a tail on Bishop and by morning I'll have more info and then I'll pay him a visit.''

"Good. Things are rolling. How'd it go with your guys?''

"Like crap. Everyone's acting all hurt and mistreated, but I told them to stuff their attitude. We got a snitch in narcotics or homicide and until the bastard is caught, no one's getting special treatment or coddling, not even Daniel Garrett.''

Before Daniel could respond, Faith, from the records department came up to them.

"Detective Garrett, I've put the files in the small

conference room as Lieutenant Tolin requested. If you need anything else, just let me know.''

"Thank you, Faith."

She walked away and Russ stared after her. Faith was in her late twenties, blond and pretty.

"Pull your eyes back in your head," Daniel quipped.

"I might ask her out."

Daniel shook his head. "Now you're going to date every woman that catches your eye?"

"Well, I've been told my social skills are lacking and dating would improve that, not to mention the grouchiness."

"In your case, Russ, I don't think so." Daniel strolled away to the conference room with a smile on his face.

He stopped short when he entered the room. Boxes were stacked almost to the ceiling. "Oh, God," he moaned, wondering how he was going to get through this in four days. Four days to find a traitor.

Where in the hell did he start?

CHAPTER NINE

SARAH JUMPED when she heard the knock on the door. Chad leaped to his feet, gun held tight with both hands.

"Who is it?" Chad asked, his head against the door.

"Daniel."

Sarah's heart pounded faster. He was back. Chad opened the door and Daniel came in with a large plastic bag.

"Hi," he said, looking directly at her. "You okay?"

"Yes," she replied, wanting to run and throw her arms around him. The impulse shocked her. She told herself she was just so glad to see him, but she knew it was much more. Daniel was working his way into her heart, a heart she'd thought would never feel this way again.

He was talking to Chad but she didn't hear their words. For the past five years she'd wanted to get far away from Daniel Garrett. Now she wanted to get as close to him as she could and she felt embarrassed and excited at her own thoughts.

Chad grabbed his coat. "See you tomorrow, Ms. Welch."

She held up her hand in goodbye, not trusting her voice.

Daniel slipped out of his jacket and threw it into a

chair. He had on jeans and a black T-shirt, the dark brown shoulder holster in plain sight, but she was staring at the muscles in his arms, the strength and power that was such a part of him. His brown hair was getting long and it curled into the back of his T-shirt, giving him a roguish, tempting quality. Daniel was handsome, as Brooke had mentioned, and she was never so aware of that fact as she was now.

"Sarah?"

She realized he was calling her name and she glanced at his face.

"What's wrong?"

"Nothing," she lied.

"Don't lie to me. We can't get through this if we lie to each other."

She was sitting on the sofa and she pulled up her knees. "It's nothing really."

"Is it what Chad said about strip poker?"

She rolled her eyes. "Of course not. He didn't mean anything by it and I'm not that touchy."

"So why are you pale and nervous?"

"Daniel, just…"

"What is it?" he persisted with a doggedness she was beginning to associate with him.

She threw up her hands. "Okay. Okay. I'll tell you." She took a slow breath. "When you came in, I wanted to run and hug you and that's not my normal reaction…especially to you. I was a little shaken by it. That's all."

He hesitated, then took a seat on the sofa. "Good shaken or bad shaken?"

She rested her chin on her knees. "Good. That means I'm feeling, and I'm happy about that."

"But not too happy that you're feeling things for

me?'' She saw the hurt in his eyes and wanted to reassure him.

"You have to be the nicest man I've ever known and I realized tonight that I've never really looked at you. I've kept the past between us like a blindfold because I didn't want to see you. But I'm liking what I see now.''

He appeared dumbstruck and she couldn't believe it. This strong man whom she didn't think was afraid of anything had a vulnerable spot—fear of being hurt. It made him very appealing to her.

To put him at ease, she asked, "What's in the bag?''

"Dinner," he said. "I called Serena to see if Mrs. Farrell had arrived safely and to tell her you were hidden away and doing okay. While I was talking to her, I asked what you liked to eat so I picked up Cobb salad with sliced chicken breast and some chocolate-fudge ice cream, which I'd better put in the freezer.''

"That was so thoughtful," she said, watching him store the ice cream.

He sat down again and they ate dinner in comfortable silence. She didn't realize how hungry she was and the food was delicious.

"How's Serena and the family?" she asked, nibbling on the last piece of salad.

Daniel took a swallow of water. "I think there's going to be a revolt in Junction Flat.''

"Why?''

"When your grandmother arrived at the ranch, Alma Ferguson was there visiting Walt. Of course the conversation turned to bridge and Alma called a couple of her friends and they got a game going this afternoon. Walt and his lady friend had plans and he wasn't too happy about the new arrangement and stomped off to the barn muttering about bossy old women.''

''Oh, my.'' A bubble of laughter escaped her.

''Needless to say things are a little tense around the Ramsey household.''

''I can imagine. I wish I was there.'' She leaned back, trying not to get bogged down in maudlin thoughts.

Daniel got up for the ice cream, setting the carton between them. ''Sorry, I didn't bring anything to scoop it into, but I brought two spoons, so dig in.'' He handed her one.

They sat there like two children eating their favorite treat.

The silence stretched and she could see Daniel was troubled. They hadn't talked about what was on both their minds. It was something they had to do.

''How did it go today? Did you find out anything?''

He looked down at a spoonful of ice cream. ''Not really.''

By the hesitation in his voice she knew he was lying or didn't want to tell her something.

''A moment ago you said we shouldn't lie to each other.''

He stuck the spoon in the carton. ''It's just not something you need to know and—''

''Daniel,'' she interrupted, ''please don't keep things from me. I'm stronger than you think and I need to know.''

He raised his eyes to hers. ''I saw Boyd today.''

Her hand went to her mouth and trembled slightly, but she quickly fought the fear rising inside her and, with supreme effort, asked, ''What did he say?''

Daniel twisted a napkin while she watched him closely. He had a somber expression on his face.

"Daniel," she prompted. "What did he say?"

Daniel looked into her eyes and seemed to make a decision. What he told her next made her blood run cold.

"Oh, my God," she muttered. "He's having these young girls raped and killed to get a new deal, to save his life."

"That's what I got out of it."

"And the note to me." She swallowed hard. "Was it from him?"

"I think so. He had someone deliver it, but we don't know who."

"You believe someone in your department still has contact with Boyd or this person on the outside? That's why you're investigating everyone."

He nodded. "We'll unravel this one way or the other."

Sarah ran both hands through her thick hair. "I thought Boyd was out of my life. I thought he couldn't hurt me anymore."

"He can't, Sarah, and I know you won't let these mind games he's playing get to you. He hasn't taken into account your incredible strength."

She looked down at her toes. "When he held me prisoner in his apartment and he forced me to remove my clothes, he enjoyed watching my fear and my revulsion. And when…when he touched me I cowered away and wanted to die. He enjoyed that, too. I think if I had fought back he would have raped and murdered me. My weakness kept me alive because it excited him to have that power over me." She sucked air into her tight lungs, hardly able to believe she was telling Daniel that deep pain she'd shared with no one but Serena.

"Your strength will keep you alive now," he said in a throaty voice.

She lifted her head to stare at him. "And you."

"I'm just doing my job." He placed the lid on the carton and she knew it was much more than that, but it was clear he didn't want to talk about it.

"Do you think the D.A. will make a deal with him?" she asked.

"No. Boyd's sentence is a done deal. They're waiting for an execution date."

"But it can be stopped."

"Sure. By the governor. The D.A. doesn't have any control over that."

"He can appeal to the governor."

"Okay." Daniel held up a hand. "Let's stop speculating. You'll make yourself crazy."

"My skin feels as if I've been stung by a hundred bees and I can't shake that sensation."

"Let's talk about something else," he suggested.

"Yes. Let's." She wrapped both arms around her legs, staring down at her pink toenails. Raspberry delight—that's what she and Serena had chosen the day they'd gone to the salon. It seemed like a lifetime ago yet it had only been two days. That day they were happy and laughing. And Sarah wanted to stay that way—intended to stay that way.

She raised her eyes to his. "Tell me about yourself. I've known you for five years, but I know very little about you."

He got up and carried the remains of the meal to the trash. "What do you want to know?"

"Do you have family?"

"Parents and a brother here in Dallas."

"Is your brother a policeman, too?"

"No." A shadow crossed his face and he told her a story that saddened her heart.

"I'm so sorry," she whispered. "Is that why you became a police officer?"

"No. I was already on the force, but he's the reason I went into narcotics. I just wanted to get that scum off the streets."

"You're very good at what you do."

His eyes met hers and from out of nowhere she found herself asking, "Have you ever been married?"

He blinked and held up his right hand. "No, ma'am."

She grimaced. "I'm prying."

"I'm just teasing you." He smiled an engaging smile and her heart wobbled. "I haven't ever been married. I was engaged once, though."

"What happened?"

"I went on a raid and there was a shootout. She didn't know for a long time that I wasn't one of the officers hit. She completely fell apart and I knew we had problems. In the end she said she couldn't be a cop's wife. That's been almost ten years ago."

"Do you ever see her?"

"Yeah, every now and then. She married a banker, had a daughter, got divorced and is now a single mom trying to make it on her own."

"Do you ever think of getting back together?" She was prying again, but she couldn't help herself.

"Not for a second. In my twenties and early thirties I was blind to a lot of things, but at forty I have my eyes wide open and what I had with Marcie wasn't the forever kind of love. It died very quickly."

She looked down at her toes again, wondering how a person knew when love was real. She'd thought what she'd had with Greg was absolutely perfect.

"I thought I would love Greg forever, but it's hard for me to remember his face. I was so shattered by his death, but…"

"But what?" he asked.

"But now I get angry."

"Why?"

"Because he knew how dangerous his mission was and he still let me go along. I shouldn't have been there."

"No, you shouldn't have."

Again she was surprised at telling him this. She hadn't even told Serena. "I'm not blameless, though. I can be persuasive sometimes and Greg had a hard time saying no to me."

"I can imagine."

She raised her head. "Can you?"

"What?" His eyes jerked toward her as if her question startled him and she wondered if he realized he'd spoken out loud.

"I don't think you're listening to me."

"Oh, I'm listening." He walked to the window and pulled the curtain back slightly to gaze outside. "I get angry at him, too, for taking you into that situation. He must have been so blind in love that he ignored the dangers."

"That's just it," she said. "If he really loved me, why would he do that?"

He turned from the window. "I don't have an answer for you." All Daniel knew was that he would never expose her to that kind of danger, even it meant he'd never see her for the rest of his life. He didn't want to talk about Greg Larson anymore or her relationship with him.

He reached for his cell phone and handed it to her. "Call Serena. She's anxious to hear from you and it will make you feel better."

She quickly poked out the number and he took off his holster and gun, then removed his shoes. He tried not to listen to the conversation but he could hear the joy in Sarah's voice just talking to Serena and he was glad. He couldn't shake what she'd told him about Boyd, though. She'd been through so much and he felt an inner rage like he'd never felt before. He'd do anything just to ease her mind and in that instant he knew that he was way in over his head with Sarah Welch. He had been for a very long time.

The concern and caring had turned into something much deeper. When that had happened, he wasn't sure. Maybe it was when she'd showed such enormous strength after her ordeal with Boyd. Or maybe when he'd seen her courage on the witness stand. It could have been all those times she'd shot him those cold glances because inside he'd known she was falling apart. She was great at helping other people, but she didn't know how to help herself.

When she got the note from Boyd, he was the first person she'd called. He should be happy about that, but he wasn't, not completely. She'd called for his help, like he'd wished for so many times in the past when he thought that she needed someone. Of course, he would help her by solving this case. He just wished she needed him for something more than that.

She talked to her grandmother and Jassy, too, and her features were animated, her beauty captivating. She and Serena were identical in looks yet their personalities were quite different. Serena was outgoing and friendly, while Sarah was quiet and reserved. Sarah had an inner softness that she hid behind a shield. It was exactly as Boyd had said. She was a combination of fire and ice and the coolness was the first thing that everyone noticed. Oddly, it was just the opposite for Daniel. He noticed her inner strength, her love for her sister, that need for love and the great pain she took to make sure no one got near the real Sarah.

She clicked off and laid the phone down, a content look on her face. "Thank you," she whispered. "I needed that. I was going to call today, but thought I'd wait until tonight when Serena was home."

He eased onto the sofa and stretched his legs out in front of him. "Everyone okay?"

"Yes," she answered. "Jassy just couldn't understand why I had to work—that's what Serena told her. I think they plug Jassy into an electrical socket every morning. She's like a live wire."

"I noticed that. She has lots of energy."

"Gran said Serena wasn't like that and Ethan said he wasn't, either. They don't know where she gets her overactive personality from."

"Were you like that?"

"Good heavens, no. I was very shy. At times, I felt isolated from the world."

"I felt that way, too." He surprised himself, telling her this.

She sat cross-legged, facing him. "Did you?"

"Not exactly the way you were. My brother and I went to boarding schools and we spent very little time at home. It wasn't exactly an idyllic childhood."

"I always dreamed of having a real family, mother

and father, brothers and sisters—a Norman Rockwell painting type thing.''

"A simple, happy life," he remarked.

"Yes. I guess that's why I feel the need to hold on to Gran's house. I'm trying to find that happy family and that is so unrealistic.''

"But it's what you needed at the time.''

"Maybe," she admitted, brushing a speck of dust from her jeans. "I can't afford to keep it much longer. Serena says I need to sell and move into something smaller, but I've been so undecided, so torn.''

"Because you don't want to disappoint your grandmother?''

"Yes," she admitted again, and that forlorn voice got him. She was like a little girl lost, desperately trying to find her way home.

"Sarah, you do realize that if you sell the house, your grandmother will still love you.''

"I realized that for the first time last night when she offered to come with me.'' She blinked back a tear.

They stared at each other. He tried to hide what was in his eyes, his heart, but he knew he'd failed.

Sarah lost herself in the warmth of his brown eyes. She'd never noticed that he had the most beautiful eyes—like dark chocolate—warm, inviting and irresistible. She saw something else, too. Daniel cared about her...and it didn't bother her. She rather liked it.

"Dan—'' His name was cut off by a bumping at the door. Before she could catch her breath, Daniel was on his feet, gun in his hand.

"Go to the bedroom," he said in an urgent whisper. "Close the door and get your gun.''

She rushed to do as she was told even though she

was trembling uncontrollably. Picking up the gun, she tried to remember how Daniel had said to use it, but her mind was short-circuited by the adrenaline pumping through her veins. She peered through the slightly open door and saw Daniel pull the curtain back to look outside. He lowered his gun and she knew everything was okay.

She released a taut breath, laid her gun down and went back into the other room.

Daniel shoved his gun into his holster. ''It was the people next door. Must have been out partying and drinking because they couldn't find their room.''

She stood there staring at him and she had the same urge she had earlier, but this time, without a second thought, she acted on it.

She walked to him and slipped her arms around his waist. He stiffened and she whispered, ''Hold me.''

His arms tightened and she rested her head on his chest, listening to the staccato rhythm of his heart. In his arms she felt safe, secure and a lot of other things. She'd never met anyone like him before—willing to give so much of himself without asking anything in return. She'd been so confused about Daniel and their relationship. No. It wasn't that she was confused—she just hadn't wanted to admit that she felt anything for him. But when she'd looked into his eyes a moment ago and seen how deeply he felt for her, she couldn't deny any longer how he made her feel. Her arms crept up around his neck as she gave full rein to everything in her.

''It's okay, Sarah.'' His voice was hoarse.

She stood on tiptoes and kissed the throbbing pulse in his neck, feeling his tension, his shock, and it drove her on. Her lips trailed to his ear, across his cheek, then to his mouth. At the first tentative brush, he groaned and covered her lips with an explosion of senses. Her hands cradled his head and the kiss deepened, both giving, both taking, and Sarah let all that fire flow through her—Daniel's fire, warming the coldest part of her.

She pressed against him, needing to feel that closeness, that masculine body. The action didn't shock or repulse her and all she could think was that she wanted more.

Daniel's fantasies didn't measure up to the touch of Sarah's lips, her voluntary touch. He was drowning, going down so fast that he couldn't think—all he could do was feel and the feeling was everything he wanted it to be and more. He'd waited forever for a response from her and it had nothing to do with protection. It was all emotion and passion.

You're too emotionally involved.

From out of nowhere Bill's words squeezed through the passion and the cop in him quickly surfaced. He broke the kiss and stepped away, holding both hands up.

"I can't do this," he said, his voice husky.

Her lips were moist from his and her blue eyes were almost purple from desire, which turned to humiliation at his obvious rejection.

"You're in my protection," he hastened to explain. "I can't take advantage of you."

She tucked her hair behind her ear. "I kissed you," she reminded him.

He closed his eyes briefly to shut out her words and her beautiful face. "I know and that makes this even harder. Please don't take this as a rejection. It isn't, but I have to keep my head clear—for you and your safety. So please go to bed and close the door.'' *Lock it. Bolt it. Put a chair under the doorknob.*

Sarah turned and walked into the bedroom, closing the door behind her. Since her life was in danger, they couldn't get distracted by something so basic. She understood that. There would be time later to enjoy each other. Two days ago if a man looked at her, it upset her. If a man touched her, it paralyzed her. Now it excited her and she knew it was because the man was Daniel.

She sat on the bed and smiled. Finally she could see everything so clearly. For years she'd been yearning for love and with Greg she'd thought she'd found it. Then Greg had been killed and her nightmare began. She hadn't wanted to ever feel love again—that's why she had so many conflicting emotions about Gran and Celia. But they loved her and she could now accept their love wholeheartedly without resentment. That realization broke the lock from around her heart and she also could see Daniel more clearly. What she'd seen in his eyes over the years was a lot more than concern—that's what had really irritated her. She wasn't ready to accept anything on a personal level from him. She touched her lips. Now she was. Her smile broadened and she lay down, cherishing this newfound freedom.

Daniel fell onto the sofa and buried his face in his hands, restraining himself from following her. His ethics kept him rooted to the spot. The needs of the man in him kept him bound in turmoil.

Fear, desire and passion were closely entwined. He'd thought that many times in his career, but tonight for the first time he'd dealt with it in a way he never had before—personally. When they kissed again, he didn't want fear involved in any way. He wanted it all from the heart and he wanted all of Sarah.

As the darkness spread outside, he wasn't sure exactly when that would be. He stretched out on the sofa and *soon* ran through his mind like a repetitive word in a nursery rhyme.

Soon. Soon. Soon.

CHAPTER TEN

EARLY THE NEXT morning Daniel peered into Sarah's room and saw that she was sound asleep. Her red hair was splayed across the pillow and she looked lost in peaceful dreams. That's what he wanted for her—to find peace and happiness and that home she wanted. Maybe, just maybe, he was beginning to believe that he could be a part of it.

A knock at the door spun him around and he whispered outside the panel, "Who is it?"

"Chad."

Daniel undid the lock and let Chad in. He had a large bag of groceries.

"Did you get something she likes?"

"Yes, sir. Lots of fruit and yogurt?"

Daniel slipped into his jacket. "Good. Like yesterday, just let her sleep and open this door to no one."

"Yes, sir."

"I'll call later."

Daniel immediately drove to the police station and started the background check of each officer, sorting through their personal files. He learned more about the people he worked with than he'd ever imagined. He thought he knew them, but he didn't. Kevin had been married three times and paid child support for three kids to three different women. Lee's wife had been arrested for shoplifting years ago and Jack's wife had actually worked in one of Boyd's strip clubs as a waitress before Jack married her. That got his attention. Daniel didn't understand why none of this had been brought out five years ago. Evidently Internal Affairs didn't think it was relevant, or they'd checked it out and found nothing. This time, though, Daniel had to dig a little deeper.

Will knocked on the door and came in. "We got Freddie," he said.

"Really?" Daniel raised an eyebrow. "That didn't take you long. Where did you find him?"

"That sleazy bar he always hangs out in. Bartender said he's been there every day. Don't understand why Jack and Tom couldn't find him."

"He probably hid from them."

"Maybe," Will conceded. "He tried to get away from us and I had to run six damn blocks to catch him."

"Have you questioned him?"

"Yes, and he said he doesn't sell drugs anymore."

"Yeah, right," Daniel replied. "Keep pressuring him. Freddie doesn't take pressure well."

"Yes—"

Before Will could finish, Tom came in. "Heard you found Freddie." He spoke to Will.

"Sure did. He was holed up in that same old bar he frequents. Don't know how you missed him."

"Goddammit," Tom exploded. "We checked there three times."

"You didn't check very well," Will shot back.

The tension became tangible and Daniel spoke up. "Keep the attitudes under control. I want information out of Freddie now."

"Yes, sir," Will said and left.

Tom looked at Daniel. "I'm sorry. He wasn't there when we checked."

Daniel's eyes didn't waver from Tom's. "I'm taking your word on that, but if there's some reason you and Jack can't work together productively then I need to know."

"It's my fault, Daniel," Jack said from the doorway. "We spent a lot of yesterday tailing my wife. I think she's seeing another man."

"Dammit, Jack. We have a rapist and murderer out there and you've got you head in the clouds. I could relieve you of your duties for this."

"Please, Daniel. It won't happen again."

Daniel sighed. "It had better not. Now get back to work before I change my mind."

Jack walked out.

"Tom," Daniel called before he could follow. "Stop covering up for Jack—that's not like you."

"Daniel—"

"Just get to work—and I mean police work. Do I make myself clear?"

"Yes."

His whole department was falling apart and he felt this was only the beginning of the upheaval that was to come.

Russ came into the room looking a little worse for wear. His shirt and jacket were wrinkled more than usual and he had a growth of beard, which was a mixture of red and brown.

"You look like hell," Daniel said.

Russ dropped a folder in front of him. "You would, too, if you hadn't been to bed." He pointed to the folder. "Run your baby browns over that."

Daniel quickly read through the contents. "Well, I'll be a son of a bitch."

"Interesting isn't it?" Russ nodded. "It took some digging, but I found Boyd still owns some clubs in several alias names. Bastard hardly ever uses his own damn name."

"We discovered that five years ago," Daniel told him. "But I thought all his holdings were seized by the feds."

"He's a slick bastard. He managed to hide a lot of money and property. I went over that list of aliases you gave me and searched until my eyes were bloodshot, and lo and behold, this is what turned up. Boyd transferred ownership of one club to Arnie Bishop after the first rape and murder and another club after the second one."

"And for what in exchange I wonder."

"That's the big question. I watched Arnie's sorry ass last night hoping he'd meet someone who'd give me that clue. He sat at one of the clubs until after midnight talking to the bouncer, who we also have a tail on. He then went home to his mansion and I mean mansion—swimming pool, tennis court, gated privacy fence with a guard. He lives there with his twenty-three-year-old wife. He's fifty-six. Charming, hmm?"

"Yeah." Daniel closed the folder. "Bishop's in this up to his eyeballs."

Russ flopped into a chair and propped his feet on the desk. Daniel stared at the bottom of Russ's shoes.

"Do you know there's a hole in the sole of your right shoe?"

"Yep. Keeps me awake on these twenty-four-hour shifts."

Daniel shook his head. Getting to know Russ was

downright scary, with a little humor thrown in for relief. Russ was exactly what you saw, though—a hard-working cop getting the job done any way he could, regardless of other people's feelings.

"Doesn't it bother you?"

"Not as much as what Boyd and Bishop are trying to get away with. Have you come up with anything?"

Daniel knew he could trust Russ. He was unsure of a lot of things, but he was positive about that. "What do you know about Jack's wife?"

Russ shrugged. "Not much. Very good-looking, was a waitress I believe."

"A waitress at Bare Babes."

"Goddammit." Russ swung his feet to the floor. "Jack never mentioned anything like that and I used to have a drink with him every now and then when he was dating her. Evidently you didn't know about this, either."

"No. He never said a word during all the raids, during all of our investigations of Boyd."

"How're you going to handle it?"

"Very carefully." He didn't mention anything about Jack's breach of duties. He'd have to tell the lieutenant first.

"You find out anything on my guys?"

"Haven't gotten to them yet so I'll probably wait until I'm through before taking action."

"That's probably best." Russ stood. "I'm going home to take a shower and sleep for a couple of hours, then I'll get back on Bishop. Joel's watching him now. Have you checked on the Wallace girl?"

"Yes. Everything's quiet there. Will's questioning Freddie Frye to find out if he supplied the party. Other than that, it's quiet, and that has me worried. Something's going to happen and I hope we're ready.''

Russ's hand went to his mouth and Daniel realized the proverbial toothpick was missing.

Daniel raised an eyebrow. ''Lose your security blanket?''

''About four o'clock this morning I jerked awake and almost swallowed the damn thing, so I threw it away. I could sure use a cigarette.''

Daniel smiled and handed him a pencil. ''Chew on that until you find another.''

Russ took it, grinning. ''Are you saying my toothpick-chewing is less offensive than smoking?''

''You got it. And when you ask Faith out, don't have a toothpick or a cigarette in your mouth.''

Russ's grin widened. ''Haven't you noticed that when I have something in my mouth I don't talk as much.''

''Good point.''

Russ twisted the pencil. ''So you think I have a better chance with Faith than with Sarah?''

Daniel stared at him. ''Definitely. Sarah is off-limits.''

''To everyone but you.''

''Don't start,'' he said, knowing Russ was only trying to get a rise out of him. ''I'm not in a mood to get into it with you.''

''Hell, Daniel, arguing with you is the best part of my day.'' Russ moved toward the door. ''I'll catch you later.''

Daniel went back to his search.

SARAH'S MORNING went smoothly. She talked to Brooke and the police had her looking at more mug shots, but she seemed in good spirits. Her parents were taking turns staying with her and that gave the girl an added sense of security. Love had amazing powers, as Sarah was discovering herself. She'd felt alone most of her life, but now at this dark time she felt truly loved by her family. And fear could not defeat that. Nor could it defeat her appreciation of Daniel.

The day seemed endless. She played cards with Chad and thought about Daniel. She kept glancing at the clock, counting the hours until he was back. For years she'd ignored her feminine side; her looks and her attitude were all tempered by what had happened to her. At last she was finding her way back to the woman in her…all because of one special man. If she closed her eyes, she could still feel his lips on hers— tender yet strong, tempting an eager, natural response from her.

When he'd stopped, she was hurt at first, but she knew he was right. This time she was going to take it slow and enjoy the crescendo before the climax, so to speak. She'd savor all these new feelings until she was ready to express them. Now she couldn't wait for Daniel's return.

"Ms. Welch?"

"Hmm?" Chad's voice finally reached her.

"I'm waiting for you to draw a card."

She laid her cards down. "I'm sorry. My mind's not on the game."

"Yeah. It's not much fun with two playing." He gathered the cards and shuffled them. "You're a counselor, right?"

"Yes."

"Can I ask you a question?"

"Sure." She curled her feet beneath her.

"I'm dating this girl and she's getting possessive. She doesn't like me going out with the guys and sometimes I need that kind of break. When I'm not working, she wants me with her. I was thinking I was in love, but now I'm not so sure."

"Why not?"

"Because I don't want to live the rest of my life like that."

"Like how?"

"If I play basketball or go bowling with the guys, she cuts off sex for two or three days or until I apologize profusely."

"This girl is manipulating you to get what she wants. She's probably insecure about your feelings and the more time you spend with her, the more secure she feels. You need to talk to her honestly, tell her how you feel and why you need some guy time."

Chad fiddled with the cards. "I'm not good at talking."

"Oh, dear," she sighed.

"How do you know if you really love someone?"

"I'd be the smartest person on earth if I could answer that."

"But you have an idea," he persisted.

She gazed toward the door. "Well, when you want to be with that person more than anyone. When you think about them all the time and can't wait to see them. And when you're with them, you're happier, content and feel a sense of belonging."

Chad stared at her.

"What?"

"You sound as if you're in love."

She shifted nervously as what she'd said seeped into her heart. Did she love Daniel? It was only last Saturday when she'd told him to stay out of her life. Now she was feeling so differently. How could that have happened in so short a span of time? Because she didn't want Daniel out of her life—she just didn't want to deal with her feelings for him.

When she didn't answer, Chad asked, "Is there something between you and Daniel?"

Her eyes narrowed. "Why do you ask?"

"Daniel doesn't handle protective custody personally, so for him to be doing this I figure you're pretty special to him. And I've seen the way he looks at you."

"How's that?"

"Besotted."

She laughed. "I don't think that's how he looks at me."

"Then you're not watching."

She felt she needed to explain to Chad before his imagination ran away with him. "Daniel has been with me ever since they arrested Boyd and got me out of that awful place. He was there for the trial and the appeal, and I've probably leaned on him more than I should have."

Chad nodded. "Daniel's that kind of guy."

"We were talking about you and your girlfriend," she reminded him, needing to switch channels, not quite ready to share her feelings with anyone but Daniel.

"I think I've got it figured out."

"You have?" she asked in surprise.

"Yeah. The sex is great." He shuffled the cards again. "You can't build a relationship on that, though, and I sure don't look at her the way Daniel looks at you."

"Okay, Chad," she said with a secret smile. "Let's play cards before we get in too deep."

DANIEL READ THROUGH the files until his eyes burned and his back hurt, but he kept going. His only breaks were to call Chad several times. It seemed as if he and Sarah were getting along fine. That's how Sarah was; she was a great listener.

Late afternoon Will came charging in. "Freddie said a man called Bear has been doing a lot of the college parties lately."

"No name?"

Will shook his head. "Freddie said Bear was a sadistic bastard and he stays away from him. I think he's telling the truth. He doesn't know his real name."

"But he knows his face. Get him to go through some mug shots."

"After that I'll have to let him go. He didn't have any drugs on him when we arrested him."

"That's fine with me," Daniel said. "Keep an eye on him after you release him just in case he's stupid enough to be lying to us."

"You bet."

BY SIX O'CLOCK Daniel had a list of people to talk to in the morning. Several of the cops had money problems, but no one had a clear connection to Boyd except Jack's wife. There was no smoking gun and his head pounded with frustration. He still had nothing.

He closed everything for the day and headed for the motel. He wanted to go to his place and shower and change, but decided to do that in the morning. The need to see Sarah was strong and he ignored everything else.

He picked up dinner and parked away from the room. He strolled toward the door, dinner in one hand, his eyes searching for anything out of the ordinary. One couple was leaving, another was driving up, the traffic hummed in the background. Everything else was quiet.

At the door, he stopped dead. Taped to the surface was a single white sheet of paper and scrawled in big letters was, *Sarah baby. You're next.*

Fear jolted through him and the bag dropped from his hand as he immediately drew his gun. He pounded on the door with his fist. "Goddammit, Chad, open up."

The door swung open and Daniel burst in. Sarah stood there wide-eyed. She was okay. He released a painful breath and pointed at the door. "Grab your things. We have to go. They know we're here."

Chad stared at the door. "What the hell?"

"Don't touch it," Daniel shouted as Chad's hand went to it. "Call Russ and get the lab over here." He turned to Sarah. "Hurry. We have to get out of here."

Sarah's eyes were glued to the door. While she and Chad had been playing cards, the killer had been not twelve feet away. Her blood ran cold at the chilling thought and for a moment she couldn't move. *Not again. Not again.*

"Sarah, hurry," Daniel repeated in an urgent tone.

She swallowed hard and ran to the bedroom.

"Did you hear anything?" Daniel asked Chad, a bite to his words.

"Not a sound."

"Did you talk to anyone?"

"No, sir. I haven't even talked to my mom or my girlfriend."

"They found her, some way, somehow."

"It wasn't me, sir. I was very careful."

"I know, Chad. Someone had a way to find us."

"How?"

"I'm not sure, but I will find out."

Sarah came back with her bag and Daniel followed her outside. "Cover our backs, then stay here and wait for Russ," he called to Chad. "I'll be in touch."

Within seconds they were in the car and driving through the night. "It's going to be okay," he told her.

"No, it isn't." Her voice wobbled, not sure if her life was ever going to be the same again. "Not until the killer is caught."

"Did you hear anything?"

"It's been quiet all day."

"How in the hell did they find out where you were? Someone had to have tailed me or…" He made a sharp turn.

She braced herself as the car picked up speed. "Daniel, where are we going?"

"To the police station."

She didn't ask anymore questions because she could sense this wasn't the time for that. He was deep in thought.

They drove into a garage with several more cars and a couple of police cars. Daniel rolled down a window. "Carlos," he shouted.

A Hispanic man appeared from a small room, wiping his hands on a grease rag. "What the hell do you want, Daniel? I'm ready to go home."

Daniel got out and talked to the man, then he opened her door. "Let's wait in here until he finishes."

Sarah stepped out and her legs buckled. Daniel caught her. "Are you okay?"

"I'm trying to be."

He held her arm as they walked to the small cluttered office. Daniel pulled out a metal chair and she sat. He knelt in front of her and she stared into those warm, concerned eyes. She needed that more than anything. The fear inside her began to subside.

"This won't take long, then we'll get lost somewhere."

"You can't do that. You have to catch this killer and find the snitch in your department. My life is not the only one involved."

"At this moment I'm only concerned about you."

Her eyes melted into his and she wanted to absorb her whole body in him until the nightmare went away, until she could breathe normally again, until...

The door opened and Carlos came in. "Found something you might want to see."

Daniel stood and Sarah followed him out to the car. The hood was up and he pointed to a small gadget in one corner. "There's your problem. Someone's attached a tracer to your vehicle."

"Goddammit." Daniel ran both hands through his hair. "Don't touch anything."

"I know better than that," Carlos snapped. "I'd say someone was mighty interested in where you were going."

"Yeah. Stay with the car until Russ arrives. I'm taking that gray sedan over there."

"Keys are in the office," Carlos said.

Sarah grabbed her things and once again they were on the highway.

"Where are we going?"

"I'm not sure," he admitted. "We're probably being watched right now."

Sarah ran her hands up her arms to shake that foreboding feeling.

"Boyd called us a bunch of Keystone Cops and I'm beginning to believe he's right. We're running in circles without a clue."

"That's only because someone close to you is feeding him information."

"Yeah, and tomorrow I'm getting up close and personal with my officers."

"So we're staying in Dallas?"

He thought for a moment. "I think we should stop hiding."

"What do you mean?"

"They seem to know where we're at anyway so we're going to my condo. That's the last place they'd expect us."

"Okay."

Daniel drove into a condo area and Sarah couldn't see much because of the darkness.

He reached into his jacket and pulled out a small remote. He pushed a button and the garage door went up. After they drove in, it immediately went down again. It was a two-car garage and she noticed a black Jeep to her left. She got her bag and they went into the house through a laundry area then into a kitchen and breakfast room.

"It has an alarm system and I've set it, so that might put your mind at rest. Have a seat. I have to check in with Russ and my lieutenant."

Sarah walked into the large den. It was light and airy, with overstuffed comfortable furniture that gave it a homey, country appeal.

She collapsed into an oversize chair and tried to gather her thoughts. She was here with Daniel and she felt safe, but she couldn't still that uneasiness inside her. Someone was trying to kill her and they'd been watching Daniel and her. Who was it? It could be anyone. That had her nerves stretched to the breaking point.

Daniel came into the room. "Lieutenant Tolin's steamed about this turn of events and he's calling a meeting of narcotics and homicide first thing in the morning. All the dirty laundry will be thoroughly aired and he won't stop until he gets an answer. Forensics is working on the door and the car."

He removed his jacket and laid it over a chair, his eyes on her white face. "What's wrong?" he asked.

"Beside the obvious?"

"Yes. You have that look on your face I've seen before—that look that says 'leave me alone.'"

He was beginning to read her so well, she wasn't sure what to say to him. She could only be honest. That's what she'd told Chad.

"I'm just so scared and I'm trying to control it."

"Me, too," he said just as honestly. "But whoever is after you will have to go through me to get to you. You do understand that I won't leave you until this guy is caught."

A change came over her face. "Last time I leaned on Serena and now I'm leaning on you. I'm tired of being weak and I'm tired of being the victim. I need to go back to my job, my life, and stop running, stop hiding. If this man wants me, then he has to come out into the open and find me. I've had karate and self-defense classes and I'm suppose to know how to protect myself. Yet I'm hiding like a coward and the killer

is watching and enjoying my fear. Well, no more."
She jumped to her feet. "I'm going home."

"Whoa. Whoa." Daniel caught her before she could
take a step. This was the Sarah he'd witnessed during
the trial, the one who'd stood in open court and
pointed a finger at Boyd and said he'd shot Greg in
cold blood three times without even blinking. He
could almost feel the fire coursing through her—the
coldness she'd mentioned earlier was completely gone.
She was fighting mad.

He held her by both arms. "Listen to me. The lieutenant gave me four days to get this thing solved. I've
got two left. Please, give me those two days."

The fire in her eyes flickered and dampened.
"Okay. But I'm going with you wherever you go. I'm
not sitting in a room somewhere. I want to help."

"Okay. Deal."

"I just want it over," she murmured, stepping
closer to him and wrapping her arms around his waist.
Her arm rubbed against his gun—a reminder of their
situation.

He did what any red-blooded male would do; he
held her tight. Pushing her away wasn't even in his
mind.

"Do you feel something happening between us?"
she asked, her head beneath his chin.

He took a deep breath. "Yes."

"A few days ago I wanted you out of my life and
now I can't imagine my life without you in it."

He closed his eyes, trying not to read too much into
her words.

"You're thinking it's out of fear, aren't you?" She
looked up at him.

He opened his eyes and the truth was there for her

to see. He did and she had to make him understand. "I knew that if I faced my feelings for you then I'd have to face my past, deal with it and get on with living. I told myself I'd already done that and it had nothing to do with you. But deep down I had all those negative feelings about you seeing me naked in Boyd's apartment. I didn't want to be a helpless victim to you." She trembled slightly.

He gently cupped her head with his hands. "As I told you, I've never, not for a second, thought of you as a slut. I think, as I did then, that you're a beautiful, brave and incredibly strong young woman. I also thought Greg was lucky to have had you in his life and I was…"

Her eyes widened. "What?"

"I was jealous that he met you first."

She smiled and his heart fluttered uncontrollably. "But we have now."

His hands slid through the thickness of her hair and he gently kissed her lips. She moaned, a sweet happy sound, and returned the kiss with an ardor he was beginning to associate with her—fiery, like her hair, and unforgettable, like her touch.

She opened her mouth and the kiss deepened as they tasted, explored and reveled in the emotions that took them away to a place of need, joy and pleasure. Daniel's hands traveled from her hair to her back and held her tight against him.

"Daniel," she breathed against his lips.

He kissed her nose, her cheek. "Hmm?"

Suddenly the alarm blasted through the condo. In a split second Daniel pulled his gun and pushed her behind him. "Where's your gun?" he asked in a hoarse voice.

"In my...in my bag."

He grabbed her bag out of the chair and handed it to her, looking at the alarm panel in the kitchen. "The front door light is blinking. Someone's coming through the damn front door." He glanced at her. "Do you have your gun?"

"Yes," she answered, her heart hammering so loud she could barely hear him.

"The alarm will go off at the police station and someone will call here in a few minutes. I'm going to the front door." He stared into her eyes. "Use the gun if you have to."

She nodded, unable to speak. She wanted this to be over and she had to stay strong to see it through. The gun was cold and heavy in her hand, but she gripped it tightly. She'd never fired a gun before and the mere thought caused her stomach to churn with a sick feeling.

To protect Daniel, to protect herself, she'd pull the trigger. She wasn't being the victim again. *Not ever again.*

CHAPTER ELEVEN

SARAH WAS BARELY breathing. She waited. The alarm continued to blare through the house, making her edgier than she already was. Then she heard voices—the high pitch of a woman and the baritone of a man.

"It's my parents," Daniel called out.

A long sigh of relief escaped her and she released her grip on the gun. She walked to her bag and slipped it back inside as the alarm cut off.

"I thought you were in France," Daniel was saying, clearly aggravated.

"We got back yesterday," the woman's voice said. "I was fed up with your father's partying."

Daniel entered the den with two older people. A well-dressed woman with blond hair cut in a fashionable pageboy, sized up Sarah with her blue-green eyes. The tall, lean gray-haired man had brown eyes and Sarah saw where Daniel got his looks. They both stared openly at her and she felt like a specimen under a microscope. She resisted the urge to squirm.

The phone rang and Daniel ran to answer it.

"Who are you, my dear?" his mother asked.

"A friend of Daniel's," she answered in a cautious manner, not liking the way the woman was looking at her.

"Are you the reason he hasn't returned any of my phone calls?"

"I wasn't aware you were trying to get in touch with me," Daniel replied as he came back. Sarah was glad. She didn't want to deal with Daniel's mother.

"I left at least ten messages on your machine. Didn't you get them?"

"I've been rather busy."

His mother glanced at Sarah. "Yes. I can see."

"Mom, Dad, this is Sarah Welch. Sarah, these are my parents, Muriel and Dan Garrett."

Muriel bristled. "Daniel, could I speak with you privately?"

Daniel walked into the dining room with his mother and Sarah stared at Dan Garrett, unsure of what to say. But she didn't get a chance because Muriel's voice could be heard, preventing any conversation.

"Isn't that Aurora Farrell's granddaughter?"

"Yes," Daniel said.

"The stripper? The one who was in all the papers?"

"She is not and never was a stripper," Daniel answered, his voice as sharp as a razor.

"I will not have you dating this woman." Muriel's voice trilled. "I want her out of this house."

"Excuse me?"

"This is the wrong type of woman for you. What are you thinking?"

"I'm thinking she's the right kind of woman for me."

"You can't be serious."

"I am, and I've heard enough." Daniel's voice grew louder. "I want *you* out of my house and I want my key back to prevent any more of these surprise visits."

"What!"

His father looked at Sarah. "I need a drink. How about you?"

"No thanks," she mumbled, her mind on Muriel's words. They ran through her head like a song in the wrong key—jarring, offensive. *Stripper. Stripper. Stripper. Wrong type of woman.*

Dan raised his glass of scotch to Sarah. "My wife's very high-strung and is known to stick her nose in where it doesn't belong. I don't pay much attention to her and you shouldn't, either."

Sarah wasn't sure what she was supposed to say to that so she said nothing.

"I resent this, Daniel," Muriel said, following Daniel into the den.

"Would you like a list of all the things I resent, Mother?"

"I can see you're in one of your moods."

"Good. Now you can leave."

"We came here to talk about Drew."

Daniel swung around. "What about Drew?"

"If you'd listen to your messages, you'd know."

"What about Drew?" Daniel repeated firmly.

"He ran away," his father answered.

"What? When?"

"Last night," Muriel told him. "That's why we were calling you. Drew listens to you."

"Tell me what happened."

Dan took a swallow of his scotch. "Your mother visited a home in France that caters to people like Drew. She thought he might like the change, but when she mentioned it, he became very upset, ranting about things we couldn't understand. Later, Claude called and said Drew had run away. He found him wandering the streets about three this morning."

"Where's Drew now?"

"He's back with Claude and I told him he didn't have to go to France. He doesn't seem to understand, though, and he wants to talk with you."

"I'll call him right away," Daniel promised. "Claude has my cell number. Why didn't he phone?"

"He probably did, but you were otherwise engaged." Muriel glanced at Sarah.

Dan downed the rest of his scotch. "I think it's time for us to go, Muriel, before you get your foot so far in your mouth that it'll require surgery to remove it."

"Why are you drinking, Dan?" Muriel snapped, turning her attention to him. "Now I'll have to drive and you know how I hate to drive at night."

"Call a cab, Muriel. That's what I'm doing. I'll be at the club." He grabbed the bottle of scotch. "I'm taking this, son."

"You're becoming an alcoholic," Muriel complained.

"That's better than being a shrew."

"How dare you talk to me like that in front of people!"

"Why?" Dan took a swig from the bottle. "You have no qualms about berating our son in front of his guest. So how does it feel? Not too damn good, huh?" He moved toward the door. "I'll call a cab from my cell phone. Good night, Daniel and Sarah. Have a nice evening. I plan to."

Muriel ran after him. "What about me?"

Dan turned to look at her. "In the words of Rhett Butler—I really don't give a damn." He raised the bottle and opened the door at the same time.

"Dan Garrett, come back here!" Muriel followed him outside.

DANIEL CLOSED THE DOOR, turned the deadbolt and reset the alarm. "So help me, if they come back I might have to use my gun," he joked, walking back to Sarah.

She sat in a chair with her knees drawn up and her arms locked tight around them. She wore a closed expression that he knew well.

"Sarah, I'm so sorry. I…"

His phone rang, cutting him off. "I'll be right back." He went to answer it. It was Drew.

"Hi, buddy."

"Sh-sh-she—"

"It's okay," Daniel stopped him. "Mom's not sending you anywhere. I promise."

"Home, Danny. Sh-she…she take me to a home for—for stupid people."

"Drew, I won't let her take you anywhere. Do you understand me?"

"N-n-no. I can't go. I have to stay here."

Drew was in such a state that nothing was getting through. Daniel wanted to strangle his mother, but then that was always his reaction to Muriel's single-minded insensitivity. The only thing Daniel knew to do was to distract Drew with something else.

"Tell you what, buddy. I'm working on a real important case and when it's over, you and I will go fishing on the coast—just you and me."

"I can't go."

"Drew, listen to me. I'm talking about fishing."

"I—I—I'm a stupid person. I can't go."

Daniel gripped the phone tightly. "You're my brother. You're not stupid and I love you."

"I'm sorry, Danny."

"Don't be sorry, buddy, think about our fishing trip. You like to go to the coast, don't you?"

"Yeah, but I can't."

"Drew—"

Claude came on the line. "Don't worry, Daniel. I'll calm him down."

"Thanks, Claude. I'm real sorry I can't come over. Please take care of him until I'm able to get there."

"I will, and if you can, keep your mother away from here. She only upsets him."

"I'll try, but Muriel is a law unto herself. I thought they were going to be in France for a while. I apologize for the intrusion."

"That's okay. Now I'd better go to Drew."

Daniel hung up with a long sigh. Could this day get any worse? He caught sight of Sarah and knew that it just had. She hadn't moved and his heart twisted at the expression on her face. It wasn't fear, it was something else, and it had to do with what his mother had said. He walked to her and squatted down in front of her.

"Sarah, what is it?" he asked softly.

"It's so hard to overcome the past."

"Please don't listen to my mother."

"She's right," she mumbled. "I was a stripper."

"Not by choice."

"What difference does it make? Some people will always think of me that way." It hurt and she was obviously having a hard time dealing with everything going on inside her. A madman was after her, trying to kill her, but it was his mother's words that cut the deepest.

"They don't matter."

Sarah locked her arms tighter.

"Tell me what you're feeling," Daniel invited.

"It's really hard to explain."

"We have all night."

She took a deep breath. "The other day I was wondering why I had the need to hold on to Gran's house and I had to admit I wanted her love. Every day I kept striving for that, but that wasn't it at all. Gran loves me. I found that out when I got the note from Boyd. It's something much deeper—I've also been striving to be accepted by society, by people like your mother—hoping I wouldn't be judged by my past."

"Sarah—"

"When I was growing up, we didn't have a lot of money for extras. I didn't have ballet or music classes or attend private schools where poise, etiquette and manners were taught."

"Like Serena?"

She nodded. "When I first lived with her and Gran, I felt as if I didn't belong, that I was out of place, and tonight...tonight when your parents walked in here and looked at me so disapprovingly I felt the same way—like I'm still trying to be accepted."

"Why?"

"Because when I hear people like your mother talking about me, I see myself through their eyes and I feel uncomfortable. I feel..."

"Did you feel uncomfortable when we were kissing?"

She glanced up, the tears in her eyes sparkling. "No. I felt good about that."

"Then let me tell you something. My parents are snobs. That's not me—until a year ago I lived in an apartment that didn't have hot water half the time. I bought this place because I like hot showers in the winter. I manage on my cop's salary and live like an ordinary working Joe. That's me. I'm not like my parents. And there are a lot of people who feel the same way I do about you—who admire your courage.''

She knew he was trying to make her feel better, but she could feel her defenses going up. She couldn't let that happen because she had fought too hard to reach this point. Daniel had come to mean a lot to her and she knew he wasn't like his mother.

"I know that," she said. "But I took my clothes off in front of men and that revulsion is always with me."

"Sometimes in life we make choices, life-changing choices, and we have to stand by them and we have to defend them. You chose to fight for your life and to fight for justice for Greg. To do that you had to degrade yourself—that took enormous courage. You said you stayed alive because you were weak and didn't fight back and Boyd enjoyed your fear. I think it was just the opposite—a weaker woman wouldn't have been able to deal with Boyd and his demands and he would have killed her. By taking your clothes off you bought time—time for the cops to find you and time for justice."

She ran her hands up and down her shinbones. "Then why do I still feel so dirty?"

"What do you tell clients when they ask you that question? What did you tell Brooke Wallace?"

"To talk about what happened to her, not to keep it all bottled up—that's the main thing—and of course to replace bad memories with happy memories."

"Have you talked about what happened to you?"

She leaned her head back. "Yes. Serena and I have

talked and I also talked with Dr. Mason. And I've been talking to you."

His face softened. "What about the memories? Have you tried to make happier memories?"

She glanced into the brown eyes she was beginning to love. Love! All of a sudden it was clear as day. The ball stopped bouncing in her head—game, set, match. She loved him. The thought was cathartic, bringing the bad stuff to the surface—stuff she had to share with him.

She inhaled a shuddering breath. "No. Up until a few days ago I covered myself completely and I'd get cold chills if a man looked at me."

"So you were letting the fear win?"

"Yes. Then I decided I wasn't doing that anymore. I'd told Brooke that it takes a concentrated effort and I knew I hadn't done that. Of course Serena always boosts my confidence."

"Getting the note put a dent in that new confidence?"

"It certainly brought back the fear, but I was surprised to find my confidence in myself as a woman was still intact. That's why I was able to kiss you at the motel."

"And we kissed a little while ago and everything was fine until my mother arrived and said those awful things."

"I felt dirty again and wanted to crawl away in shame."

His eyes caught hers. "You have nothing to be ashamed of."

Daniel's faith and belief in her was uplifting. It had been there for years and she'd blocked it out. He was right. She had nothing to be ashamed of and she had to prove that to herself and no one else. *She had nothing to be ashamed of.*

For the first time she really believed that. She slid to the floor to face him. "No, I don't," she said with confidence. "Your mother and people like her can't demean me anymore—not unless I let them. I'm taking my life back and I need your help."

"What can I do?"

"Help me to make happy memories, to erase the bad ones."

"How do I do that?"

Her eyes held his. "Touch me."

He swallowed. "Where?"

"Anywhere, everywhere."

His eyes didn't waver from hers. "Are you sure? Kissing is one thing, but…"

She picked up his hand and linked her fingers with his. "I'm very sure. I want to forget everything that's happening outside this house and I don't want to think. I just want to feel—feel you touching me." She noticed his gun. "Preferably without your gun on."

He quickly slipped out of the shoulder holster. She watched the muscles rippling in his arms and her lower abdomen stirred in a familiar way. She saw all the looks she'd witnessed in Daniel's eyes for the past five years—those looks of caring. She went to him and he wrapped his arms around her, tight and strong, yet gentle and comforting. She breathed in his masculine scent and let herself go with the moment.

He ran his hands up her back, feeling her softness, taking it slow, not wanting to hurt or to frighten her in any way, even though he was about to detonate from the emotions coursing through him. He'd dreamed of this moment, holding her, loving her, but it was never like this, so potent, so real and so very dangerous. She was under his protection and he shouldn't be touching or kissing her at all. He'd just told her that adults make choices and he'd just made a conscious choice that he knew was right. He would defend it with everything in him. She needed him and for once in his life he wasn't going by the book.

They held on to each other with tender caresses. Slowly he slid a hand beneath her T-shirt, touching the smoothness of her bare skin. She moaned and kissed his neck, his chin. He turned his head and their lips met urgently, hungrily, and Daniel tried to slow the pace, but her hands were in his hair, on his skin. Thought was impossible.

They were on the area rug on their knees, face-to-face, and striving to get closer. Sarah melted into his arms with an eagerness that surprised her. There was no revulsion, just desire between a woman and a man. She was high from Daniel's touch and the feeling was euphoric, enticing her to take the next step.

"Oh, Daniel," she moaned. "I have to see myself in your eyes, see your reaction to my body—that's the only way to erase the bad memories."

He rested his forehead against hers. "You know what you're going to see."

"What?"

"Sarah, you know how I feel about you."

"How?" she asked, wanting to hear him say the words.

He got to his feet and reached out a hand to her. "Let's continue this upstairs." She placed her hand in his and stood. He scooped his gun up with the other hand and they made their way to the stairs and to the bedroom.

Inside the room, Daniel clicked on the lamp and laid his gun on the nightstand. He still held her hand and pulled her to him. "Now, what were we talking about?"

"How you feel about me."

He cradled his hands at the back of her waist. "I think everyone knows that but you."

She ran her hands up his chest. "Yes. I was so confused and struggling with emotions about myself, my family, that I couldn't see much of anything. And I didn't want to admit what I was beginning to feel for you."

"What do you feel for me?" he asked with a catch in his voice.

She looked into his eyes. "I love you."

He stepped back, his eyes wide with shock. "Sarah, please don't say that if you don't mean it."

"You've known me for a long time. Have you ever known me to lie?"

"No." He ran both hands through his hair. "But you've been through a lot and a few days ago you hated me."

She shook her head. "I've never hated you. I hated the way you were making me feel and I didn't want to have those feelings for a man again, especially after what happened with Greg."

He paled.

"What I feel for you doesn't even compare to that. It comes from here." She placed her hand over her heart. "It comes from knowing you and the kind of man you are—the kind that loves unconditionally even after the way I've treated you. You haven't said it, but I know you love me. I've seen it in your eyes."

"Sarah." His voice was uncertain. Still, it didn't stop her.

She pressed her body against his. "It's so good to feel again and I want to make love—with you," she whispered. "I want to. I need to."

"Sarah, be very sure about this. You said you didn't like to be touched and I don't want to frighten you."

"Take off my T-shirt," she breathed against his lips.

"Sarah."

"Daniel, make love to me." Any resistance he'd had vanished with the huskiness of her voice. He pulled the T-shirt over her head and threw it on the bed. Unsnapping her white bra, he gazed at her porcelain skin, her round, firm breasts. Almost in slow motion, she removed her sneakers, jeans and panties. Her movements were graceful, evocative, and he thought she was the most beautiful woman he'd ever seen. Freckles, like fairy dust, were lightly sprinkled across her breasts and other areas of her body. He saw all her beauty, but he saw a lot more—he saw her heart and courage. All he wanted was to take her in his arms and obliterate the bad memories.

"You know what I see in your eyes?" she asked, her voice a thread of softness.

He shook his head, his pulse jolting like a faulty engine.

"I see love, not lust, and that's the way I will see myself—feminine, attractive and very human."

In slow motion, he reached out and pulled her against him, holding her, breathing in the scent of her hair, her skin. "Sarah, Sarah, Sarah," he groaned into her neck.

She kissed his cheek, his chin. "Love me, Daniel. Love me tonight."

"Sarah."

She placed a finger over his lips. "Shh. Don't think about duty, the killer or Boyd. This night is ours and let's make the most of it, then we can face tomorrow—together."

He stroked the smoothness of her back and her body responded, ached for more. She turned her face to his and his mouth took hers gently, stoking the fire, and she opened up for Daniel as she had for no other man. All he had to do was to take what she was offering.

Their lips and tongues touched, tasted and discovered each other. Sarah was beyond thinking and she knew that finally she was ready to love again.

Daniel pulled back only to slip out of his T-shirt, but he couldn't stay away long, taking another kiss as he kicked off his shoes while undoing his belt and jeans. Soon all his clothes were on the floor and he gathered her body against his and she reveled in his masculine body against her. They fell backward onto the bed and neither seemed to notice the impact.

Daniel gazed down at her with heavy-lidded eyes and caressed her breasts, her stomach and lower, touching sensitive, moist and intimate places. His hand was like a salve on a wound, cleansing, healing, until the old fears completely vanished and her fingers became bold, kneading, stroking along his chest, flat stomach and male hardness until breathing became an effort.

"Sarah, Sarah, Sarah," he moaned raggedly.

"Yes, yes, yes," she answered in the same tone. She didn't even know what the question was. All she knew was that she wanted Daniel with everything in her.

Daniel rolled on top of her, his mouth on hers in fevered elation. She opened her legs, welcoming him.

"Protection?" he gasped against her.

"No."

He pulled away for a second and reached into the nightstand for a plastic packet. "I don't like these damn things," he mumbled as he ripped it open and sheathed himself.

Sarah watched, her breathing labored. Soon he was back with her, kissing, caressing, stroking until she could take no more. "Now, Daniel." A long sweet breath left her as he entered her, filled her. With each thrust her breath became sweeter and sweeter until her body moved in perfect harmony with his. So long denied, so long ignored, her body convulsed with such intense pleasure that she cried out his name and clutched his back.

She kept holding on to Daniel, not wanting the sensation to ever go away, not wanting to ever leave his arms.

Daniel's release shook his whole body and he knew the world had stopped turning. It had to because nothing would ever match this moment, this time out of time, except loving her over and over and....

CHAPTER TWELVE

DANIEL DRIFTED IN AND out of sleep with his arms around Sarah and he felt truly blessed. He'd never witnessed such strength and courage in one person. He knew she could face whatever lay ahead. And he'd be right beside her.

The blaring of the alarm brought him fully awake. He jumped out of bed and quickly slipped into his jeans then grabbed his gun.

Sarah sat up, brushing hair out of her eyes. "Daniel, what is it?"

He glanced at the alarm panel on the wall. "Someone's coming through the back door. Get your gun."

"It's downstairs in my handbag," she cried, scrambling to her knees.

Daniel raced to a dresser, opened a drawer and pulled out another gun. He handed it to her, trying not to stare at her loveliness. He had to stay focused. "The safety's off, so be careful."

His cell phone beeped and he clicked it on. "It's Russ," he said to her. "The alarm has gone off at the police station." He turned his attention back to Russ. "It's the back door. Send a car. I'm going down to check it out. Keep talking to Sarah so you'll know what's going on."

Daniel gave her the phone and her hand trembled

slightly. He kissed her briefly. "It will be okay." Then he was gone.

She bit her lip and got out of bed, searching for her clothes. She was in her jeans in a matter of seconds and she could hear Russ's yelling for a response. "Yes," she said into the receiver, shimmying her way into her T-shirt.

"Do you hear anything?"

"No. Just the alarm." As she said the word, the alarm cut off. Then she heard Daniel's voice.

"Sarah, it's okay. It's my brother Drew. Tell Russ."

"It's his brother," she said to Russ, her heart rate slowing.

"What the hell is it with his family?" Russ bellowed.

"I don't know."

"Tell Daniel I'm posting a guard outside and the first Garrett that shows up is gonna get shot. This is like some Mickey Mouse show. Do these people know we're after a rapist and a killer?"

She suppressed a retort because it would be wasted on Russ. He was a cop to the core and if anything got in the way of him doing his job, he became unbearable. For once, she was glad he was on her side.

"Tell Daniel to call me."

"I will," she said, clicking off. She put the gun back in the drawer and made her way downstairs.

Daniel was in the den with a younger man in jeans, sneakers and a big coat. His hair was dark like Daniel's, but otherwise they didn't resemble each other much. Drew was shorter and very thin.

"How'd you get here, buddy?" Daniel was asking in a soothing voice.

"I—I—I walked."

"It's over three miles."

"I—I—I have to see you."

"I know, buddy." Daniel put his arm around his trembling little brother. "But it's five o'clock in the morning and I don't like you walking the streets at this hour. Are you cold?"

"N-n-no. I'm hot."

Daniel helped him off with his coat. "How did you get into my garage?"

"I—I—I remember the code. I—I—I'm not stupid."

"No, you're not." Daniel nodded. "You remembered it from that time you stayed with me when Claude took a vacation."

"Yeah, and when…when Claude say I c-couldn't go fishing, I waited until he fell asleep and I—I came here." Drew twisted his hands.

"Come on, Drew, sit down," Daniel said as he led him to the sofa. Drew was very agitated and nervous, and Daniel wondered if he'd missed taking his medication.

Drew made a face. "Claude made me mad."

"Why?"

Drew plopped down. "A-a-always telling me what to do."

"I know that's hard, buddy, but we'll go fishing when I'm through with this case. Do you understand?"

"You after a bad guy?" Drew asked, his voice excited.

"Yeah. A real bad guy."

Drew fidgeted. "I—I—I wanna go fishing."

Daniel didn't want to disappoint his brother. "Me,

too, but think what fun we'll have when we do go. Half the fun is in the planning.''

''I—I—I can't go. Have to stay here.'' Daniel didn't understand what he was talking about and he feared Drew was close to having another seizure. He had to find out if he'd taken his medication.

''I'll call Claude and ask him to pick you up. Okay?''

''Okay.'' He seemed to calm down a little.

Daniel called Claude, who was driving around searching for Drew. ''He's at my place,'' he told him.

''I'm so sorry, Daniel.''

''He's very agitated. Has he had his medication?''

''No. I found his pills on the bathroom counter. He's been very good about taking them, but your mother has him so upset.''

''Yeah,'' Daniel sighed. ''He seems more upset than usual.''

''I'll come and get him. Once he takes the medicine, he'll calm down.''

''Okay, Claude,'' Daniel said. ''Drew can be a handful, but please be diligent about him taking his pills.''

''I will.''

Daniel hung up. ''He's on his way,'' he told Drew.

Drew plucked at his jeans. ''H-h-he's gonna be mad. Call me stupid.''

''No, he…''

''I—I—I'm not stupid,'' Drew shouted. ''I'm not and Mom can't make me go.''

Daniel squatted in front of Drew realizing just how much turmoil Drew was in. ''Look at me,'' he said, and as Drew raised his head, Daniel saw his eyes were feverish. *Hurry up, Claude.* ''You're not stupid.

You're special and I love you and I promise you don't have to go anywhere you don't want to. But you have to take your medicine."

Drew thought about it for a second. "I—I—I want my medicine."

"Claude will give it to you when he picks you up."

"Okay. I—I—I want to stay in Dallas."

"Okay, then." Daniel patted his knee, realizing Drew was out of it.

Daniel glanced up and saw Sarah standing at the foot of the stairs. He caught his breath at her natural beauty. She had her jeans and T-shirt on and her feet were bare. Her red hair was in disarray and her features serene, but he focused on her eyes. Despite everything, she looked happy and he felt a moment of sheer joy.

"Buddy, I'd like you to meet someone," Daniel said, getting to his feet, his eyes on Sarah.

"W-w-who, who, Danny, who?"

Daniel held out his hand and Sarah came to his side and gripped it tightly.

"This is Sarah Welch. And, Sarah, this is my brother, Drew."

"Nice to meet you, Drew," Sarah said.

"You're pretty," Drew replied.

"Thank you."

"A-a-are...are you Dan-ny's girlfriend?"

Daniel squeezed her hand. "Yes, she is."

"Danny's got a girlfriend." Drew put a hand over his mouth and giggled.

The phone rang and Daniel went to answer it.

It was Russ again. "There's a man outside your condo and he says he's there to pick up your brother."

"It's Drew's caretaker. I'll send him out."

"Daniel, I'm not quite sure how to say this since my social skills are lacking, but get your family the hell out of this picture. Do they not comprehend what the hell's going on?"

"They don't know what's going on," Daniel replied, realizing things were getting more complicated with every interruption.

"Your security has been blown to hell."

"I'm not sure it makes a difference. Someone knows our every move anyway."

"That sure gets to me, but maybe today we'll find some answers. I'm on my way to wake up Arnie Bishop and haul his ass to the station for questioning. Do you want to be there?"

"Yes. I'll be there in about an hour. When I leave the condo, have the guard follow me."

"So you're bringing Ms. Welch to the station, too?"

"You bet. I'm not letting her out of my sight."

"This could be a problem."

"It had better not be, Russ, because I honestly don't see any other way to do this. If anyone is dumb enough to come into the police station for her, they'll have an army to contend with."

"Yep. You're right. I'll have Chad on hand if you need him."

"Thanks."

"I'll see you at the station for Bishop's questioning, then we'll go to Lieutenant Tolin's show-and-tell, which should be interesting."

"Okay. Tell the guard that Drew's coming out."

"Will do."

Daniel hung up and heard Sarah talking to Drew.

His face was animated as he watched her. Daniel noticed that he wasn't stuttering.

"Daniel catches lots of fish and we drink beer and do guy things. Daniel says we can only drink two beers. I want more and I sneak it when Daniel's not looking."

"Why do you do that?" Sarah asked.

"Because everyone treats me like a baby and I'm not a baby. I'm a man and I can do what I want."

"Does Daniel treat you like a baby?"

"Sometimes. He's my brother, my best friend, but he…"

"He what?"

Drew linked his fingers together. "He wants me to be careful, responsible."

"That's how adults should be—careful and responsible."

"Yeah," Drew said, his eyes bright. "Daniel wants me to be an adult."

"Yes."

"I'm an adult," Drew pronounced loudly. "And nobody tells me what to do."

"Just people who care about you." Sarah smiled.

"Daniel does and he…"

Daniel hated to break up the conversation, but the guard was waiting and if he didn't send Drew out, Russ would be calling. There would be plenty of occasions later for Drew and Sarah to get to know each other—when things weren't so dangerous.

"Time to go, buddy," Daniel said. "Claude's waiting."

Daniel helped him into his coat and walked him to the door.

"'Bye, Sarah," Drew called.

"'Bye," Sarah called back.

Daniel hugged him. "Love you, buddy. Please take your medication."

"I get my medicine now. 'Bye."

Daniel opened the door and the guard escorted Drew to Claude. He closed the door, turned the dead-bolt, set the alarm and went back to Sarah.

She went into his arms as if she belonged there.

"I like Drew," she said. "I think counseling would help him."

"He likes you, too. He doesn't open up to many people, but you had him talking up a storm. You're a damn good counselor."

"Thank you."

He cupped her face and kissed her tenderly, then deepened the kiss to a level he needed. "I've been wanting to do that since I saw you on the stairs."

She ran her fingers across his naked shoulders, loving the freedom to touch him at will and loving the need in her to want to do it. "You feel so good," she murmured, her eyes dreamy.

He kissed her nose, her cheek. "Oh, sweet lady, it's only started. I wish we had all day, but we have to get to the station."

"Mmm." She rested her head on his chest and listened to the steady rhythm of his heart. "I just want to hold you before the chaos of this day starts."

They stood holding on, both knowing that the events of this day would change their lives forever and both hoping they had the strength to face it.

THE DRIVE TO THE STATION went without incident. Sarah stayed in the conference room with all the files and background checks Daniel had been researching.

Chad stood guard outside the door. At Daniel's request, she went through the files to see if she might catch something he'd missed—anything that would tie an officer to Boyd.

Daniel met Russ and Joel in the hall outside a questioning room with a two-way mirror. He looked at Russ. He had the same wrinkled clothes on that he'd worn the last time Daniel had seen him and his beard was thicker.

"Have you had any sleep in the last two days? Not to mention a shower and shave?" Daniel asked.

Russ scratched his beard. "I've had a couple of hours' sleep in the car and I've been showering in the officers' locker room—haven't had time to shave, been busy chasing your damn relatives and covering your ass."

"I appreciate it, Russ. I really do."

The two men stared at each other, both knowing their relationship was changing—they were now friends.

Russ grinned. "So you trust me now, huh?"

Daniel met his eyes squarely. "With my life...and Sarah's."

Russ held out his hand and seemed at a loss for words, which was definitely a first. Daniel shook his hand. Neither said a word. They didn't have to.

Homicide Lieutenant Charles Bauer, Narcotics Lieutenant Bill Tolin and Hannah Corbett, an A.D.A., walked up.

"Do you have anything?" Lieutenant Bauer asked.

"No," Russ replied. "We're letting him stew for a bit."

"Let's see what he has to say," Hannah said.

"Russ, go by the book," Lieutenant Bauer warned.

"Ah, Lieutenant, I'll be a model cop." Russ winked and turned to Daniel. "Ready for Bishop?"

"You bet. And I promise not to interfere with your questioning."

"Hell, Daniel, don't take the fun out of everything." He straightened his jacket, which was a lost cause. "Just be prepared for a lot of attitude. He's pissed at being brought down here at this hour."

Russ opened the door and they went in.

"Detective Garrett," Arnie sneered. "You went to see my client without my permission."

Arnie reminded Daniel of a toad—slippery, fat, with eyes that bulged out of his bald head. "A lot of things are done without your permission, Arnie."

"Not as many as you'd think," Arnie snickered.

Russ pulled out a chair and sat across the small table from Arnie. He chewed on a toothpick and watched Arnie, then he placed a folder in front of him. "Let's get down to business."

"I'm not telling you a goddamn thing. I'll have your badges for daring to arrest me."

Russ laughed. "Tell you what, Arnie. You can have my badge as long as you're on death row with Rudy Boyd."

"You son of a bitch. You got nothing on me."

Russ opened the folder and laid some papers in front of Arnie. "Boyd transferred the ownership of clubs after each rape and murder to you. Of course, the clubs were in one of Boyd's fictional names, but we still found the transfers. Why?"

"Because he owed me the money, dammit. I'm an attorney and I don't work for free."

"You sure don't." Russ placed more papers in front of him. "Boyd gave you power of attorney over his bank account—the only one that wasn't seized by the cops five years ago. There's a tidy sum in the account, more than enough to cover your services.''

''Where did you get that information?'' Arnie pulled out a handkerchief and mopped his forehead. He was getting nervous. That was good, Daniel thought. Now maybe they could get some straight answers.

''Does it matter?'' Russ asked. ''You're in these rapes and murders up to your bugged-out eyes. Unless you want a cell next to Boyd's, you'd better tell me who's doing this.''

Arnie mopped his forehead again. ''I want an attorney.''

''Really.'' Russ raised an eyebrow. ''Earlier you said you didn't want one—that you could represent yourself.''

''I've changed my mind.''

''That's your prerogative.'' Russ stood. ''All I want is a name. An A.D.A. is out in the hall and she might take the death penalty off the table if you cooperate.''

''I didn't kill anyone. You can't scare me and you can't prove a damn thing.''

Russ moved away and nodded to Daniel.

Daniel stepped forward. ''If I were you, I'd be very scared, Arnie. In Texas it doesn't matter if you committed the murders or not. All that matters is that you ordered them. Two young girls are dead and one's in the hospital and another's life has been threatened. Boyd's signature is all over this. He's ordering the rapes from prison through you, trying to finagle a new deal, trying to save his sorry ass. That's not happening. Neither the D.A. nor the governor is dealing with Boyd. His execution is going forward and you'll be left holding the bag. We're being pressed to make an arrest and right now you're our number one suspect.''

"I want an attorney."

"Think about what we said."

Arnie raised his head, his eyes narrowed. "Maybe you should think about it, Garrett. If Boyd dies, a lot of innocent people will, too."

Daniel frowned. "What do you mean?"

"Sarah Welch is very beautiful and Boyd's not gonna let her live." The words were meant to taunt and goad him. It worked.

Before Daniel knew what he was doing, he'd jumped across the table and had Arnie by the neck. Russ pulled him off.

"Now you're really pissing me off, Arnie," Russ said.

"I'm filing charges against him for police brutality." Arnie rubbed his throat.

"File away, you slimeball," Daniel said, getting himself under control. "Before this night is over, I'm going to nail your ass to the wall."

He could hear Arnie laughing as Russ ushered him into the hall.

"That wasn't very professional," Hannah said to Daniel. "I expect that kind of behavior from Russ, but not from you, Daniel. Get your priorities straight."

"I'm sorry. I lost it. That creep knows what's going on. He knows everything and he's calling the shots."

"Still that doesn't…"

"Can it, Hannah," Daniel shouted. "I'm not in a mood to listen to Arnie Bishop's rights."

"Calm down," Bill ordered. "Or I'll take you off this case."

Daniel turned away, taking several deep breaths.

The moment Arnie'd mentioned Sarah's name he'd seen red and he'd wanted to shake the life out of him. That was the first time he'd lost it with a suspect. He was in too deep. He wasn't being taken off this case, though. He had to apologize.

Bill held up a hand, stopping him. "Get this case solved—today—without losing your temper."

"We'll have to let him go by tonight," Hannah said. "We don't have anything to hold him on."

"Don't you worry." Russ spoke up. "I'll find something—littering, his dog doesn't have a leash, anything."

Hannah frowned. "I want real charges."

Russ bowed. "Yes, ma'am."

She ignored him and spoke to Bill and Charles. "Call me if you get anything." Saying that, she strolled away, her high heels clicking on the floor.

"Bitch," Russ muttered.

"Don't start," Charles warned.

"The meeting's in a few minutes," Bill said. "Charles and I will see you in the conference room." The two lieutenants walked down the hall.

Russ patted Daniel on the back. "We've been around each other too long. You're starting to act like me."

"Oh, God," Daniel groaned.

Russ grinned. "Don't worry, it'll pass." His face became serious. "We've clashed a lot over the years because we do our jobs differently. You're always calm, factual and methodical, but sometimes I have to be brusque and insensitive to stomach this job, or else it gets to me."

"Yeah," Daniel agreed, seeing a side of Russ he thought he never would—his vulnerable side. "It takes

a lot to stomach this job on a good day and vermin
like Arnie just..."

"We'll get Arnie," Russ vowed. "With a little
more pressure, he'll crack like a rotten watermelon."

"I hope so." Daniel turned away. "I have to check
on Sarah before the meeting."

Daniel found her reading through the files. Her red
hair was pinned at the back of her head and several
tendrils hung around her face, softening her features
that were once so tight. She wore a white knit top and
jeans, an outfit so unlike the business suits he was used
to seeing her in. But then, their lives had changed
drastically.

She looked up and smiled. "Hi."

He smiled back. "How you doing?"

"Better now that you're here."

He sat beside her, his pulse quickening from her
nearness. "The meeting's in a few minutes. Chad's
outside the door and policemen are up and down the
hall. That's about as secure as it gets."

"Did Arnie Bishop say anything?"

"No, but we'll keep pressuring him. I'm just hoping
for something to happen in this meeting."

She tapped a file. "All I see are hardworking cops
with problems like everyone else."

"Whoever the snitch is has made sure that he'll
never be found. He's covered all his tracks, but he's
going to slip up and I'm hoping today is his day." He
stood. "I'd better go."

At the door he stopped. "If you need anything, just
tell Chad."

She looked into his eyes. "I don't need anything
but you. I need you."

He wavered slightly. "If I come over there, I'll never leave this room."

"I know." She tucked a tendril behind her ear. "I just wanted to tell you that."

He nodded and left the room.

Sarah sat in silent wonder at the changes in her life. A few days ago she was suppressing her emotions and in complete denial. Today she was talking, sharing and loving, and maybe soon she and Daniel would be free to get on with their lives. They hadn't talked about the future—they were too busy fighting to have one— but she knew their future would be together. First they had to stop Boyd.

She heard voices and got up and went to the door. She opened it a crack and Chad immediately appeared.

"Do you need anything, Ms. Welch?"

"No. I was just wondering what the noise was."

"Officers summoned by Lieutenant Tolin and Lieutenant Bauer are filing into the big conference room for the meeting."

"Oh," she murmured, seeing men in plain clothes and in uniforms making their way into a room down the hall. She didn't see Daniel, but she saw Russ, Joel and a few other cops she was acquainted with. Then her breath lodged in her throat. She saw a gun in a holster she'd seen before. The holster was on a man's hip and the leather was worn through from many years of use. She remembered it clearly and she knew exactly where she'd seen it.

"Chad," she said. "Get Daniel."

"They're closing the doors and I can't go in unless it's an emergency."

"This is an emergency."

Chad seemed perplexed. "Ms. Welch…"

"Do it—now."

"Yes, ma'am," Chad responded, and called down the hall. "Ray, come here." A uniformed officer walked over.

"What do you want?"

"Guard this door until I get back."

"Where you going?"

"Into the meeting."

"You're not allowed in there."

"Guard the damn door. I'll be back in a sec."

Sarah pushed the door to and leaned against it, her heart hammering wildly. *Hurry, Daniel, hurry. I know who the snitch is.*

CHAPTER THIRTEEN

SARAH PACED BACK and forth. What was taking so long? She went back to the door and looked out again; the hall was empty except for the uniformed cop who was looking rather confused. She continued her pacing, her nerves ready to snap. *Hurry, Daniel.*

The door opened and she swung around. Daniel walked toward her, wearing a worried frown.

"What is it? Chad said it was an emergency."

She took a deep breath. "I think I know who the snitch is," she said in a rush.

"What! How? Did you find something in the files?"

She took a gulp of air, feeling as if she'd run a marathon. "No. I glanced out the door and saw some men walking down the hall to the meeting. Who's the tall man, almost bald, with nice starched clothes and a pistol on his hip that has a worn leather holster?"

Daniel frowned. "That's Tom Hudson. He's been with me on narcotics for years."

"He could be the snitch."

Daniel seemed shocked. "No, he can't..." He took her arm and led her to a chair. He sat facing her, holding both her hands. "Tell me how you know this?"

"When Boyd was making me strip, there was always guards to escort me back to my room. I never looked at anyone's face. I looked down, trying to pretend that I wasn't there, but I remember seeing a gun on a man's hip—the leather was really worn—just like Tom's. He was talking to Boyd, so I assumed he was one of his henchmen. It's the same holster and gun. I remember it.''

"Was this man there every night?"

"No. I only saw the holster a couple of times."

"Sarah, be very sure about this."

"I am."

He wanted to deny it—didn't want to believe that Tom, his friend of many years, was the snitch. But Daniel saw that Sarah was dead serious.

"We've all razzed him about that holster, but it belonged to his father, who was also a cop, and he didn't want to get rid of it. He's a family man with three kids. I've eaten at his and Carol's house many times. His kids are in all kinds of sports and he coaches baseball. This is so out of character."

"Maybe he loaned his gun to someone?"

Daniel shook his head. "No. He'd never let anyone have that gun."

"Maybe he was there pressuring Boyd to find out what happened to Greg."

He shook his head again. "I never ordered him or anyone to pressure Boyd. We were watching Boyd, hoping he'd slip up and lead us to Greg. There was no reason for him to be talking to Boyd late at night. No reason unless…" He couldn't say the words, even as anger quickly overtook his shock.

There was a tap at the door and Chad poked his head around. "The lieutenant wants you in the conference room—pronto."

"I'm on my way." He got to his feet and stared down at Sarah. "I've been looking for something to link one of my guys to Boyd—I never thought it'd hurt so bad.''

"There has to be a reason he'd do this."

"There's not any reason on this earth good enough.'' He walked to the door and didn't look back. Tom had finally slipped up.

As Daniel entered the room, Bill said, "Nice of you to grace us with your presence."

"Sorry, sir,'' Daniel replied, taking his seat next to Bill, Russ and Lieutenant Bauer at the long table facing the men. "I had to take care of something."

Bill gave him one of those looks that said "get your act together,'' then he got down to business. "As all of you know, we're looking for a snitch in narcotics or homicide, someone who had information that was valuable to Rudy Boyd. This sticks in my craw like a wad of chewing tobacco and I'm here to tell you it ain't no fun.'' Bill glanced at Charles. "Lieutenant Bauer is here to support the men from his squads. This is an in-house investigation handled by myself and Detective Garrett."

Bill opened a big folder. "I'll start with Daniel first. You're all aware that Mr. Garrett was born with a silver spoon in his mouth and he traded it in for a badge. Most of us are looking for that easy lifestyle, but Daniel's running from it. He lives off his detective's salary and spends more hours in this police station than anyone I know. He's loaned or given money to almost everyone in this room. If Daniel has a secret life, I didn't find it."

"I think we need to contact the Pope and nominate Daniel for sainthood.'' Russ spoke up.

"I second that,'' Will said and several more officers added their comments or jokes.

Daniel was uncomfortable, but he'd started this investigation so he had to endure the digs.

"Enough," Bill ordered. "Let's move on." His words drummed on inside Daniel's head as Bill went through the detectives and officers, each offering satisfactory answers to the questions Bill asked.

All the while Daniel kept watching Tom. He sat on the end of the front row, right in front of Daniel, cool as a cucumber, not even breaking a sweat like Kevin, Jack and Lee. He thought he was home free. He thought his secret was safe.

The past few years flashed through Daniel's mind. He remembered Tom and Carol having financial problems. They'd bought a new home and with three kids they were having a hard time making the payments. Then suddenly things had changed—Daniel didn't hear any more complaints about money. Carol's mother had passed away and Tom said she'd left them some money. They'd bought a bigger house with a pool and went on expensive vacations. He should have been more astute and asked questions. But then, they were friends; he'd believed him.

When Boyd was arrested, Bill appointed Tom as a liaison to aid Internal Affairs when needed. Bill believed, as Daniel did, that Tom was above reproach. Daniel had been busy with the trial and getting Sarah ready to testify. He'd checked in with Tom from time to time, but he'd never had anything substantial. Now Daniel knew why. He'd been protecting himself. Why hadn't he delved deeper? Loyalty. Friendship. The cop bond. Everything was staring him in the face and it was a chilling truth. He should have known Tom couldn't afford the new house, new vehicles and expensive trips. He'd bought it all with blood money—Greg's blood and the blood of those two young girls.

Tom sat with a smug expression on his face, knowing Bill had nothing on him. If not for Sarah, it would probably stay that way. Daniel felt a moment of failure in his job as a detective for not recognizing the signs. He had his eyes wide open now, though.

"Daniel," Bill said. "Do you want to add anything?"

"Yes, sir," Daniel replied, and got to his feet. He had a lot to say. He walked around to the front of the table and leaned back against it. "The lieutenant's right. I've loaned or given money to almost every person in this room." He gazed out at the men nodding their heads, then his gaze settled on Tom. "Everyone but you, Tom."

"You know I don't like borrowing money." He brushed the remark away.

"Then how did you afford that big house and the BMW you just bought Carol?"

"It's no secret that Carol's mother died and left us some money and I got a loan from the bank for the car."

Daniel folded his arms across his chest. "Really? The lieutenant just went through your expenses and I don't remember hearing a note for a BMW."

"It's a new car and it's probably not on file yet."

Daniel nodded. "Yep. That could be it." He stared directly at Tom. "But I don't think so."

"If you have something to say, Daniel, spit it out," Tom said, still cool, still thinking he had everyone fooled.

"You're very proud of that gun you wear."

"You know I am. It was my dad's."

"Not many like it, especially the holster with the leather worn through like that."

"Is that suppose to mean something?"

"Yes. You see, I have Sarah Welch in a room down the hall."

"We're all aware of that."

"But what you don't know, Tom, is that she was watching everyone filing into this room and she noticed something familiar."

Tom didn't answer and for the first time Daniel saw fear in his eyes. The room became very quiet and no one moved or spoke.

"What the hell did she see?" Russ broke the silence.

Daniel pointed to Tom's gun. "She saw Tom's gun."

"So?" Russ raised an eyebrow.

"She also saw that holster at Teasers, the strip club where Boyd made her strip. The man wearing it was talking to Boyd."

The room became painfully quiet.

"Were you at Teasers talking to Boyd after Greg was killed?" Daniel asked point blank.

The fear in Tom's eyes became vivid. "Okay." He shifted uncomfortably. "I had a little visit with Boyd hoping he might slip up and mention Greg."

"Why? I specifically gave orders to stay away from him."

"I didn't follow orders," he snapped. "That's not a crime."

"You're lying your damn head off."

Tom didn't say anything and avoided looking at Daniel.

"Were you selling information to Boyd?" Daniel leaned in toward Tom.

Tom still didn't answer. He stared down at his shoes.

"I asked you a question."

"Of course not," Tom denied.

Daniel took a controlled breath. "There wasn't anything about an inheritance in your file, but I can find out how much money Carol's mother left you or if she left you any at all. Do you want me to do that, Tom?"

No response.

"Did you sell information to Rudy Boyd?" Daniel shouted.

"I—I—I—" Tom stammered.

Will jumped out of his seat and made a dive for Tom, knocking him to the floor. Lee and Kevin pulled him off, but Will got in several punches.

"You goddamn bastard. You traded Greg's life for money. You low-down bastard. I'll kill you!" Will tried to break free. Kevin and Lee held him tight.

"Knock it off," Bill yelled.

"I'll kill him, Lieutenant. I will."

Bill nodded to Kevin and Lee. "Take him outside and help him cool off. I'll take care of this."

Lee and Kevin dragged Will out the door. All the while he was screaming, "I'll kill you, Tom. I'll kill you."

Jack stared down at Tom. "You said you saw my wife with a younger man. You lied, didn't you?"

Tom rubbed his jaw.

"Why?" Jack asked angrily. "Why would you do that to me?"

"Because you're a fool."

Daniel got between Jack and Tom. "He didn't want

you working the case." Daniel enlightened him. "If your focus was somewhere else, then you wouldn't find out who was selling drugs to the college kids. And evidently Tom knows who is."

Jack tried to get past Daniel. "You low-life bastard. I'll help Will kill you."

"Tom will get his, I promise," Daniel said to Jack, who was breathing heavily. "Take a deep breath."

"He knew how jealous I was and he played on that. Angie said she wasn't seeing anyone else and that she loved me, but Tom kept…"

"You're so damn gullible," Tom sneered

"Not as gullible as you," Jack shot back. "I'll be sleeping with my wife and you'll be rotting in a cold, dark cell like the vermin you are."

"Go call Angie and cool off." Daniel gave him a push toward the door and he slowly walked through it.

"Everyone clear the room," Bill said.

Lieutenant Bauer got to his feet. "I'll leave this to you, Bill. Russ, you and Joel stay behind if Lieutenant Tolin needs any help."

"I wasn't planning on going anywhere, Lieutenant, not when we've got a traitor in our midst," Russ said.

"Put a sock in it," Charles ordered as he left.

Daniel was trying very hard to keep from doing what Will and Jack had wanted to do—to beat Tom to within an inch of his life. He gritted his teeth and watched Tom crawl into a chair, his nose bleeding.

Daniel pulled out his handkerchief and handed it to him, out of desperation not courtesy. If he hadn't, he probably would have taken out his gun and shot him. He didn't want to sink to that level.

Bill walked up to Tom and held out his hand. "Let me have your gun and badge."

"That's my dad's gun," Tom mumbled, doing as Bill asked.

"Where you're going, you're not going to need it."

"You don't understand."

"I'm listening," Bill said. "And that's a big concession on my part."

"I didn't want to, but I had no choice."

"Boyd had something on you?" Bill asked.

"Yeah." Tom wiped his nose. "I went into Teasers one night looking for Vinny, that snitch that brings us information. He wasn't there, but the strip show had started and I got caught up watching the women. Carol and I were fighting and it was just a relaxing thing. Later, one of the strippers came to my table and we got to talking and she invited me upstairs. Boyd taped the whole thing and a couple of weeks later he showed me the video and he threatened to show it to Carol if I didn't give him information. He just wanted to know when Daniel was planning the raids. That's all he said. I couldn't let Carol see that tape—she'd leave me." He looked at Daniel. "You know how it is. We arrest them one day and they're out the next. I didn't see the harm."

"Why did you tell him about Greg?" Daniel asked in a voice like steel, trying to stay calm.

"I didn't. I just got myself in so deep I couldn't get out. I had a twelve-year-old daughter and Boyd said that if any undercover cops came into any of his establishments and got information on him that he knew some boys that would love to have a good time with her. I couldn't...all I said was not to tell Greg anything. I didn't know he was going to kill him. I didn't.''

"What did you think?" Russ asked, each word dripping with sarcasm. "That he was gonna have a picnic with him?"

"I didn't think, okay?" Tom shot back.

"No, it isn't okay," Daniel shouted and he knew he was close to losing it. "You saw what he did to Sarah. Wait a minute." Daniel frowned. "You weren't there when we arrested Boyd and you stayed away from the trials. I thought you'd had enough of Boyd. Hell, we all had. You were just afraid Sarah might recognize you. That's it, isn't it?"

Tom fidgeted nervously.

"Good God," Daniel exploded. "You told him where we were hiding Sarah before the trial." A rage filled him, but he managed to continue. "Do you remember how many officers were hit that day? Do you remember that Ethan Ramsey took a bullet meant for Sarah and Serena?"

"I try not to remember."

"How very convenient." Daniel's hands curled into fists. "I remember every day seeing my friend and fellow officers lying in their own blood. I remember Serena covered in Ethan's blood and shaking. I remember Sarah scared out of her mind and all because of you, you piece of trash."

"I had to protect my family."

"You were protecting your own ass and now you're going to give me the name of the man who murdered those young girls."

"I didn't have anything to do with that."

"You're lying," Daniel yelled. "You're now feeding information to Arnie Bishop."

"I didn't. I just…"

"What? You might as well tell me because I'll find out all the sordid details and it will go a lot easier on you if you tell me now."

Tom gulped for air. "Arnie called and said Boyd had a plan to beat the death sentence and I had better cooperate. Boyd wanted young girls to be killed and he wanted to know how to get Daniel involved in a murder. I just told him narcotics had to be found—that's all."

Daniel frowned. "Boyd wanted me involved?"

"Yeah."

"Why, Tom? Why did Boyd want me involved in those cases?"

"He blames you for everything that's happened to him. You made his life difficult when he was on the outside by never letting up on him and now that he's on the inside he wants to make your life a living hell. You should have turned a blind eye to his illegal activities, Daniel, and we all would have been better off."

Daniel pulled back as if Tom had struck him. "Do you honestly believe that?"

A uniformed officer knocked on the door and Joel let him in. "Lieutenant, the chief wants to see you."

"I'll be right there." Bill handed Daniel Tom's gun and badge. "Watch his gun and keep things under control. I'll be back as soon as I can." He hurried away.

Russ took Tom's gun out of Daniel's hand and Daniel didn't stop him. He was still reeling from Tom's take on the law. Russ sat in a chair and propped his feet on the table. "Now, Tom, let's get down to the nitty gritty. And remember, I'm not as nice as Daniel.''

''I've told you all I know.''

''Well, you see, I don't think so.'' He removed the gun from the holster. ''I like these old revolvers. Six bullets in the cylinder. One shot does it all. Of course, that is if you're a good shot. And you're a good shot, aren't you, Tom?''

''Yes. Please put down my gun.''

''Tom, boy, I don't take orders. Do I, Daniel?''

''Not very well,'' Daniel replied, knowing Russ was playing one of his cat and mouse games. He should stop him, but again he didn't.

''You see that hole in my shoe, Tom?''

''Yes.''

''I got it from pounding the pavement searching for a murderer. I haven't had a good night's sleep in days and I haven't had time to shave. You might say I'm pretty pissed at this point. I'm busting my ass to catch a killer and you're helping one. That pisses me off even more.'' Russ slowly removed five bullets and laid them on the table in plain sight, then he spun the cylinder.

''Ever play Russian roulette, Tom?''

''No.''

''Well, today's your lucky day.'' He pointed the gun at Tom. ''What's the killer's name?''

''I don't—''

Russ pulled the trigger and it snapped.

Tom jerked back. ''You're crazy.'' He glared at Daniel. ''Do something.''

Daniel shrugged. ''He doesn't take orders from me.'' Daniel had seen Russ do this before and he hadn't liked his tactics, but now he thought that Tom should sweat a little. And he knew Russ had everything under control.

"That was for the first girl that was raped and murdered," Russ said, spinning the cylinder. He pointed the gun again at Tom. "This is for the second girl. Give me a name."

"Russ, if I—"

Russ pulled the trigger and it clicked. "Damn, you're lucky." Before Tom could catch his breath, Russ said, "This is for Brooke Wallace. Give me a name."

"Please—"

Click. "Goddammit, Tom, you're a lucky bastard." He pointed the gun again. "This is for the officers that were hit five years ago at the hotel. Give me a name."

"Please, I—"

Click. The blood drained from Tom's face.

Russ spun the cylinder again. "We're down to two. How lucky are you feeling, Tom? This is for Sarah Welch. Wouldn't it be the sweetest irony if you were killed with your own gun? I want a name."

"Russ, please—"

Click. Tom stiffened, his face a pasty white.

"Well, I'll be damned. Now you'll know when it's coming. This one's for Greg and it's from every officer in this building. A name—now."

"All I know is that Arnie called him Bear. That's all I know. Put the gun down, please."

Russ pulled the trigger and Tom jolted backward as if to brace himself for the blow, but none came—only another click.

"Oops." Russ smiled in a sly way. "Guess I removed all the bullets."

"You bastard," Tom hissed, visibly shaking.

Russ jumped to his feet, but Daniel got in front of him before he reached Tom. "Are you afraid, Tom?" Daniel asked. "That's the way Sarah's been feeling the past few days. Did you put that note on her door?"

"No."

"Did you put that tracer on my car?"

Tom didn't answer.

Before Daniel knew what he was doing, he reached out with his fist and knocked Tom from the chair.

"What the hell's going on here?" Lieutenant Tolin demanded as he came back.

Daniel rubbed his fist, appalled at his own actions.

Russ spoke up. "Well, sir, Tom here is having a hard time sitting in his chair. The floor must be un-leveled or something."

Bill saw the gun and bullets lying on the table. "What are the bullets doing out of Tom's gun?"

"Now, sir, that's another story," Russ replied.

"And I don't want to hear it." He grabbed the bullets and the gun. "Read him his rights, book him and get him in a cell—now. Or the next fist flying will be mine." He walked toward the door. "Daniel, Russ, in my office when you're through."

"I'm sorry," Tom muttered.

"Yeah. That's going to get you a cell right up there with Boyd." Russ caught Tom by the arm and pulled him to his feet.

"I'm sorry, Daniel," Tom muttered again.

Daniel turned away.

"Okay, Joel. Read Tom his rights and don't leave out a word. We want this tied up nicely." Russ and Joel led him from the room. "I'll catch you later," Russ said to Daniel.

Daniel felt betrayed, empty and angry. Angry that

he hadn't seen what was going on under his own nose. He saw Tom almost every day and he'd never suspected a thing. They were friends. Or so he'd thought.

He ran both hands over his face. He hated this job. He hated everything about it and he knew it was time to quit—to hand in his gun and badge. He'd failed miserably as a cop, as a leader. He'd had the same feelings a few days ago, but now there was no doubt in his mind. His career was over. He wouldn't leave, though, until the killer was caught.

Now he had to see Sarah.

CHAPTER FOURTEEN

DANIEL OPENED THE door and Sarah ran into his arms. "What took so long? I heard yelling and screaming."

"Will, Greg's partner, isn't taking this well. Hell, none of us are."

Sarah looked into his eyes. "Then it was Tom?"

"Yes." Daniel sank into a chair. "He's been Boyd's informant all along. He tried to deny it, but he knew it was over. He told Boyd about the raids, about Greg, where you were staying before the trial. He even put that tracer on my car. Why couldn't I see what that bastard was doing?"

Sarah sat facing him, her knees touching his. "Because you trusted him."

"Yeah," he sighed, his eyes meeting hers. "And that makes me a very bad detective."

"Don't you dare say that," she said with fire in her eyes. "You're the reason Boyd is on death row."

He stood. "He's still controlling things from his cell. Tom said Boyd wanted to make sure that I was investigating the rapes and murders. That's why the heroin was put in the girls' arms—to get back at me for all the years I persisted in getting something on him that would hold up in court."

Sarah watched the turmoil on his face and her heart ached for him. "Daniel, please don't..."

"Those girls died because of me—because I wanted Rudy Boyd behind bars."

She got to her feet. "Those girls died because of Boyd and his warped mind. That has nothing to do with you."

"But he's sending me a message and I have to stop him before someone else gets hurt." His eyes caught hers. "I can't let anything happen to you."

"I'm in a police station," she told him. "I feel safe."

He slipped his arms around her waist and held her tight. "This is going to be a long day and I hate that you have to sit in this room."

She pulled back. "I'm fine. Just catch the killer."

"I have a meeting with the lieutenant and then we'll apply pressure to Bishop and Tom. We need a name. Right now all we have is Bear."

Her eyes grew big.

"What?"

"One of the guards at Teasers was called Bear. I'm sure of it. I heard Boyd shout that name several times. Oh, God. It's probably someone I've seen before."

Daniel caught her arm. "Are you sure?"

"I'm positive."

"Then his name would be in the files we have on Boyd. Every employee is listed." He moved toward the door. "This'll help tremendously. I'll check in later."

"Be careful."

"I will."

Daniel hurried down the hall to Bill's office. He knocked and entered. Bill was popping antacids into his mouth.

"Where's Russ?" Bill demanded, munching.

"Right here," Russ said from behind Daniel.

"Is Tom in a cell?"

"Yep," Russ replied.

Bill shook his head. "This isn't good. Before I can even think about the repercussions for my department, we have to catch the killer, and the chief wants it done today. Do either of you have an idea how to accomplish that?"

Daniel told him what Sarah had said.

"Damn. Instead of hiding Sarah Welch, I should have her working on this case. Get every man on this pronto and I want names on my desk in less than an hour. Understand?"

The narcotics squads went to work with homicide and within an hour they had the names of twelve men that worked as guards for Boyd. Then they set out to find them.

Daniel was energized just knowing the killer would soon be caught. He was beginning to see a ray of light at the end of the dark tunnel and felt sure they were now on the right track.

THE DAY DRAGGED for Sarah as she waited patiently for news. She talked to Brooke for an hour. The confinement was getting to her and Sarah tried to bolster her spirits.

A woman named Faith came and gathered up the files and Sarah helped her. At least she was able to do something. Later, Faith brought lunch and ate with her. Sarah was grateful to have someone to talk to, but she wished it was Daniel. He was out there now searching for a crazy person who was capable of anything—even killing Daniel. A chill spread through her and she prayed the nightmare would soon be over.

BY SIX O'CLOCK they had nine of the twelve suspects in custody. Two were already in prison and the last one seemed to have disappeared off the face of the earth. Daniel was hoping they had the one they were looking for and that Sarah could identify him.

As Russ and the others were getting them ready for a lineup, Daniel went to get Sarah.

"We have nine of the twelve that worked as guards for Boyd," he told her as they walked to a room with a two-way mirror. "Do you think you can identify the one called Bear?"

"I'll try."

Sarah noticed that Daniel looked tired and on edge. She knew how hard he was working to solve this case and she would do anything to help him.

Russ was waiting with Lieutenant Tolin. The men were brought into a room on the other side of the mirror but Sarah didn't recognize any of them.

"Dammit." Daniel swung away from the mirror. "I thought we had him."

"I'm sorry," Sarah said. "I never really looked at their faces. I just wanted to block everything out."

"It's not your fault," Daniel was quick to reassure her. He turned to Russ. "Bring Brian Colley in. He knows his face."

Daniel pulled Sarah to one side as Joel brought in a young man. He stared at the men behind the mirror then shook his head. "I haven't ever seen any of those men," he said.

"Look real good," Russ instructed.

"No, sir," the man replied. "He's not there."

Russ said a foul word as Joel led the man away.

"Who's number twelve?" Bill asked.

Russ opened a folder he was holding. "Melvin Jenkins,'' he read. "Dishonorable discharge from the army.'' Worked as a bounty hunter until Boyd hired him. We checked his last known address and he moved out four years ago. Not a trace since then.''

"Step up the pace,'' Bill said. "We have to find him.'' He looked at Daniel. "This is going to be an all-nighter so it's best if Ms. Welch went back to your place. We'll post guards inside and out and everything should be fine. This guy's probably on the run now.''

"Okay,'' Daniel replied, staring at Sarah. He wanted to stay with her, but he had a job to do. He took her arm and led her away from the others.

"Are you okay with that?''

"Yes,'' she answered. "Like your lieutenant said, this guy knows the cops are on to him and he's on the run.''

"I'll check in when I get the chance.''

"I don't guess I can kiss you.'' She gave a small smile, glancing at the other officers.

Daniel guided her down the hall and around the corner and kissed her deeply. He leaned his forehead against hers. "I'll be back as soon as I can.''

"You better,'' she whispered and saw Chad coming down the hall. She pulled back and Daniel gave Chad his orders. She walked away with Chad, but looked back at Daniel and had an eerie feeling that she couldn't shake.

WITHIN MINUTES it seemed, she was in Daniel's condo sitting on a sofa hugging a pillow and longing for Daniel. Chad and Ron, another officer, were searching the house. Two other officers were outside. They conversed through two-way radios so everyone would know what was going on inside and out.

Sarah was drained and went upstairs, planning to take a shower, but decided to lie down for a bit. She kicked off her sneakers and curled up on the bed, thinking about Daniel and hoping he was safe.

She must have dozed off because she woke up to loud voices.

She charged down the stairs. "What is it?"

"Daniel's brother is outside wanting to see Daniel. We can't make him understand that Daniel's not here," Chad said.

Drew probably thought he and Daniel were going fishing. "Let him in and I'll talk to him. Maybe I can get him to understand."

Chad hesitated, then, "Okay, but make it quick." He went to the front door, turned off the alarm and spoke to Mac, an officer outside. Ron stood a few feet away. Chad opened the door and Drew came in.

"I—I—I come to see Daniel," Drew said, looking at Chad, Ron, then Sarah. "W-w-why...why are cops here, Sarah? Where's Daniel?"

She went to him. "He's at work."

Drew frowned. "Make them put their guns away. They scare me."

"It's okay, Drew," she tried to pacify him. "It's late and you shouldn't be out. Where's your caretaker?"

Drew shrugged. "Don't know. I—I—I ran away— have to talk to Daniel." The look on Drew's face bothered her. He was on something. She knew that drugged look; she'd seen it before.

Sarah was struggling for a way to handle this without bothering Daniel. "We'll call you a cab to take you back to your place, then I'll phone Daniel and have him get in touch with you. Will that be okay?"

"I—I—I guess."

Sarah nodded at Ron and he went into the kitchen to call a cab.

"Daniel will phone as soon as he can," she told Drew.

"H-h-he's mad at me."

Sarah smiled at him. "No, he isn't. Daniel's not like that."

"He's a good guy," Drew stated.

"Yes, he is," Sarah agreed, watching Drew closely. He kept looking around as if he didn't know where he was.

"Time to go," Chad said, then spoke into the radio, "Mac, he's coming out."

There was no response.

"Mac, is everything okay?"

Still nothing.

"Mac…"

A loud boom sounded and the front door flew open. Everything happened so fast that Sarah didn't have time to do anything. A man rushed in and fired two quick shots, one at Chad, the other at Ron. Sarah's whole body froze in abject fear. It was him—the guard from Teasers. Bear. She recognized him. He was a big, heavily muscled man with hair sheared close to his head. The gun was now pointed at her. A scream solidified in her throat. It all happened in a split second.

"W-w-why'd you shoot them, Claude?" Drew asked, his voice thick.

"Shut up, you stupid idiot!"

Sarah was trying to stay calm. She glanced at Chad and saw blood oozing from his chest. She had to help him. Bending down, she checked his pulse to see if he was breathing. There was a faint heartbeat. He was still alive. Thank God. Ron was in the breakfast area, lying perfectly still. She made a step toward him.

"Stay right there, you bitch," Claude snarled.

"These men need a doctor." She was amazed how calm her voice sounded.

Claude smiled a sinister smile and her skin crawled. "Don't worry about them, baby. You should be worried about yourself."

"Y-y-you can't hurt her, Claude," Drew said, his words becoming thicker. "S-s-she's Daniel's girlfriend."

"You stupid idiot," Claude hissed.

"Y-y-you say I get in Daniel's house you give me more heroin."

"Here's your heroin." Claude backhanded Drew across the face and knocked him against the wall.

Drew crumpled to the floor, whimpering, "Y-y-you mean."

Her gun was in her purse, which was in a chair about six feet away. She took a step in that direction. Poor Drew! Evidently Claude, or Bear, or whatever he was called, was manipulating him with drugs. She took another step.

Claude turned to her. "Now, Ms. Sarah Welch, you and I are gonna have some fun."

She fought the nausea churning in her stomach. To stay alive until Daniel got here, she had to keep him talking. She had to use all her skills to do that since revulsion was in every beat of her racing heart.

"Why are you doing this?"

"For money, baby, and lots of it."

"Boyd's paying you?" She took another step.

"Not exactly," Claude sneered. "He's in jail, as

you well know, but he has some valuable holdings that will be mine and Arnie's.''

''And for that you're raping and killing young women.'' She couldn't keep the horror out of her voice.

It didn't faze him, though. ''Rudy's a smart dude. He wouldn't give it all to us at once. After I did each girl, we got so much. You, Sarah baby, are the big payoff. Rudy wants to know every little detail of what I do to you and the cops will have nothing to trace it to Arnie or me.''

She swallowed hard. ''Why did Boyd want Daniel to investigate the crimes?'' She had to keep the questions coming—to keep him busy.

''The needle in the arm was brilliant. Garrett, the heroin expert, was all over it.''

''Was it because of Drew?'' She took another step toward her purse.

''You're pretty smart, Sarah baby.''

She shivered but she didn't let it show.

''Boyd was Drew's drug connection in college.''

Sarah gasped, unable to stop herself.

''Yeah. Drew had plenty of money and Boyd sold him all he wanted. The more his parents pressured him about his grades, his future, the more heroin he took until finally, well, you know the rest.'' He glanced at Drew's slumped form. ''He's a blubbering idiot.''

''Did Boyd sell Drew drugs after the overdose?''

''Yep. As soon as Drew went home from the hospital, he called Boyd. His brain doesn't work too well, but he knows he wants drugs.''

''Why didn't Boyd mention this to Daniel after he was arrested? It would have been a way to get back at him.'' She was trying to get all the information she could. Daniel would need it.

Claude's lip curled back. ''Boyd ain't stupid. He had a plan to really stick it to Garrett. After what happened to Drew, Garrett was gung-ho about getting the big drug dealers. When he made detective, his number-one goal was to put Rudy behind bars and he never knew Rudy was Drew's drug source. Rudy liked it that way. Drew was very profitable and he didn't want Garrett stopping that. Rudy always managed to stay one step ahead of Garrett. He knew about the surprise raids, he knew every move Garrett and his boys made.''

Sarah took a breath. ''How?''

''Shut up, you damn bitch!'' Claude shouted, the questions getting to him. ''Boyd should have shot you like he did your boyfriend, but he wanted you in the worst way and he wanted you to suffer before he slit your throat. Everything snowballed after that—your sister came looking for you, Ethan Ramsey got involved and Garrett was there to finally nail Rudy. It should've been over, but Rudy's been waiting to even the score with Garrett.''

''How?'' she asked again.

''The plan was for me to get close to Drew and get him so hooked on drugs that he'd take another overdose. The plan changed slightly when Rudy decided he might be able to beat a death sentence by trading his life for the young women of Dallas.''

''How did you become Drew's caretaker?'' She'd thought the Garretts were more astute than to hire a criminal.

''I took my cousin Claude's identity. He was a male nurse and died in a car accident seven years ago.

He had an impeccable record and the Garretts didn't check for a death certificate and neither did Mr. Detective. He was so busy tying up all the loose ends with Rudy that he left a door wide open.''

And like a vermin you slipped right through. She took another step closer to her purse. ''You won't get away with this.''

''I have so far.''

''They'll catch you,'' she insisted.

His lips curled back again. ''Sarah baby, nothing is gonna interfere with this night. I watched you take your clothes off at Teasers and I watched Rudy drool all over you, but tonight you're mine.''

She made a dive for her purse, her hand finding the gun immediately. She gripped it tightly and released the safety. Before she could aim, Claude was on top of her.

''You bitch,'' he snarled.

The weaker Sarah of five years ago would have crumbled easily, but this Sarah was determined to fight. A man wasn't taking advantage of her again. She'd fight to her last breath. She kicked out with her arms and legs and they tumbled to the floor. The fall jarred the gun loose from her fingers. It spun a few feet away. She clawed to reach it before Claude.

''D-d-don't hurt her,'' Drew muttered, coming out of his stupor. He clutched Claude's feet and Claude turned the gun on Drew and fired. Drew's body jerked then went limp, blood seeping from his stomach.

''Ohmygod! Ohmygod!'' The fight went out of Sarah and she tried to get to Drew, to help him. Claude grabbed her around the waist and hauled her toward the stairs. His arms were solid and strong and she could barely breathe, but she knew she had to stay alive so Daniel could know the truth. Like five years ago, she'd use her body any way she had to to accomplish that.

Any way.

IT WAS AFTER ELEVEN and Daniel and Russ still had no trace of Melvin Jenkins, so they decided to question Arnie again. He knew where Bear was and they intended to get an answer. Hannah hadn't pressed them to release him and spending a few hours in jail made Arnie surlier than usual.

"I'm not telling you bastards a goddamn thing," Arnie spat.

Daniel laid some photos in front of him. "Take a look at your guy's handiwork. These are the two girls he raped and murdered."

Arnie turned his head. Russ caught Arnie's head with both hands and turned it so he had to look. "Take a good look," Russ demanded.

"The one on the left is Janet, twenty-two, just received a degree in journalism and was working for a newspaper," Daniel informed him. "The one on the right is Lori, twenty-one, a student in elementary education. Two beautiful young women with their whole futures ahead of them, but it was snuffed out just like that." He snapped his fingers in Arnie's face.

"I didn't have anything to do with those murders," he mumbled, and Russ released his head.

"You ordered them," Daniel said.

"You can't prove it."

Daniel placed both hands on the table and leaned in close to Arnie's face. "Tom Hudson," he spoke the name slowly.

"Is that suppose to mean something?"

Daniel nodded. "He's the snitch in our department working for Boyd—and now working for you. He's talking his head off to save his own hide."

Arnie didn't say anything, but Daniel could see he wasn't quite so pompous anymore so he pushed further. He tapped the photos. "When a jury sees these photos and hears Tom's testimony, there'll be a cell on death row with your name on it."

"I want to see my lawyer," Arnie spouted.

"Well, Arnie," Russ said. "That high-powered attorney from Austin you called hasn't shown up. Guess you're not his number one priority." Russ opened a door and a man stepped in. "This is Wendell Groves, a court-appointed attorney."

"Get that idiot out of my sight. He doesn't know the first thing about being a defense attorney."

"Are you refusing counsel?"

"You're damn right."

"You heard the man," Russ said to Wendell. "Your services aren't required."

"Are you sure, Mr. Bishop?" Wendell asked.

"Damn sure."

Wendell quietly left.

"I wanna go back to my cell," Arnie muttered.

Daniel got into his face again. "Listen, you sleazebag, you're not going anywhere until you tell me where Bear is. Do you understand me?"

"It's too late anyway." Arnie glared at him.

"What?" Daniel strained to catch what he was saying.

"It's too late," Arnie shouted. "Can't you hear?"

"Why is it too late?" Daniel asked.

Arnie glanced at the big clock on the wall. It was

eleven forty-five. "He was supposed to kill her by midnight."

"Kill who?"

Arnie stared directly at Daniel, a sly smile on his thin lips. "Sarah Welch."

The blood drained from Daniel's face and he could feel it seeping from his body, leaving him defenseless and weak. He jerked up and tore out the door with one thought on his mind—to get to Sarah.

He ran out the building to his car. As he backed out, Russ yanked open the passenger door and leaped in. Daniel turned the siren on and they blared through the night.

"Slow down, Daniel," Russ said. "You'll kill us both. I'm trying to get Chad on the phone." Russ frantically poked out numbers on his cell phone. There was no answer.

Daniel pressed his foot down, praying, hoping she was still alive.

Hang on, Sarah.

CHAPTER FIFTEEN

DANIEL WAS OUT of the car before it came to a complete stop. He went in with his gun drawn; Russ was a step behind and backup was on the way. They found Mac and another officer first. Daniel felt for the pulse in the officer's neck.

"He's dead," he murmured in a stiff voice.

"Mac's still alive," Russ said, and called for an ambulance.

Daniel ran toward the house, not thinking, just reacting with steel-like precision.

"Let me go first," Russ appealed. "We don't know what we'll find in here."

"No. I have to do this. Cover my back."

"Daniel…"

Daniel wasn't listening. He wasn't feeling, either. He was frozen inside and he let his training, his cop instincts, take over. Slowly he moved to the front door. The lock was broken and swung open easily. He stepped inside the foyer, looking around, an eerie quiet permeated the place and he moved to the den then… He stopped dead at the scene in front of him and a sharp, paralyzing pain shot through him.

"My God," Russ uttered as he took in the bloody sight.

Daniel fell down by Drew, trying to keep his emotions at bay. "Drew, buddy," he whispered, feeling for a pulse. He was still alive. Air gushed from Daniel's lungs.

"Chad's alive—barely," Russ said as he checked him and moved to Ron. "Goddammit. Ron's dead."

"Buddy, can you hear me?" Daniel asked.

"D-D-Danny."

"Yes." Daniel swallowed. "It's me."

"H-h-he killed her. I'm sorry."

Daniel had to swallow again. "Where's Sarah, buddy?" *Where is Sarah!*

"He killed her," Drew said again.

His heart slammed into his chest, restricting his breathing. "Who killed her?" he asked with a tremor in his voice.

"D-D-Daniel," Drew gasped. "I'm sorry."

Sirens could be heard in the distance. "Hold on, buddy. The ambulance is coming."

"I'll check upstairs," Russ said.

"No." Daniel got to his feet and took the stairs two at a time. The bedroom door was locked and he kicked it in with his foot. He took the room in at a glance. Claude stood with an arm around Sarah's neck, a gun pointed at her temple. Sarah had a bra and jeans on and her hair was in disarray. She was alive, was all he could think. *She is alive.*

"Hello, Detective," Claude sneered. "You're a little early."

"Melvin Jenkins," Daniel said, holding his gun squarely on him. It finally came together in his head as Boyd's words played out a sickening echo. *In ways you'll never imagine.* The rapist and murderer was Claude, alias Melvin Jenkins, alias Bear, Drew's caretaker. A violent scenario put together for revenge— revenge against him. The thought threatened to cripple him, but he fought it. He had to get Sarah away from him.

"Let her go," he said, his words sharp. "This is between you and me."

"Wrong, Detective." Claude laughed. "It's between you and Rudy. I'm just the messenger."

"And you'll die his messenger."

"Don't think so. I'm walking out of here very much alive."

"Hear those sirens?" Daniel brought his attention to the sirens that were getting closer. "For you to walk out of here alive you'd have to be God."

"No one's going to touch me as long as I have her." He tightened his arm around Sarah's neck.

Sarah's face was sickly white and Daniel refused to look at her. He couldn't. He had to stay focused on Claude. "You're not walking out of this room so you might as well let her go."

"Come on, Detective." Claude laughed again. "You think I'm scared? You saw what I did to those other girls and I'll blow Sarah baby's brain all over this wall right in front of you. Now put the gun down."

Daniel's gun never wavered. "You shoot her and I'll shoot you. You're not getting out of here."

"You're not fooling me, Daniel, with your tough-cop act," Claude said, his eyes glittering with contempt. "You wouldn't harm a hair on Sarah's head. You've had the hots for her for so long it's pathetic."

"Let her go and we'll settle this man to man."

Claude grunted. "In your dreams, Detective."

"Why'd you drag Drew into this?" Daniel had to have an answer to that.

"He was always calling Rudy for drugs so he decided to make good use of Drew's habit—to get back at you.''

Daniel frowned. ''Drew's on drugs?''

''Heroin, big brother, his real medication,'' Claude told him. ''He's never been off of it except for the time he was in the hospital.''

''But...''

''Got you, hmm, Daniel? Rudy's been Drew's drug source since college and you never suspected. You never questioned why Drew wore long-sleeved shirts even in the summer, even when you went fishing. He was getting so thin and you worried he wasn't eating enough. Hell, he wasn't. He was shooting up heroin all the time. When Boyd wanted me to finagle my way into Drew's life, Drew was doing the stuff every now and then. But I made sure he was able to get it every week, then every other day and now the poor thing is hooked so bad what brains he had are totally fried.''

A rage swelled inside Daniel.

''What's the matter, Mr. Narcotics Cop, the truth too hard to take? Little brother might be an idiot but he knew how to hide his habit, especially from you.''

''Why did you have to shoot him?''

''Bastard has a soft spot for Sarah baby and tried to stop me,'' Claude replied. ''Drew does exactly what I tell him as long as I reward him with heroin, like last night. I had to find out if Sarah was here so Drew pretended he'd run away, but I drove him. You thought Drew needed his medication because he was nervous and jittery. All he needed was a fix and he wasn't getting it until I had my information.''

The rage turned into a blazing inferno. ''You've been giving him heroin instead of his medication?''

''You got it.''

"You son of a bitch."

"Your mother almost ruined our plans with her crazy idea of a home for Drew. I told him he'd better change her mind or he'd never get any more heroin. Enlisting your help is Drew's solution to everything because he knows you'll do anything for him."

The rage burned out of control.

"I'm the one who took care of the idiot while you and your parents went on with your lives. You were more than happy to hand over the responsibility and now I'm getting my reward—more money than I ever dreamed about and I don't have to put up with the idiot anymore."

"Stop calling him that, you bastard."

Sarah could see Daniel was close to the edge and she knew she had to do something. Claude's arm was so tight around her neck that she could barely breathe, but her legs were free. She tried to gauge if she could get her heel into his crotch. She didn't think she could with any degree of force.

"Drop the gun," Claude shouted and tightened his arm even more.

Sarah gasped a ragged breath and Daniel slowly laid his gun on the floor.

Even though breathing was difficult, Sarah managed to turn her head slightly. She opened her mouth and bit into his bicep as hard as she could.

Claude jerked, cursing, "Goddamn bitch." He didn't release her, but it gave Daniel the opening he needed. He made a dive for Claude and they tumbled backward onto the floor—Claude's gun landed on the carpet. Sarah crawled away, frantically trying to reach it.

Claude drove his fist into Daniel's stomach. He

withstood the blow and landed a punch to Claude's jaw. Back and forth they exchanged blows. Claude was bigger and stronger and Sarah didn't know how long Daniel could last. She reached the gun and picked it up.

Daniel was on his stomach, his arm outstretched to reach his gun. Claude had both of his hands linked together and applied blow after blow to Daniel's head. Daniel kept inching toward the gun.

Sarah closed her finger around the trigger and a loud boom resounded in the room, then another. Claude slumped to the floor, blood running from his torso. Daniel grabbed his gun and swung to his feet, staring down at Claude.

Russ squatted and checked Claude's pulse. "The bastard's dead. Good riddance."

Sarah didn't even realize Russ was in the room. She sat on the floor still holding the gun, unable to move, then she started to shake.

Daniel dropped down beside her and gently took the gun from her. She flew into his arms.

"You okay?" he asked in a shaky voice.

She nodded. "Did I...did I..."

Russ shoved his gun into his holster. "No, Ms. Welch, I shot him."

"Oh." She wasn't sure. She heard the sound but couldn't remember pulling the trigger.

Daniel helped her to her feet and picked up her blouse from the floor. She immediately slipped into it, not even feeling embarrassed that Russ had seen her this way. She was just glad they were all alive.

Russ headed for the doorway. "The ambulance is here."

Daniel and Sarah hurried down the stairs. At the

bottom Daniel swayed and Sarah wrapped her arms around him.

"Are you okay?"

"I'm fine," he lied.

"You are not," she said. "He hit your head repeatedly."

"I'm fine," he insisted and rushed to Drew. The paramedics had Drew on the stretcher, trying to get him stabilized.

"Daniel," Drew mumbled.

"I'm right here, buddy."

"I—I—I'm sorry. I—I—I had to have…the heroin. Y-y-you wouldn't understand…couldn't tell you."

Daniel couldn't speak.

"We have to go." A paramedic spoke up.

"I'm coming with you." Daniel found his voice and turned to Sarah. "I have to go with him."

"Go," Sarah replied. "I'll get Russ to bring me to the hospital."

Daniel ran after the stretcher.

Sarah wrapped her arms around her waist, feeling so exhausted that she didn't know how she was still standing. Russ walked up to her.

"Ms. Welch, are you okay?"

She glanced at him. "I'm not sure. I, uh, could you please take me to the hospital?"

"My pleasure."

Not much was said on the drive. Sarah was just worried about Daniel, wanting to be with him as soon as possible. It had been a horrific night and she prayed it didn't get any worse, but as soon as she walked into the emergency room she knew another nightmare had just begun. Daniel stood outside the double doors, his skin white, his gaze disoriented. She immediately went to him.

"He's dead," he said in a trembling voice. "He died on the way, saying, 'I'm sorry' over and over."

"Oh, Daniel. I'm so sorry." She slipped an arm around him.

Daniel's whole body was stiff and he didn't respond to her words or her touch. She wasn't sure he'd even heard her. He pushed back. "How could they do this? He was innocent. He didn't deserve this." Tears filled his eyes and he moved off down the hall. Sarah followed him. Russ watched from a distance.

"Daniel." She reached out to touch him but he swung away and her heart pounded with alarming force. He was putting distance between them; she could feel it. He wasn't letting her get close to him. The pain was controlling him totally.

"They killed him because of me."

"That's not true," she refuted, looking into his watery eyes. "Drew is not as innocent as you think. He started this years ago with his drug habit and it escalated into violence. Even when he almost died, he still went back for more. He kept it a secret from you, from your parents, because he knew that you would disapprove and seek help for him. He didn't want help. He wanted to live the way he was. That was his decision, not yours."

"They used him."

"Yes. That's the sad part, but Drew never said a word to you about Boyd. That was his decision, too. He did try to stop Claude, though, and that's why Claude shot him."

Daniel swayed slightly and she immediately caught

his arm. "You have to see a doctor. You probably have a concussion."

"What the hell does it matter?" he cried. "Nothing matters anymore."

"Daniel—"

"I have to tell our parents," he cut in. "I'm not quite sure how to do that."

"With the truth."

"Yeah." He let out an angry breath. "I'll tell them that through our negligence and insensitivity to Drew's needs that he's dead."

He ran both hands over his face. "I guess I'd better do it before they hear it on the news." He sucked in a long breath. "It's all over, so it's safe for you to go home."

"I suppose," she said, not liking that detached tone in his voice.

His eyes held hers. "I mean it's all over. Whatever we had between us is over, too. I'm not the man for you. You'd have been better off if you had continued to hate me. I'm sorry—that's just the way I feel."

His words were like a blow to her chest and it took a moment to catch her breath. "Daniel…"

"I didn't want anyone to ever hurt you again and I'm the one who's hurt you. By being who I am I've put you through hell once again. So get as far away from me as you can."

"Daniel." She tried again.

"It's true," he stated. "Get on with your life. You deserve one."

She bit her lip to still her emotions. He was hurt beyond belief and didn't know what he was saying.

"So do you," she said, hoping to reach him. But he didn't even seem to hear her.

"Russ will drive you home. I have to check on Chad and Mac." He strolled off down the corridor toward Russ.

Her insides trembled then convulsed with the worst pain she'd ever felt. She knew in that moment that she loved Daniel Garrett more than she'd loved anyone in her life. Through the pain she held on to that truth. Daniel would change his mind. He had to.

Russ walked up to her. "You ready?"

She blinked. "What?"

"Daniel said to drive you home. Chad and Mac are in surgery, so he's going to see his parents."

"Oh. Yes."

They made their way to the entrance. "Daniel's not thinking too straight right now."

"Don't tell me about Daniel," she flared.

He held up both hands. "Sorry."

They got into the car and she apologized. "I'm sorry. You've been very nice and I'm being rude."

"Hell." He grinned. "That's the first time anyone's called me nice. It's usually the other way around."

"Yes. I've seen that other side and it's definitely not nice."

"Ah, now don't go and hurt my feelings."

Some of the tension eased in her, but the pain was still there. "Please watch out for Daniel. He needs to see a doctor."

Russ backed out of the parking space. "I'll be there, but getting him to see a doctor is another thing. I'll tell the lieutenant—that's all I can promise."

Silence ensued.

Then Russ said, "Give him some time. That's all he needs."

She wished she could believe that, but Daniel's

words were so final. She knew him well enough to know that he'd meant everything he'd said.

When they reached her house, Russ searched the place and deemed it safe, then he asked, "You sure you feel safe here?"

She bit her lip. "Yes. All the demons have been slain tonight." *And more created.*

"Sometimes life is hard to take, but I've been told there's always a brighter tomorrow. And, Ms. Welch, you've had more than your share of dark days so your tomorrows should be as bright as—" He frowned. "What does my kid say? As bright as the stars in the skies. I'm not very good with words."

She tried to smile, but failed miserably. "Thank you. And please call me Sarah."

"Okay."

"You don't have a toothpick in your mouth. I don't believe I've ever seen you without one."

He scratched his beard. "It's kind of dangerous to have one in your mouth when you're in a life or death situation—swallowed, they could puncture a lung. I started chewing them when I stopped smoking. My wife, now my ex-wife, said she'd leave me if I didn't stop. I quit and she left anyway. Go figure women…"

Russ's words drummed on inside her head, but she didn't hear anything—just Daniel's words. *It's over. Whatever we had between us is over, too. I'm not the man for you.*

"I'd better go." She heard Russ's voice. "My lieutenant's probably screaming his head off for me. If you need anything, here's my cell number." He scribbled it on a piece of paper and handed it to her.

"Thank you," she said. "And…"

He held up a hand. "I know. Be there for Daniel."

"Yes."

"As I said, tomorrow will be better, and when you feel up to it, we need to get a statement."

Russ left and she collapsed onto the sofa in her living room and took a couple of deep breaths. She was home and for the first time she felt an incredible joy in that. But home wasn't a place—it was a feeling in the heart that came from love. Gran, Serena and Celia loved her. She knew that and had gained confidence from it. And now she loved Daniel and wanted to be with him. But he didn't want her.

Tears streamed down her face and she didn't try to stop them. The events of the past few days caught up with her and she cried until there was nothing left, only an empty, lonely feeling. She'd lived through the nightmare, endured the horrifying outcome and she wasn't going to fall apart. Her reactions were normal and she could handle the aftereffects. She couldn't handle losing Daniel, though.

She grabbed some tissues and blew her nose, then she picked up the phone. Staring at the grandfather clock she slowly replaced the receiver. It was 5:00 a.m. and Serena would still be sleeping. Ethan was probably up, though. No, she had to talk to Serena.

She stretched out on the sofa. She should take a shower, but she didn't have the strength. She'd rest then call Serena again. Once she heard her voice she'd be able to face the future. "Daniel," she murmured as she drifted into sleep.

The ringing of the doorbell jarred her awake. She glanced at the clock—9:00 a.m. It had to be Daniel. He was back. She flew to the front door and yanked it open. Sarah's mouth fell open. Serena, Ethan and Gran stood there. Daniel was nowhere in sight. Her heart sank for a brief second before she embraced her sister then her grandmother.

"What are you doing here?" Sarah asked.

"Daniel called us," Ethan replied. "We caught the first flight out of San Antonio."

Daniel had called—that meant he was thinking about her. "Did Daniel tell you everything that happened?"

"Yes," Serena said. "Are you okay?"

Sarah brushed back her hair. "I'm not sure. I'm just so worried about Daniel. What did he say when he called?"

Serena glanced at Ethan. "After he told us what had happened, he said he felt you didn't need to be alone and I agreed with him."

Aurora smoothed Sarah's hair. "Darling, you look so tired. I should have stayed with you."

Sarah rested her head on her grandmother's shoulder. "I just need some rest and now that you and Serena are here, I'm much better."

Ethan cleared his throat.

"You, too," Sarah added quickly.

"Just didn't want to be left out." He grinned and hugged her. "I'm going to try to find Daniel." He kissed Serena and walked toward the door.

Sarah looked at Gran and Serena and felt their love. Why had she ever questioned it? Insecurity, fear, but those things were now gone and she embraced her family with love…real love…family love.

Gran hugged her tightly and kissed her check. "I'm going to unpack. I know you and Serena want to talk." Aurora wiped a tear from Sarah's cheek and went upstairs.

Serena linked her arm with Sarah's and they made

their way into the study. "Where's Jassy?" Sarah asked as they sat on the settee.

"She's at home with Pop. We woke her up at six this morning and told her that you were sick and we had to come and take care of you. And that she had to stay at home because we didn't want her to catch what you had. It was a lie, but Ethan and I agreed it was the best thing to do. We weren't sure how things were here. I'll call her in a few minutes. We've talked to her twice already. Alma's coming over and they're going to make tea cakes and have a tea party, so she's excited."

Sarah twisted her hands and they were quiet for a moment.

"Tell me everything that happened." Serena's voice was soft.

"It's a nightmare."

Serena caught her hands. "We've been through those before."

"It was almost like last time. Claude broke in and shot Chad and Ron and..."

"Oh, Sarah."

"I didn't fall apart like before, though. I fought back until he shot Daniel's brother."

"You saw all this?" Serena asked in a shocked voice.

Sarah nodded. "Yes. I tried to help them, to help Drew, but..."

Suddenly, Sarah grabbed her sister and they clung together. "I'm so glad you're here."

"I wouldn't be anywhere else—not when you need me."

Sarah pulled back and brushed away tears. "I need Daniel, too."

Serena blinked. "Oh."

"The past few years you've been trying to get me to date and I have stoutly resisted saying I wasn't like you, that I didn't need a man in my life. But I realized I'm more like you than I ever thought. I want a man who loves me—a home and kids. And I want Daniel."

Serena took Sarah's hand again and settled close to her. "Tell me how all this came about."

Sarah told her everything that had happened since she'd last seen her, but she didn't go into detail about that night in Daniel's condo. She was sure Serena could put two and two together.

"All this time I've been suppressing my real feelings for Daniel—out of betrayal to Greg, guilt, whatever. I know now I've been falling in love with him for a very long time."

"And he feels the same way?"

"Yes. His brother's death has hit him hard, though, and he's pushing me away."

Serena shook her head. "I just feel so sorry for what he's going through."

"I do, too, and I want to be there for him, to help him through this but…"

"But what?"

"I keep remembering back to that time when we were rescued from Boyd and you wanted me to talk. I just wanted to be left alone and that's how Daniel is feeling now. He's shutting the whole world out… including me."

"The trauma of last night will fade and Daniel will think more clearly," Serena promised. "He's probably already regretting what he said."

"Always the optimist," Sarah remarked.

"You bet. I believe in happy endings and I know

they're real every time I look into Ethan's eyes. And when I look into Jassy's there is absolutely no doubt.''

"I love you." Sarah smiled, realizing she'd been yearning for family and roots and she had all that by being part of Serena's life, by being her twin. As a woman, though, she needed so much more.

"I love you, too." Serena smiled back. "We'll get through this just like before."

Sarah wasn't so sure. She couldn't survive this without Daniel and that shook her. Through sheer will-power she'd overcome the past braver and stronger; she wondered how long she could sustain that strength without him. He might want her to forget about him and their love, but she knew she never would.

Not ever.

CHAPTER SIXTEEN

DANIEL SAT IN Drew's apartment trying to piece together the shattered remnants of his life. He'd told his parents about Drew and his mother had become hysterical. They'd called the doctor and he'd sedated her. His father had been drowning himself in a bottle of scotch when he'd left.

The room was dark, but outside the sun was heralding a new day. He glanced at the watch on his arm. It was after nine. How long had he been here? He didn't remember nor did he remember how he'd gotten here. All he knew was that he had to be close to Drew. His things were here—the pool table, big-screen TV, video games and a state-of-the-art stereo system. Everything was here but Drew.

There wasn't a sound in the room. He listened to his breath—in, out. He shouldn't be breathing. Claude should have shot him. Boyd should have killed Daniel instead of Drew. But then, Boyd wouldn't have gotten what he wanted. He'd wanted to hurt Daniel and he had. He was hurting worse than he'd ever hurt in his life.

In ways you can never imagine. Boyd's words kept torturing him.

He got to his feet and flipped on the light. A picture of him and Drew stood on a table. The two of them were fishing and Drew looked happy. Happy? How well did he know Drew? Claude was right; the Garrett family had been eager to hand over the responsibility for Drew. A week of fishing did not make up for years of closing his eyes to Drew's problem.

When Drew would run away, he'd come to Daniel. He often looked dazed, Daniel had thought from the medication. But it wasn't that—he'd been doing heroin. As a narcotics detective, he should have been able to see that. He hadn't. He hadn't seen a thing. He'd ignored the signs, he'd ignored everything and now Drew was dead.

An overpowering helplessness gripped him and he picked up the picture and threw it against the wall, a vase followed, video games, movies—anything he found, he slammed against the wall.

"Hope you're getting it out of your system because you're making a damn mess." Russ stood in the doorway.

"Get out of here, Russ," Daniel shouted.

"Ah, Daniel, you know I don't take orders very well."

"Shut up and leave me the hell alone."

"Sorry, can't do that, either. I promised Sarah."
Sarah. Sarah. Sarah.

He stuck out his hand as if to ward off the power of her name, but it seeped through his defenses. *Oh, God, Sarah, no.* Weak and empty, he sank to the floor and rested his back against the wall. As exhausted as he was, he couldn't let her memory take control. He couldn't. She was better off without him.

Russ sank down beside him on the floor. "I'm sorry about Drew."

"Thank you," Daniel mumbled. "I should have seen what was going on. There were signs and I ignored them. Claude had scratches on his arms. He said it was from a cat he rescued out of a tree and I believed him. They were Brooke Wallace's scratches as she'd fought for her life. I didn't suspect a thing, just like I never suspected Tom. I've lost my edge. I shouldn't even be a detective.''

''Hell, Daniel, you're not God. No matter how hard you try, you can never second-guess a corrupt mind.''

''Boyd planned all this in prison.'' The diabolic plan was clear in Daniel's head but the details were sketchy.

Russ stretched out his legs. ''Yep. I've been at the police station and Arnie's talking his head off. We can't seem to shut him up. He said Boyd started telling him about all the money he had stashed away and how he could get it and the clubs if Arnie did what he wanted. The plan at first was to get to you through Drew—seems Drew's been involved with Boyd for a long time.''

''I don't understand that,'' Daniel said. ''How could my brother be involved with that lowlife? He knew how hard I worked to get him off the streets.''

Russ rubbed his beard. ''Well, Daniel, you might not like to hear it, but Drew was a drug addict and you've been in narcotics long enough to know that addicts will do anything to get their drug, even betray someone they love.''

Daniel's throat muscles closed up.

''Something else you might not like to hear,'' Russ went on. ''Drew was more than a little involved in this. Arnie said the plan was to start killing young women to get the police in a frenzy. With the heroin in the arm, Boyd was counting on you to pay him a visit. Then with his help to solve the crimes, he was betting that the D.A. would pull some strings to lighten his sentence. Arrogant bastard evidently doesn't understand the judicial system. And to put the screws to you, Boyd wanted Drew to kill the first girl, but he couldn't, so Claude took over. Drew was there for the first rape.''

A tortured moan left Daniel's throat. Russ stopped for a second, then continued. ''Arnie said Drew was so upset that Claude had to give him more heroin than usual, then later he withheld it from him because he didn't do what Boyd wanted him to. Drew went into deep withdrawal and Claude was afraid you'd stop by unannounced so he gave him an injection.'' Russ paused again. ''Claude supplied drugs to college kids. He chose girls from the parties who wouldn't take drugs. The plan was just to kill the first girl. When Drew couldn't, Claude dragged her into the bushes and raped her. That was his personal spin on this evil scheme.''

Daniel felt the anger in him turn to disillusionment then denial, but he couldn't close his eyes anymore. He had to face the truth.

''For each rape and murder, Arnie and Claude received money and titles to property. Sarah's death was to be the big payoff. Boyd wanted her dead in the worst possible way and he knew you had a thing for her. It was just ironic that she happened to be counseling Miss Wallace instead of Dr. Mason. Claude checked at the hospital to see if Brooke was still alive and he saw Sarah coming out of her room. He told Arnie and Arnie relayed the news to Boyd who thought the plan was coming together better than expected. Claude left the messages.''

Daniel's insides churned as if he was on the high

seas, each rolling wave, each news flash, hitting him with such velocity that all he yearned for was a measure of peace.

"You taking her into your personal protection probably saved her life. Tom didn't know where you had her so Arnie forced him to put the tracer on your car."

Daniel couldn't think about what could have happened to Sarah. She was safe—away from him. He wanted to say so many things, but what came out of his mouth was, "I don't understand how Claude fooled my parents."

"Daniel." Russ sighed with fatigue. "Open your eyes. Claude didn't fool them. Drew did. Drew went through caretakers like cheap toilet paper. He never liked any of them because they watched him too closely. He didn't like those restrictions. He liked going out and doing what he wanted without it being reported back to your parents. Claude coaxed Drew into persuading your parents to hire him. Drew knew about the rapes, he lied to you about the scratches on Claude's arm and he got Claude into your house past the alarm and the guards, knowing what Claude had in mind for Sarah. Drew didn't care as long as he got the heroin."

Daniel clambered to his feet in an angry movement. "For heaven's sake, don't even try to spare my feelings."

Russ got to his feet more slowly. "When you start blaming yourself, it's time to take a reality check. You can't help someone who lies and deceives you at every turn. Drew's mind was messed up bad and there's no way you could have known what he was doing unless he wanted you to—and he didn't."

"I was his brother, his best friend," Daniel mumbled.

"No. Heroin was Drew's best friend."

Daniel paled as the truth hit him like an avalanche, taking him down into a dark hole where there was no light, no air. He was suffocating.

"That's hard, but it's the truth, so stop beating yourself up over this. Grieve for your brother, then get on with your life. There's a woman just waiting for you to call her, so pick up the phone and get your ass over there."

Daniel pressed his hands against the sides of his head, trying to breathe normally and trying to block out Russ's words. "Get the hell out of here. You're not helping. You're making me angry."

"Good. That means you're feeling and if…"

"Get the hell out of here!" Daniel swung around as he heard a knock on the door. It was Ethan.

"Is it okay to come in?" Ethan asked.

"Ethan Ramsey." Russ walked over and shook his hand. "Damn good to see you."

"Good to see you, too." Ethan glanced at Daniel. "I heard shouting."

"That's Daniel's response to my lack of social skills," Russ said. "So I'll let you handle it from here." He glanced at Daniel. "Chad and Mac are out of surgery and the lieutenant wants to see you as soon as possible."

Daniel nodded and Russ left.

Daniel stared at his old friend and wanted to ask how Sarah was, but if he did, he'd fall apart completely. Right now he was walking a tightrope and he didn't know how much longer he could stay balanced.

Ethan took in Daniel's haggard appearance. "You don't look good."

Daniel fell onto the sofa and buried his face in his hands. "That's an understatement."

"I'm not going to say I'm sorry about your brother because you'll hear that a hundred times in the next few days and you know how I feel. I'll do whatever I can to help you."

"I'm not sure that's possible."

"Why?" Ethan sat in the chair opposite him.

"I'm not sure it's possible to live through this kind of pain." He glanced at Ethan and knew he'd been through similar circumstances. "How did you get over losing your son Ryan?"

"I won't lie to you. It wasn't easy—the healing has to come from within. Somewhere deep inside you'll find the strength to survive, to go on. You don't have much of a choice. I could have drunk myself into oblivion but that wasn't the epithet I wanted for my son. I wanted him to be proud of me just like you wanted Drew to be proud of you."

Daniel grimaced. "Drew would always ask if I was going to catch the bad guys. I thought he was proud of my work and I..."

"I went by the station," Ethan said when Daniel stopped talking. "Bill told me some of what Arnie Bishop was telling them. Since no one's heard from you, he's worried and sent Russ over here. That's how I found you."

"I treated Drew like a child," Daniel murmured as if Ethan hadn't spoken. "But he was an adult and understood a lot more than I gave him credit for. He lied to me, Ethan. He lied for Claude and I'm having a hard time accepting that."

"I didn't know your brother, but I know what drugs can do to the mind."

Daniel jerked to his feet and started to pace. "I thought Drew had learned his lesson with the overdose. Hell, I went into narcotics because of Drew, to get the scum that sold drugs to kids off the streets. My brother was working with the creeps! Drew knew exactly who Boyd was when we busted him. He was Drew's source. When I visited with Boyd in prison he said I would pay in ways I'd never imagine. He knew he had my brother under his control and he was holding the winning hand."

"Not quite," Ethan said. "Bill said Boyd's execution date has been set."

Daniel stopped pacing. "His death won't bring back Drew or those young girls or Greg or alleviate the hell he's put Sarah through. Boyd's death won't make any of this right."

"Maybe not," Ethan admitted. "But his reign of terror will be over."

"Everything is over," Daniel muttered.

"What do you mean?"

Daniel took a deep breath and looked off to the windows and the sun streaming through. "I've loved Sarah for what seems like forever and it was very clear she hated me. I hung in there, though, waiting, hoping until finally she told me to stay away from her because I reminded her too much of the past. Boyd's note brought us back together, but it would have been better if she still hated me."

"Why?"

"We became very close in the past few days and I could see all my dreams coming true—I just had to keep her safe. Now I have this empty hole inside me and there isn't any room for anything else. I just feel the pain—that's all—and Sarah doesn't need any more pain in her life.''

"No, she doesn't,'' Ethan agreed. ''Serena and I didn't know what to expect when we got here, but we didn't see any of the old Sarah. She wasn't withdrawing into herself or cowering away in fear like the last time. She's stronger and braver than any woman I know and that includes my wife.''

''I've always admired her fighting spirit.''

Ethan stood. ''Then let's go to the house so you can tell her that.''

''I can't,'' Daniel said. ''I have to check on my parents, then the guys at the hospital and I have to see Bill.''

''Those are excuses.''

Daniel didn't answer. He picked up his jacket from the sofa and slipped into it. ''I'll talk to you later.''

As he walked past, Ethan caught his arm. ''You will talk to Sarah?''

Daniel inhaled deeply, not wanting to lie.

''Why don't you admit what's really bothering you?'' Ethan said before he could reply.

''What?'' Daniel asked in a low voice.

''You're blaming yourself for what happened to her. You're thinking that you're the reason she had to go through this nightmare again and you can't live with that thought.''

''She's better off without me.''

''Let her make that decision.''

Daniel didn't respond and Ethan continued. ''You once told me when I was unsure about my relationship with Serena not to mess up something that could be good for me. I'm telling you that now—don't deprive yourself or Sarah of something that could be good for both of you.''

Daniel moved away and walked out the door heading for he knew not what. All he could see was darkness.

SARAH SPENT THE REST of the day visiting with Serena and Gran and it was exactly what she needed. Ethan came back, but he didn't say a whole lot about Daniel, just that he was going through a difficult time. He told them about Boyd's plan and a chill ran up her spine. She wanted to go to Daniel and to comfort him because she knew how much he loved his brother. She restrained herself knowing he needed this time with his family, but her heart ached for him.

Serena and Ethan left late afternoon to catch a flight back to San Antonio. It was just her and Gran again. Aurora embraced her granddaughter.

"I'm so happy you're okay, darling. I couldn't stand to lose you a second time."

Tears filled Sarah's eyes. "Thank you, Gran."

"I made so many mistakes with your mother and I promised myself I wouldn't do that with Serena. She turned out so beautifully that it's hard to believe I raised her."

"Serena's sweet and compassionate and everything a woman should be."

Aurora stroked Sarah's cheek. "So are you, my darling."

Sarah smiled, feeling so much love she thought her heart would burst.

"All those years Serena was growing up, I tried not to think about you because if I did I wouldn't be able to live with myself. But now you're here in my life, and you always will be. I love you, precious grand-daughter.''

''Oh, Gran.'' Sarah hugged her tightly. ''I love you, too.''

Sarah was home. There was just one other place she had to be before she was completely home—with Daniel.

She stepped back. ''I'm going over to the hospital to check on the cops that were shot and a patient.'' Sarah reached for her jacket.

''That's fine, darling,'' Aurora said. ''I have to call my friends and let them know I'm back.''

''I'll pick up something for dinner on my way back.''

'''Bye, darling.''

MAC WAS RESTING comfortably and was expected to have a full recovery. Sarah walked down the hall to Chad's room and knocked lightly. There was no response so she pushed the door open and glanced in. Chad was propped up on pillows, his chest bandaged, and blood dripped into his arm through an IV. His heart was also being monitored. He was asleep, as was the young woman sitting by his bedside, her head resting on their clasped hands.

Sarah started to close the door when Chad opened his eyes and saw her.

''Ms. Welch,'' he muttered in a weak voice.

''What?'' The young woman immediately jumped up as if something was wrong.

Sarah had no choice but to enter the room.

''It's okay, honey,'' Chad said. ''This is Ms. Welch, and Ms. Welch, this is Niki, my girlfriend.''

''Nice to meet you,'' Sarah said, and Niki tried to

smile, but Sarah could see how incredibly exhausted she was.

"Why don't you go get some coffee and something to eat," Chad suggested.

"I…"

"I'll stay until you get back," Sarah offered.

Niki rubbed her eyes and stood up. "Okay. I won't be long." She kissed Chad and quietly left.

"Gosh, Daniel said you were fine, but it's good to see with my own eyes," said Chad.

"It's good to see you, too. The nurse said you were doing great."

Chad glanced away. "I should never have let Drew in the house. I just never dreamed he had anything to do with all of this. I feel so responsible—as if I've let Daniel down."

"Don't blame yourself. I told you to let him in, remember? And if you hadn't, they'd have found a way to break in. I'm sure Daniel doesn't blame you for anything, either."

"I suppose."

Sarah thought she should change the subject. "I like Niki."

Chad raised his eyes. "She's been here since they brought me in. My friends and parents have been in and out, but Niki hasn't left and I can't get her to go home." He looked at Sarah. "She really loves me and we talked for a long time. I guess I had to get shot to do that, and you were right, she was insecure about my feelings. I finally have this love thing figured out."

"Have you?"

"Love is when you want to be with that person more than anyone and you're there for that person no matter what. Even if I was paralyzed, Niki would still be here. I know that beyond a doubt.''

''You have that besotted look in your eyes,'' she teased.

He grinned. ''Yeah.''

They were silent for a moment.

''Daniel was here earlier and he looked like his heart had been ripped out.''

Sarah's chest tightened, but before she could say anything, Niki came back and Sarah said her good-byes.

In the hall she paused to gather herself. *Daniel, where are you? Please talk to me.*

She hurried to Brooke's room before she got bogged down in crippling thoughts. Brooke and her parents were getting ready to leave.

''Oh, Ms. Welch,'' Brooke ran to her. ''You're okay.''

''Yes.''

''Detective Devers said the rapist was killed and it was safe to go home.''

''Yes. It's over.'' Sarah wasn't sure how much Russ had told her, but from what she knew of Russ, probably not much.

Brooke heaved a long sigh. ''I'm glad. I'm ready to go home.''

''That's a good sign.''

''I've talked with Dr. Mason and I really like her. Not as much as you, though,'' Brooke added quickly.

''It's okay, Brooke, as long as you're talking to someone.''

''Dr. Mason said Brooke could go back to classes whenever she wanted.'' Brooke's mother spoke up. ''What do you think?''

"That's up to Brooke," Sarah replied. "The sooner you get back into life, the sooner you can put all this behind you."

"But it never really goes away, does it?" Brooke asked. She sounded so sad.

"Honey, let's go." Brooke's father tried to stop Sarah from answering and Sarah understood why.

"Did Dr. Mason set up some appointments for you?" she asked instead.

"Yes."

"Then we'll talk about your question in those sessions. Just remember you did nothing wrong and you have nothing to be ashamed of." *Like I have been for so many years.* That had been the root of all her insecurities. But not anymore—thanks to Daniel and her many talks with Brooke. She'd stripped because she'd made a conscious choice to stay alive. That was nothing to be ashamed of—if anyone didn't understand that, then they didn't deserve to know her.

"Dr. Mason said there's a rape victim's group that I could join."

"Yes. That would be very helpful."

Brooke looked down. "I don't know if I can talk about it in front of other people."

"If you don't feel like it, you don't have to. You can just listen. Sometimes it helps to hear what other people have been through."

Brooke gave her a shaky smile. "I'm glad I got to meet you. You helped me more than I can tell you."

"Thank you," Sarah said. "I'm glad I met you, too."

"I'll see you in the office," Brooke said as they left.

Brooke was going to be fine, Sarah thought as she

made her way down the corridor. She kept looking for Daniel, hoping he'd be here. She asked at the desk and they said he'd stopped by earlier.

Russ had said she had to give a statement so she decided to do it now. Maybe Daniel was at the station and she could talk to him.

When she got there and asked the officer at the desk, he said Daniel wasn't in. She then asked for Russ and was shown into the same room she'd been in earlier. She took a seat and waited. She glanced around—all the files were gone, there were only a couple of desks and chairs. A few hours ago she'd sat in this same chair waiting for a killer to be caught, but it was tolerable because Daniel had been with her. Now everything had changed. The killer was dead, Drew was dead and Daniel was suffering. That she couldn't reach him was intolerable.

Russ came charging in. "Sarah," he said in surprise. "What are you doing here?" He still wore the same rumpled clothes of the night before. His beard was now almost full and the toothpick was back in his mouth.

"You said I needed to give a statement," she reminded him.

"Don't you want to give that to Daniel?"

"Yes, but he's not here." She frowned. "Russ, have you been here all night and all day?"

"Yep. We finally got everything out of Arnie and Tom and the A.D.A. feels she has enough to get an indictment and conviction so I'm fixing to go home and crash for a few hours. Hell, I might crash for two days."

"Has Daniel been in?"

"For a little while, then his father called and he had to leave."

"I see," she replied, then bit her lip. "I might as well give you my statement. Daniel needs to be with his family."

Russ hesitated for a second. "Okay. I'll get a tape recorder."

For the next thirty minutes she told Russ everything that happened after she'd left the station. She didn't leave out a thing, not even the part where she started to strip to keep Claude occupied, hoping to catch him off guard.

Russ clicked off the machine. "I'll get it typed up and you can sign it tomorrow."

She stood. "Okay. I'll see you tomorrow."

"Sarah." She glanced back at him. "I apologize for ever calling you Colder Than Ice. It took a lot of courage to do what you did last night."

More courage than she'd thought she had. "Don't shatter all my illusions, Russ. Let me go on thinking you're a macho, insensitive, tough guy."

He grinned. "I can do that because most of the time it's true."

"Good night, Russ."

He followed her to the door. "I'll give the A.D.A. a copy of your statement and if she needs you to testify, I'll let you know."

"She won't be testifying."

Sarah swung around to face Daniel and her heart sank to the pit of her stomach. Like Russ, he still had on the same clothes of the night before and they were more wrinkled than Russ's. His hair was tousled and he had a growth of beard, but the pain in his eyes was vivid and strong and it took everything in her not to reach for him.

"That's not your call," Russ said.

"She's not testifying," Daniel repeated.

Russ held up both hands. "Okay. I get the message and now I'm going home before I have to punch you in the mouth." He walked off down the hall.

"You won't have to testify," Daniel said. "I'll see to that."

"I'm fine," she told him. "I can handle it."

"No." He shook his head. "You're not putting your life on the line again."

She took a deep breath, not knowing if Daniel was thinking straight or if he was thinking at all. "Daniel, that's not like you. You believe in justice."

"Justice? There is no justice."

She touched his arm and he jerked away. "Don't touch me."

She fought for a measure of control. "Talk to me," she pleaded.

"Talking won't help. Talking won't solve anything."

"Daniel, please…"

"I'm tired, Sarah, and I've completely used up every resource I have to continue this fight against evil. Evil always wins."

"No, Daniel. Love always wins."

His eyes caught hers and they were glazed over with an emotion she couldn't describe. "You're wrong. I loved you with everything in me and look how I've hurt you. I can't…"

He turned and quickly strolled away.

"Daniel," she called and ran after him, but he disappeared too quickly. She stopped, her heart pounding in her chest.

No, Daniel, no. Love will win. I promise.

CHAPTER SEVENTEEN

DANIEL WENT STRAIGHT to his desk, picked up his resignation letter, walked into Bill's office and laid it in front of him. Bill glanced at the letter then at Daniel's face.

"We've been through this, Daniel."

"This time it's final."

"The case is not finished. There's a lot of paperwork to do and loose ends to tie up."

"Russ is capable of handling all that. It's his case."

"He's also involved in the shooting and will be busy answering a lot of questions until it's ruled a clean shoot."

"Joel will take up the slack."

Bill watched him for a moment. "I'm sorry about your brother."

"Thanks," Daniel muttered.

"Take some time and…"

"No," Daniel stopped him. "I'm through as a cop. I'm completely burned out and I'm not any good to anyone like this."

"There's so many things I could say to you right now, but I have a feeling you don't want to hear them."

"No, sir, I don't."

Bill leaned forward and rested his arms on the desk. "How's Ms. Welch?"

Daniel's stomach tightened. "She's holding up." He caught Bill's eyes. "And just so we're clear, she will not be testifying."

"That's up to the D.A."

Daniel's eyes darkened. "You're not listening to me. She's not getting on a witness stand to put another bastard behind bars. What good does it do? The bastard can still go on with his illegal activities and make her life a nightmare in the process. She's done enough for this stinking system."

Bill got up and walked to Daniel, putting his arm around his shoulder. "The system stinks. I agree with you. Having a traitor on our force hasn't helped. Our department will undergo a thorough investigation by Internal Affairs, but you did a great job on this case. You insisted on taking Sarah Welch into your personal custody and even though it went against the rules, I agreed. If you can't see anything else, see that you saved Ms. Welch's life. Right now you need some rest." He pointed to a box on a chair. "I had Kevin and Will bring some of your things over—shaving kit and clothes for a few days. The condo has been sealed off by the crime lab until Internal Affairs finishes its investigation. It's probably not a good idea to go back in there just yet anyway." He patted his shoulder. "Get some rest and we'll talk again."

Daniel picked up the box and walked out, feeling numb.

He checked into a motel, removed his clothes and fell across the bed. The horror of what had happened still had control of him, but the lieutenant's words sneaked through. *If you can't see anything else, see that you saved Ms. Welch's life.* That Sarah was safe was his last thought as exhaustion claimed him.

SARAH SET THE SALADS on the table and put the ice cream in the freezer, trying not to think about Daniel. She'd try again tomorrow to talk to him. She wasn't giving up.

Gran came into the kitchen. "Oh, you're back."

"Yes, and I brought chef salads and double-fudge ice cream."

"Yummy," Gran replied, sitting at the table.

"Coffee or tea?" Sarah asked.

"Tea, please. It's in the refrigerator. I already made it."

"Oh." Sarah was a little surprised because Gran was used to being waited on. It had been a big problem between her and Serena. These days, though, Gran helped out a lot. They were all going through changes.

"Thanks, Gran." She filled the glasses and brought them to the table.

"Serena called and said they made it home fine."

"Good. I'll call her later."

Sarah handed Gran silverware and a napkin.

"When I was at the ranch, Jassy and I had ice cream every night. Serena would eat about a tablespoon and Ethan would tease her, but Serena's always been very conscious about her diet, her weight and her looks." Aurora opened the napkin and placed it in her lap. "I'm afraid she got that from me. You're different, more adventurous and accepting. I guess you got that from Celia. Oh, my." Gran put a hand to her cheek. "I forgot. Celia called and said for you to call her right away."

"Oh, no," Sarah groaned. She'd been so worried about Daniel that she'd forgotten to call Celia to let her know she was home. She got up and reached for the phone. "I'd better call her now."

Celia answered on the first ring. "I'm sorry, Celia. Things have been rather hectic," Sarah immediately apologized.

"That's fine, honey, as long as you're okay."

"Yes. I'm fine and back at home with Gran."

"I'm sure Aurora's pleased."

Sarah closed her eyes at the undisguised sarcasm and she wasn't in a mood to get into this tug of emotional war.

"I just wanted to let you know I'm going to a bird show in Houston for a few days," Celia was saying. "Why don't you come along for the ride? It will get your mind off things."

"Thanks, Celia, but I can't leave right now."

"Are you sure you're okay?"

Why did everyone keep asking her that?

"Yes."

"I love you, honey. Take care of yourself."

Sarah took a soft breath, feeling blessed that she had so many people who loved her. "Love you, too. Have a good trip. I'll talk to you when you get back."

Sarah hung up, took her seat and picked up her fork. They ate for a while in silence.

"She's off with those birds again?"

Sarah slowly laid down her fork, knowing she and Gran had to talk. "We have to talk about Celia."

Gran glanced up. "Why? I'd rather not discuss her at all."

"That's just it," Sarah told her. "I'm tired of being caught in the middle of you and Celia and I'm tired of being made to feel guilty because I love both of you."

"Oh, darling, I didn't mean to make you feel that way."

"But you do, and Celia does, every time one of you says something nasty about the other."

Gran dabbed at her mouth with her napkin. "It's just that Celia and I have a past."

"Yes. Serena and I are the results of that past. You and Celia were best friends in high school and she slept with and married your boyfriend, John Welch. Then many years later, Jasmine, your daughter, our mother, stole John from Celia. It's like a badly written soap opera, but it's my life and I just can't take any more resentment. Life is too traumatic to keep this up."

Gran got up and hugged Sarah. "Darling, don't get upset."

"I just want some peace."

She kissed Sarah's forehead. "I'll try to curb my resentment toward Celia, but it's hard for an old person to change years of habits. For you, though, I'll try."

"That's all I ask."

"Where's that ice cream?" Gran asked, obviously trying to lighten things up.

They ate ice cream and talked about Jassy, one of their favorite subjects. But Sarah knew they had something else to talk about. It wouldn't be easy.

"How do you feel about this house?" Sarah broached the subject.

Gran swallowed a spoonful of ice cream. "I've lived here most of my life. It's big and familiar. It's home."

Sarah bit her lip. Gran's answer made this even harder.

"It's your home, too, isn't it?"

Sarah licked ice cream from her lips, trying to think

of the right words. "I've tried real hard to feel a connection to my mother, to Serena and to you in this
house, but I've always felt out of place, as if I didn't
belong here."

"Darling…"

"Please, Gran, let me finish," Sarah stopped her,
needing to say her part. "Through the trauma of the
past few days, I realize that belonging has nothing to
do with this house. It's in here." She placed a hand
over her heart. "It has to do with love. I now feel that
love and I feel part of this family."

"I'm so happy, darling."

"I just can't afford for us to stay here any longer.
The upkeep is astronomical."

"Serena mentioned this, but I haven't said anything
because I wanted you to stay here as long as you
wanted."

"I wanted us to stay here, too," Sarah admitted. "I
needed to feel close to my mother and my new family." She turned to face her grandmother. "How do
you feel about moving into something smaller? Maybe
a two-bedroom condo with no yardwork."

Gran looked thoughtful—not at all upset. "You
know Gladys moved into a retirement villa last month.
Opal is already there. It's a very nice place with separate apartments and access to a pool and all kinds of
recreational activities."

Sarah pulled back. "You mean, you want to move
into the villa with your friends?"

"Yes. I think I'd like that."

"I thought we'd live together." Try as she might,
she couldn't keep the hurt out of her voice.

Aurora reached for Sarah's hand. "Darling, you'll

be making your own life with Daniel and I'll be happier out of your way and with my friends."

"You won't be in the way," Sarah disputed, then quickly asked, "How do you know about Daniel?" She hadn't mentioned a word about her personal relationship with Daniel.

"I'm not completely deaf. I hear what's going on and even at my age it's not hard to figure out how he feels about you."

"Daniel is suffering and I'm not sure about the future."

Aurora squeezed her hand. "I am. Your future is with Daniel. He may not realize it just yet, but he will. Now I'm going to call Gladys and get the details on that villa."

Words died on her lips as Gran hurried away, excited as a child with a new toy. Sarah never dreamed the discussion would go like this—so easy. She put the ice cream back in the freezer and wondered where Daniel was. Maybe with his parents. Maybe at the station. Most likely somewhere alone letting the pain control him. *Daniel, please, let me help you.*

DANIEL AWOKE TO A pounding headache as all the pain came flooding back, drowning him in a sea of misery. He gave in to it for a few minutes then got up, showered and dressed. He was at his parents' within thirty minutes. His mother and father were in the sunroom having breakfast. Muriel was better and was planning Drew's memorial. His father's eyes were bloodshot and he was gulping down coffee.

"I'm glad you're here, Daniel," Muriel said. "Reverend McFee will be here shortly. Is there anything you'd like said at the service?"

''No. I want to get this over with as quickly and easily as possible.''

''My sentiments exactly,'' Dan said.

''How could this happen to my baby?'' Muriel cried, tears streaming down her face. Esther, the maid, handed her a fresh handkerchief and she dabbed at her eyes.

''Would you like anything, sir?'' Esther asked Daniel.

''Coffee, please,'' he replied.

''Muriel, don't cry anymore,'' Daniel's father barked.

''I'm not as strong as you.''

''You're the one that always wanted to put him in a home somewhere,'' he told her. ''I wanted him with us.''

''Blame me, Dan, if it makes you feel better. Blame me for everything that's happened with Drew, but I didn't know how to care for him in his condition. He needed professional help.''

''You didn't care for either of our sons when they were small. You left their care to nannies to follow me around the country afraid I might sleep with another woman and, believe me, it's crossed my mind more than once.''

Muriel sobbed into the handkerchief.

Daniel's nerves were close to the breaking point. He didn't know how to deal with two people he felt he barely knew. He'd always seen his parents through the eyes of a child and now he had to see them as an adult, with all their faults. He'd always wanted different parents, parents like he saw on TV, with a mother that cooked and took her children to school and a father who played baseball in the backyard and helped his sons build go-carts or hot rods. His home life was nothing like that. It was reminiscent of the scene he was witnessing now, with his parents more involved with each other's faults than in their children or creating a loving atmosphere. Today he didn't want to listen to it.

Esther handed him a cup of coffee and he took a couple of sips. "There's enough blame to go around so let's try to get through this the best that we can." He placed the cup on the table. "I'll be back later."

Muriel sat forward. "Where are you going? I need you here."

I needed you for so many years that I've forgotten the feeling, Daniel thought, but he didn't say the words. His mother was hurt enough and he couldn't inflict any more pain.

"I've got guys in the hospital I have to check on."

"Why you have to do this cop thing I don't know. It's only brought pain and misery. Can't you see that?"

"Yes, Mother, I see it very clearly."

"Why don't you alienate the only son we have left?" Dan spat. "I need a drink." His father headed for the bar in the den and Daniel left.

He went to the hospital then the police station. He wanted to get the things off his desk. After the service, he wouldn't be going back. His career as a cop was over—he'd accepted that and Bill would have to, as well.

Everyone stopped what they were doing when he walked into the room, then Will and Kevin came forward to shake his hand, to offer their condolences. Jack and Lee came next and several other officers.

Daniel didn't know what to say so he mumbled a quick "Thank you" and hurried to his desk.

He sat because his legs were shaky. He'd come here for a reason. Now he couldn't remember it.

Russ walked up and plopped some papers in front of him.

"What's that?"

"Sarah's statement. Thought you might like to read it."

He picked up the paper and started to read. His whole body began to tremble as he read her words and through the cobwebs of pain his fear for her became a palpable thing he could feel again. *Oh, God, no, no, no.* He rose to his feet and tore toward the door.

"Daniel..." Russ called, but Daniel kept walking. He had to see her.

SARAH CAME IN FROM WORK feeling exhausted. She'd spent the morning with Karen, playing catch-up with clients that she hadn't seen and spending time with those that needed her.

Gran wasn't home. She'd gone to visit Gladys at the villa then she had a bridge game. Sarah would give her a few days to see if moving close to her friends was what she really wanted before putting the house on the market.

She got bottled water out of the refrigerator and thought about calling Daniel. She had all his numbers, but she wanted to give him the time he needed. Time to...she reached for the phone as the doorbell rang.

Something about the doorbell ringing when she was alone unnerved her, but she went to answer it. First she looked through the peephole and her heart rate accelerated. She opened the door quickly.

"Can we talk?" Daniel asked.

"Yes," she answered without hesitation, noting that he'd shaved and cleaned up. But what she noticed most was that his eyes weren't so glazed over with pain.

She followed him into the living room. "Did you have the doctor check you over?"

"Yes. The lieutenant insisted. My neck is bruised, but I'm fine."

"Good."

He turned to face her. "I'm not sure where to start." He looked more nervous than she'd ever seen him.

She sat on the sofa. "Start anywhere you want to."

"I just read your statement," he blurted out. "When I broke the door in and saw Claude with his arm around your neck, I think I stopped feeling at that moment. My goal was to get you out of there alive, but I was aware that you had only a bra and jeans on. That wasn't my main concern, though, then Drew died and I felt as if I was detached from everything and I couldn't quite make the connection to bring me back. I've been so angry, disillusioned and hurt." He paused. "When I read what happened before I got there, I could feel myself coming back from that awful place and the fear I had for you was renewed. I'm sorry you had to see Claude shoot Chad, Ron and Drew, then…then he made you strip. I'm so sorry you had to go through all that again."

"You gave me the strength to survive."

"What?"

"If Claude killed me, you wouldn't know what happened to Drew. I had to stay alive any way I could."

"My God." He closed his eyes briefly.

"When he shot Drew, I thought I'd fall apart. I had this déjà vu feeling and I fought it."

"I don't know how."

"That night we were together was all I could think about. Claude kept talking about how he used to watch me strip at Teasers and how there was no one to stop him from taking what he wanted. I knew I had to stay alive until you came and the only way to do that was to stall. He wanted to touch me…"

"Oh, God," Daniel groaned.

"It's all right, Daniel," she said in a strong voice. "I'm all right. I said he couldn't touch me until I took all my clothes off and he was so hyped up he agreed. I didn't intend to remove all my clothes. I just wanted to catch him off guard so I could get away, but then we heard the sirens and he knew he'd been caught."

Daniel eased down beside her. "I'm sorry I got you involved in this."

She raised an eyebrow. "How did you get me involved in this?"

"By pressuring you to testify against Boyd. By telling you it was the right thing to do."

She turned sideways to face him. "It *was* the right thing to do."

"How can you say that? Look at the terror you've been put through."

She scooted closer. "Daniel, listen to me."

He looked down at his hands.

"Look at me, please." He turned tortured eyes to her. "You are not to blame for what happened. If anyone is to blame it's Drew and me."

He frowned. "You?"

"Yes. I'm the one who convinced Greg to let me go with him to learn about the strippers. And Drew's liaison with Boyd has culminated into the events of the past week. You had nothing to do with any of that. You're just the nice cop that has always been there for both of us.''

''I'm not so nice.''

She scooted even closer, until her knees were touching him. He didn't move away. ''Yes, you are.''

''I don't feel nice. I feel as if I've taken advantage of you.''

She tilted her head to one side, knowing exactly what he was talking about. ''Really? I have only happy memories and I think we could use those right now.''

Unable to stop herself, she slipped her arms around his waist and rested her body against him. He took a deep breath then wrapped his arms around her tightly, burying his face in her hair. ''Help me, Sarah. I can't deal with all this pain.''

Her throat constricted painfully. ''Talk to me. Tell me what you're feeling.''

For the next two hours Daniel poured out his heart. He told her about Drew, their childhood, their parents and about the discontentment in his work. Everything came out—even his feelings about her. Once he started, the words came fast and furious and Sarah listened with her heart.

''A few days ago we had each other and the future was dazzling, but now all I see is an empty darkness ahead.''

''That will change,'' she promised.

''I…''

Gran came in and Daniel stopped.

''Oh, Daniel,'' Gran said in surprise. ''I didn't realize you were here.''

Daniel stood. "Hello, Mrs. Farrell."

"Don't mind me," Aurora said. "I'm just going upstairs."

"That's okay," Daniel replied. "I should be going."

"You talk to Sarah. It's what you both need." She disappeared up the stairs.

Daniel ran both hands through his hair. "I don't have anything else to say. I'm empty."

Sarah got to her feet. "It's normal to feel that way and you don't have to promise me anything or feel guilty because you can't. Just keep talking to me is all I ask. Take each day at a time. Grieve for Drew, be there for your parents. That's all that's expected of you."

"My parents." He sighed in frustration. "That's a nightmare. Every time I'm in the room with them I want to scream."

"But you won't." She gave him a little smile.

"You're amazing."

"Thank you."

He touched her lips with his fingers. "Your kisses are happy memories."

"Yes," she whispered.

"I wish I could say we'd have them again, but I..."

She placed her finger over his lips. "Remember? You don't have to promise me anything."

He swallowed. "I'll be rather busy the next few days dealing with my parents. After the memorial, I'm leaving town for a while. I have to put Dallas behind me, to find my perspective again."

Ask me to go with you.

"Take all the time you need," she said with every

ounce of courage she possessed. "I'll be waiting for you."

He looked deep into her eyes. "Don't wait for me."

"I'll wait forever."

"Sarah…"

"For so long I've denied my feelings for you, but I'm very clear about what I want. Now you have to decide what you want. Do you want to spend the rest of your life wallowing in guilt and pain or do you want a life…with me. When you make up your mind, I'll be here."

He slowly made his way to the door and Sarah resisted the urge to run after him. He had to find peace within himself before they could have a future. She'd wait forever if she had to, just as she'd said.

Forever.

THE DAYS THAT FOLLOWED weren't easy but Daniel wasn't pushing Sarah away and that was the most important thing. He called to tell her when and where the funeral was and she'd told him that she would be there. He'd said he'd like that.

Serena and Ethan flew in for the service and they all went—even Gran. Muriel and Gran knew each other, having supported several of the same charities over the years.

The Garretts had a crypt and the service was in a small chapel that was attached to the building. The place was full—most of the police department was there. Sarah was unprepared for the sight of Muriel and Dan. Muriel was impeccably dressed and accepting condolence graciously, but her eyes were filled with pain, as were Dan's. They both looked as if they'd aged ten years.

Sarah's eyes were focused mainly on Daniel. He wore a dark suit and a look of torment. She wanted so badly to make all this better for him, but she couldn't. Daniel had to find his own kind of peace.

It was a closed casket and the service was short. They waited until everyone had spoken to the Garretts then they made their way to the front. Muriel's tear-filled eyes grew big when she saw Sarah and Serena together. They both wore dark suits and their red hair was up.

"Oh, my, Aurora," Muriel said. "What beautiful granddaughters you have."

"I think so," Gran answered, hugging Muriel and offering some consoling words.

Muriel dabbed at her tears. "I'm afraid I don't know which one is Sarah."

"I am," Sarah said, also hugging Muriel, then Serena and Ethan followed.

When Sarah reached Daniel, he took her elbow and led her to a small alcove.

"How are you?" she asked, her heart in her eyes, wanting to hold him so bad her arms ached.

"Trying to be strong for my parents," he said, fighting back tears.

She stroked his arm. "It's okay to hurt and it's okay to cry."

"Men don't cry, Sarah."

Then what is that I see in your eyes? But he was trying to be the strong one in his family when he didn't have any strength left.

He took a long breath. "I wanted to let you know that my parents are leaving in the morning for France and I'm going with them. I hadn't planned to, but I feel I need to be with them."

Ask me to go. Just ask.

But again he didn't.

"Please understand that I have to go. I can't stay here."

"I understand, Daniel," she said. "Just try to find a way to forgive yourself."

He frowned. "What?"

"That's your problem. You can't forgive yourself for what happened to Drew."

"Yeah." He blinked. "I hear what you're saying yet I feel as if I'm floating, detached from everything. I'm not anchored and I can't get beyond that feeling."

She reached for his hands and held them in front of her. "That's normal. It takes time."

"Everyone keeps saying that."

"Because it's true." She kissed his knuckles. "When you're thinking of Drew in the days ahead, think of his responses to everything you did for him and I think you'll find that Drew was never very honest with you."

He said nothing.

"You once told me that your major fault was that you wanted to help everyone. Sometimes that's not possible."

They stared at each other for endless seconds then Daniel softly kissed her cheek and walked away.

She held her hand to the spot he'd touched with his lips. She didn't know if they'd ever have happy memories again but she prayed that wherever Daniel went that he'd find the peace he was looking for. Most of all, she prayed he'd find his way back to her.

CHAPTER EIGHTEEN

THE DAYS STRETCHED painfully for Daniel. He tried to fit in with his parents' friends in Paris and found he couldn't. He didn't want to socialize—he wanted to be alone. Yvette didn't understand. She was in her late twenties and she liked to party. Their parents had gone out for the evening and Daniel sat on the terrace nursing a glass of wine.

Yvette pulled up a chair close to his. "Daniel." He liked her accent. Sometimes it was soothing. "I know a really nice nightclub. We can make a night of it." She wiggled in her chair. "I feel like dancing."

"Sorry, Yvette. I'm not really in the mood."

Her eyes grew dark. "What is it? Am I not attractive enough?"

"You're very attractive," he told her.

"Then why do you keep pushing me away?"

He glanced at her blond hair and blue eyes and all he could see was Sarah.

"Why, Daniel?" she persisted.

"Your hair's not red," he said.

She frowned. "Is that American slang for something?"

"No. It's the truth."

She scooted closer. "So you like redheads?"

He took a sip of wine. "One particular redhead."

"Your mother didn't say you had a girlfriend." She pouted.

"My mother doesn't know a whole lot about me."

She stood and flounced to the door. "I'm going to the club. You can drink your wine and think about your redhead."

The door slammed loudly and he took another sip. He wouldn't think about Sarah. He was still floating, lost in a maelstrom of pain, yet he could see her beautiful face and that saved him.

The next day Daniel left his parents in Paris and flew to Spain. He had a friend, Diego Valdez, who lived in Madrid. They'd been in boarding school together and had stayed in touch. Diego was a businessman with a wife and three kids. They were very hospitable, but Daniel felt in the way and soon left. He spent a week in London just walking. It seemed to always be raining, but he didn't mind the rain. How he wound up in Mexico City he wasn't sure.

He met a guy in a bar who was going to work on a big cattle ranch. He said the rancher was still hiring so Daniel went, too, and worked until he was exhausted. He rode a horse until his butt and legs were numb, but that didn't bother him. He welcomed the physical activity. In the evenings, the cowhands frequented a local cantina. Daniel went along because he wanted a beer. He spoke some Spanish so he was able to converse with the locals.

A young girl not more than eighteen sidled up to him at the bar. "I speak English," she said with pride.

"That's nice," he responded.

"You need woman?"

Daniel was taken aback for a second. She was so young. "No, thanks."

She edged closer. "I very good. I make you happy."

He looked into her dark eager eyes. "No, thanks," he said again.

"You no like women?" She was getting angry.

"It's not that."

"You no like me?"

"You're very beautiful, but you don't have red hair." *And you don't have Sarah's inner strength.*

Her eyes narrowed. "What that mean?"

He swallowed back the rest of his beer. "It means I'm not interested." He walked outside and stared up at the dark sky and the million twinkling stars—the same stars that were shining over Texas, his home. And over Sarah. Thoughts of her were constantly with him. Despite the horror she'd lived through, she'd still managed to put her life back together and to help other people. Her strength was an inspiration to him and he kept that thought close to him. Now he had to find that same kind of strength. He recognized he wasn't going to find any answers thousands of miles away from home—away from her. He had to go back to Texas to face his demons. He was now ready to do that.

So MUCH WAS HAPPENING in Sarah's life, but thoughts of Daniel were always with her. They'd put the house on the market and got a contract the first week, which made things rather hectic. The retirement villa didn't have an apartment for Gran until the end of the month and Sarah had to find a place to live. She signed the contract to sell with the stipulation that they'd be given the time they needed to get out of the house.

She, Serena and Gran had talked about the sale in

length and agreed it was the right thing to do. Serena came one weekend and they sorted through years of belongings. They soon realized it would take more than one weekend.

Through all of this Sarah waited for a call from Daniel. Days turned into weeks and still he didn't call. Wherever he was, she hoped he was safe and finding the inner strength to go on.

Please come home, Daniel.

SARAH WAS GETTING READY to leave her office to look at a town house when she heard loud voices outside her door. Suddenly the door opened and Muriel and Dan stood there. Wendy, the receptionist, was behind them looking flustered.

"She said we needed an appointment to see you," Muriel said with more than a touch of irritation. "Surely we don't need one just to talk to you."

"No. Please come in," Sarah invited, eager to hear news of Daniel. She walked to the door and spoke to Wendy. "Please reschedule my appointment with the Realtor for tomorrow."

"Yes, ma'am," Wendy replied, and closed the door.

"Have you heard from Daniel?" Muriel asked.

Sarah blinked. "No. I thought he was with you."

"He was for about two days," Dan said. "He got fed up with Muriel's matchmaking tactics and left. We haven't heard from him since."

Matchmaking. It took a moment for Sarah to digest this.

"I don't understand why he doesn't like Yvette," Muriel complained. "She's very beautiful."

"The answer is standing in front of you," Dan replied, his tone blunt. "But as always you ignore the obvious."

"Oh," Muriel said, staring at Sarah. "I didn't realize that you and Daniel were that serious."

Sarah bit her lip and walked to her desk refusing to give Muriel any information. *Who was Yvette?* "I haven't seen or heard from Daniel since the funeral."

Muriel sank into a chair and began to cry. "I feel as if I've lost both my sons."

"I've had enough of these tears." Dan plopped into the other chair and Sarah had a feeling she was in for a long visit.

"And I've had enough of your drinking," Muriel spat, reaching into her purse for a handkerchief.

"Then leave, Muriel. The door's always open."

"You want me to leave?" Muriel asked in a shocked voice.

"I want the same thing Daniel wants—a measure of peace. But no, after the funeral instead of grieving privately we had to go to France. You wouldn't listen to anything I was saying."

"Because you're always drunk."

Sarah realized this was about to get out of control and she didn't want to interfere, but she sensed these two people needed help, needed someone to listen.

"May I say something?" She took her seat.

"By all means." Dan waved a hand.

"You've been married for over forty years and you seem to be at each other's throats constantly. Yet you've stayed together. Why?"

"Marriage is forever, that's why," Muriel snapped.

"Yeah. Marriage is a golden ring prison."

"See how he talks to me?"

There was so much underlying resentment and hostility that Sarah could actually feel it. She told herself they weren't her clients, they hadn't asked for her help and she should ask them to leave. They were Daniel's parents, though, and she'd do anything she could so they could find some harmony in their marriage. For Daniel she would try.

"Yes, Muriel," Sarah agreed. "Dan is rude and seems to have no respect for you. Yet you continue to stay with him. Why?"

Muriel hung her head.

She turned to Dan. "You continue to put up with Muriel's constant nagging and insensitivity. Why?"

"It hasn't been easy," Dan muttered. "But like she said, marriage is forever."

Neither was going to admit a thing, so she had to push. "So you do have feelings for each other?"

"Ha," Dan grunted. "I'm not sure Muriel knows what feelings are. We've been married for forty-two years and not once has she told me she loves me."

Muriel gasped, but she didn't deny it and Sarah knew they were getting to the root of the problem.

"Have you ever told her?" Sarah asked Dan.

"On our wedding night." Dan shifted uncomfortably. "She never answered me and I never made that mistake again."

Sarah was shocked, to say the least, and knew some blanks had to be filled in. "How did you meet?"

Dan shifted in his seat again. "My father owned a construction company and Muriel's was an architect. They joined forces and started building shopping centers. The business became very profitable. I was an only child and so was Muriel and our parents decided we should get married."

"Because you were sleeping with every woman in

Dallas and your father was afraid you'd get some girl pregnant.'' Muriel twisted her handkerchief.

"So it was an arranged marriage?'' Sarah asked before Dan could retaliate.

"I wasn't a raving beauty like Dan's other girlfriends and he didn't want to marry me.''

"I never said that.''

"I felt it every time you looked at me.''

"Good God.'' Dan crossed his arms in anger.

Sarah had to bring this conversation back to the real problem. "Muriel, why haven't you ever told Dan you love him?'' She threw the question out there and it was dangerous, but the way they were living was more dangerous.

"I, uh, I'm just not able to do that.''

"Why?''

Sarah waited and she thought Muriel would refuse to answer, then her words came. "Every night as my mother put me to bed she'd tell me that she loved me and I'd say I loved her, too. When I was six, she died. My father was a cold man and I wanted him to hold me and tell me he loved me. He said there was no such thing as love and I was never to say the word again. As I got older, I realized he was just hurting because his wife had died, but still, the damage was done. I couldn't say those words—not even when my sons were born. I was afraid they'd be taken from me, too. I know that's crazy because I've lost Drew and I never told him I loved him. I—I...never...'' She sobbed loudly into her handkerchief.

Dan got up and knelt by her chair. "Muriel, look at me.''

She raised her tear-stained face.

"I married you because I loved you and when you wouldn't say those words, it almost killed me."

"You loved me?"

"Yes. If I didn't want to marry you, I could have changed my father's mind. I actually gave him the idea because I grew tired of trying to get your attention. The question is, how do you feel about me?"

"I'll leave you two alone." Sarah got up and left the room, but not before she heard Muriel's choked, "I—I…love you."

Sarah waited outside the door. Since everyone had gone home, the offices were quiet and empty. She glanced at her watch. Ten minutes. She wanted to give them all the time they needed. She never dreamed that with a little pushing so much emotion could erupt. Muriel had been suppressing destructive feelings for so long that it was way past time.

She could only imagine Daniel's childhood, but then, hers hadn't been idyllic, either. Everyone needed a deep, binding family love and she vowed that when Daniel came back she was going to say those words to him every day. First, he had to come home.

Finally they came out of the room. Muriel wasn't crying anymore; her eyes were sparkling with happiness as she stared up at her husband.

"Thank you, Sarah," Dan said. "Muriel and I are going home."

"I'm going to fix my husband dinner," Muriel said in a proud tone. "I used to make a good omelet."

"Could we come back tomorrow?" Dan asked.

Sarah was taken aback. "You mean, as clients?"

"Yes. Muriel and I need to keep talking."

"You both could benefit from marriage counseling. I'll see if Dr. Mason can fit you in."

"No, Sarah, please," Muriel pleaded. "I'd feel more comfortable talking to you."

Sarah hesitated. She was closely involved with their son and they needed therapy from someone who—

"I'm sorry for my crassness," Muriel's voice cut through her thoughts. "I think you're a beautiful, courageous young woman and I apologize for my rudeness to you."

"Please, Sarah." Dan added his pleading.

She found she couldn't say no. These were the parents of the man she loved. "If you come tomorrow at four, I'll be glad to help you."

"Thank you." Muriel smiled.

"We'll see you then," Dan called as they walked away arm-in-arm.

Sarah went home feeling better than she had in a very long time. If only Daniel was here. *Please come home, Daniel.*

ONE MORNING when she went in to work, Russ was waiting in her office.

"Russ," she said, startled.

"Have you heard from Daniel?" he asked.

"No, not a word." She laid her purse and briefcase on the desk.

"Boyd's execution is on Wednesday. I thought you might have heard from him."

"No."

"Since Daniel's not here, I'd take you if you wanted to go."

She bit her lip to still the agitation in her. "Thank you, Russ. I appreciate it, but I was notified and I declined. It's not something I really want to witness."

"I understand. Just thought I'd make the offer."

Russ fidgeted and she'd never seen him do that in all the years she'd known him. He was always very self-assured.

"Is there another reason you stopped by?"

He shoved his hands into his pockets and the tooth-pick slid to the other side of his mouth. "I, uh, been talking to my ex. She heard about the shooting on the news and that I was involved and she called. We've been talking without the anger and the tension."

"That's very good," Sarah said.

"You see, the big problem in our marriage was my job. She said I brought it home and she wanted us to go to counseling together. I flatly refused. A real man doesn't need counseling. He can solve his own prob-lems."

"Have you changed your mind?" She had a feeling that this was the reason Russ was here.

"I see death every day and sometimes it's hard to shake. That's not easy for me to admit, but I want to kiss my child good-night and see her shining face in the morning. And when I've witnessed a horrifying death, I want to hold my wife at night. I'm tired of being alone. I want my family back. If I have to go to counseling to accomplish that, then I'll do it." He glanced at her. "I think I can talk comfortably to you."

"Russ Devers, you've shattered all my illusions."

He grimaced. "Thought that would make your day."

"I'd be glad to help you and your wife," she told him, amazed he trusted her so much. "Have your wife make an appointment."

He let out a long breath. "Thank you." Then his

eyes narrowed. "You won't try to change me, will you?"

She hid a secret smile. "Outwardly, no. I'll leave that to your wife. Inwardly, maybe a little."

"Daniel said I needed an attitude adjustment."

This time she grinned. Daniel had influenced a lot of the people he'd worked with and hearing his name was uplifting. "The fact that you're willing to try means a lot."

"Thanks, Sarah." Russ moved to the door. "I'm going to call my ex and maybe soon she won't be my ex anymore."

At the door he stopped. "If you change your mind about Wednesday, just let me know."

She didn't. On Wednesday evening she turned her radio on at the appointed time. She just wanted to know it was over. She listened carefully. "At six-seventeen Central Standard Time, Rudy Boyd was pronounced dead."

The words did not generate a good feeling. They made her sick—too much hate, pain and suffering in the world. There was nothing good about that.

DANIEL LANDED IN Corpus Christi, Texas, rented a Jeep and headed for the coastline. This is where he and Drew went fishing, from the beaches of Padre Island to the bays of Rockport, Aransas Pass, Matagorda Bay and Port O'Connor. It was just the two of them being brothers, doing fun stuff. All the times they'd been here and he'd never seen any signs of Drew's drug use. Or maybe he hadn't wanted to.

He glanced at his watch and turned on the radio. He was well aware of what day it was and when he heard the news of Boyd's death, he felt no victory.

Death was never a victory. As Ethan had said, though, his reign of terror and violence was now over, but the aftermath of Boyd would be with everyone for a long time to come.

He was sure Sarah had heard the news and he should drive straight to Dallas to be with her. In his condition, though, he wasn't any good to her…or himself. Here, where he'd spent time with Drew, he hoped to find the forgiveness he needed. For it was clear to him now that Sarah was right. He needed forgiveness—from himself. He yearned for it, struggled for it, yet he was still bound by guilt and pain.

FINALLY THE MOVE OUT of the house was complete. Gran was at the retirement villa and Sarah was settled into a town house. Gran, Serena and Sarah said a poignant goodbye to the old house, but a family with four children had bought it and they knew that happy laughter would soon fill its walls. They were content with the arrangement.

Sarah saw the Garretts regularly and she was amazed at the change in both of them. They were like two teenagers finding love for the very first time and it was fun for Sarah just to watch them. They were always touching each other. Muriel had taken up cooking and Dan teased her about her efforts. She also started playing golf so she could go with Dan when he played. The earlier resentment was gone and they were trying to be a family.

They talked a lot about Daniel, and Sarah enjoyed those times. Talking about Drew wasn't so easy, but they decided they wanted to build a memorial for him. They were undecided, though, of exactly what and they wanted Daniel's input. They needed him to come home.

She did, too.

DANIEL SAT ON THE DOCK in Rockport, Texas, watching the boats come in from a day of fishing. Life went on, people around him seemed busy. This was the way it should be. Then why did he still feel like crap?

He swung to his feet and walked across the street to a restaurant. He headed for the bar and sat on a stool.

"Scotch, neat," he said when a waitress asked.

She set the drink in front of him and walked away. The bar was dimly lit and some music played in the background, but all Daniel was aware of was the big knot in his stomach.

"Mr. Garrett, is that you?"

Daniel raised his head to stare at a familiar face. Leo Thayer, the owner of the restaurant, smiled at him. He and Drew had come in here many times to eat and to get a beer and had become friends with Leo.

Daniel rubbed his beard. "Yeah. It's me."

"Didn't recognize you with all that hair. Looks like you been out fishing for a few days."

"No, not really."

Leo looked around. "Drew in the bathroom?"

Daniel's stomach clenched. "No."

"Is he outside?"

"No."

"Where is he?"

Daniel gripped his glass until his fingers were numb. "He's dead."

"Oh, no. I'm sorry."

Daniel took a long drink of scotch. "Thank you," he mumbled.

Leo watched him for a second. "Drew was so confused and…"

Daniel's eyes narrowed. "And what?"

"Nothing." Leo nervously began to wipe the bar.

"Go ahead, Leo, finish what you were going to say."

"It doesn't matter now."

Daniel reached over and grabbed the towel, stopping Leo from wiping. "And what?"

Leo swallowed. "I was just going to say that Drew was so confused most of the time and it was probably due to the drugs he was on."

"How do you know he was on drugs?"

"I shouldn't have said anything. I only saw y'all a couple of times a year and…"

"How do you know?" Daniel asked again, feeling the anger churning through him. Did everyone know Drew was on drugs but him?

"From the times he was here," Leo said in an undertone.

"You saw Drew do drugs?"

Leo shook his head. "No, but I saw him buy them."

Daniel swirled the liquid in his glass. "When?"

Leo mopped his brow. "When the two of you would leave, Drew would come back later asking for Willie Wong."

Daniel frowned. "Drew would come back?"

"Yeah, and I'd tell him that Willie wasn't allowed in here and he'd get all nervous and jittery. I tried to call you one time and he got real upset saying that you were sleeping and he was grown and could do whatever he wanted. I saw him several times out back talking to Willie. He'd give Willie money and Willie'd give him something in a baggie.''

"Why did you never mention any of this to me?"

"You're a cop and I wasn't about to tell tales out of school. I just didn't want Willie in my place."

"He was selling drugs, dammit. You should have contacted the police."

"I have," Leo shot back, "and Willie's out a month or so later doing the same thing and threatening me to keep my nose out of his business. I have a family and I wasn't about to jeopardize them. If the police can't do anything with Willie, what am I supposed to do?"

The swinging door of justice. He was well acquainted with that system—he'd spent a lot of his life fighting it. Sometimes he won and got people like Rudy Boyd, other times he felt was a waste of his time.

He swallowed back the rest of the scotch. "I don't have an answer for you, Leo. I work narcotics and yet I had a brother who I didn't even know was still on drugs. I kept my eyes closed. It was easier that way." He stood and laid some bills on the counter.

"Mr. Garrett."

Daniel looked up.

"Maybe I shouldn't say anything else, but when Drew came in with you he was laughing, happy and silly—childlike. Later he was sullen, angry and demanding. It was almost like he was two people."

"It was the drugs, they do that to a person. He just needed a fix and he'd do anything to get it." *Even deceive his brother.* Finally he could admit that.

He left the bar and strolled to the water, walking along its edge. Waves lapped at his feet and the mist sprayed his face, but he kept walking. The darkness shrouded him in his own thoughts and they beat at him as heavily as the waves—repetitive, tedious thoughts that he had to face.

He sank onto some rocks and stared across the wide, black expanse of water. It moved, rocked and soothed until he heard Sarah's words. *Think of Drew's responses.* He remembered when he'd visited Drew in college and caught him smoking pot. Daniel had flushed it down the toilet and told him if he ever caught him doing that again, he'd kick his butt. That was harsh of him, but he'd been angry at Drew for following along with the college crowd. Drew had promised he wouldn't do it again—that it was the first time and he was experimenting. *Drew was lying.* Daniel could see that now. Daniel had been eager to believe him and Drew had been eager to have him believe him. The deceit started then.

So many times he'd intervened with their parents, at Drew's pleadings, to not pressure him and to give him time to get his grades up. All the time Drew had been working him, playing him, using him. When Drew accidentally overdosed, Daniel had intervened again when Muriel wanted Drew to go to a clinic in Philadelphia for rehab. Drew wanted to stay in Dallas and Daniel had helped to make his parents see that Drew would be better off at home. *So he could get drugs. From Rudy Boyd.*

Daniel drew the salt air into his lungs feeling it burn like bad whiskey.

When Daniel had arrested Boyd, Drew kept saying that Daniel got the bad guy. He'd always wanted Daniel to get the bad guy. That's the way he wanted Daniel to think and it was exactly the way Daniel had thought. He was getting the bad guys for his little brother. But the brother was a master at deception.

All of Drew's responses had been false. *That's what Sarah wanted me to see.* There was nothing Daniel could have done to change that. *There was nothing I could have done.* He couldn't have saved Drew because Drew hadn't wanted to be saved.

You can't help everybody. He could hear her words now and he believed them. The spray from a crashing wave drenched him and he felt the coolness of the water as the wind whipped around him. He also felt a cleansing of the demons, the blame and the guilt. All that turmoil was gone. *There was nothing he could have done.*

He stood and for the first time in months he felt his feet touch solid ground. He was anchored; he could think clearly. Through that clarity he knew what he wanted.

He strolled down the beach heading for a future he now believed he deserved.

I'm coming home, Sarah.

SARAH STUFFED PAPERS in her briefcase, eager to leave the office early. She was having dinner with Muriel and Dan and she wanted time to go home and shower and change. Muriel was trying a new recipe and she wanted Sarah's opinion. When Muriel had called, Sarah could hear Dan in the background joking, "Bring hamburgers. We might need 'em."

Sarah knew that they wouldn't. Muriel was a very good cook and she enjoyed it. She ate at least one meal a week with them and with Gran and with Celia. The tension between them had eased somewhat. Sarah now insisted on having dinner together with the two ladies in her town house. She didn't know why she hadn't thought of it before. Being a guest in her home, they both behaved beautifully. They were actually talking civilly to each other, sharing memories from their girlhood, even sharing memories of John Welch. They would never be best friends again, but they were getting along for Sarah's sake. Sarah couldn't have loved them more. Her evenings were full and she was glad of that. She didn't want to be alone to think about Daniel.

Her intercom buzzed and she grimaced. Not a problem, please, she thought. She had to leave to make it on time. She pushed the button.

"Mr. Garrett wants to see you," Wendy said.

Sarah frowned. What was Dan doing here? She was expected at their house in a little over an hour. Something had to be wrong. Maybe they'd heard from Daniel.

"Send him in," she replied, her heart hammering.

In her agitation, she knocked a pen on the floor and bent to retrieve it. She heard the door open. "Is something wrong? Did you hear…"

The words died in her throat as she straightened and caught sight of the man standing in the doorway. His dark hair was past his shoulders and he had a full beard with gray highlights. He looked vaguely like Dan, but it wasn't Dan. It was Daniel!

"Are you still waiting?" he asked in a husky voice.

She flew around her desk and into his arms. He enveloped her in a tight bear hug. He kissed her hair, her forehead, her cheek, then her lips. Her arms crept around his neck as she kissed him with all the love she had for him. The kiss went on and on as each took what they needed to ease the pain of separation.

"Yes, yes, oh, Daniel," she finally breathed against his lips. "You're back. You're back. You're back." Her hands stroked his face, his hair, almost in reverence.

"Yes," he whispered, cupping her face. "I'm back—really back."

She stared into his eyes and saw that he was, all that pain had disappeared, leaving a lingering sadness.

"I couldn't help Drew because he didn't want my help. You told me that, but I couldn't accept it. Now I can."

"I'm so glad," she said, her heart about to burst with happiness.

"I don't have a place to stay or know what I'm going to do with my life, but I know I want to be with you."

"You'll stay with me." She kissed his cheek.

"What about your grandmother?"

"Oh, that's a long story." She took his hand. "I have my own place now and I'm taking you home to see if I can find you a razor."

He rubbed his beard. "Don't like the beard, huh?"

She shook her head, her eyes twinkling, and he kissed her again. For several seconds they were lost in each other. She took a much-needed breath. "I have to call your parents first."

He leaned back, his eyes wide. "My parents? Muriel and Dan Garrett?"

"Yes. That's a long story, too." She picked up the phone.

Daniel watched her as she talked to his mother and she could see he was puzzled. She would explain—much later. As she talked, her eyes never left his face. The worry inside her suddenly dissipated and she experienced a giddy, bubbly feeling. She couldn't believe how much she loved this special man who'd given her back a vital part of herself—her femininity. He wasn't getting far from her ever again.

"They're so excited you're home," Sarah said as she hung up. "They wanted us to come right over, but understood we wanted to be alone."

"My parents understood?" he asked in disbelief.

She grabbed her purse. "Yes. You're going to see a big change in them." She went back into his arms. "I promised we'd be there for breakfast." She kissed his lips leisurely, just enjoying the taste and feel of him. "Tonight it's just you and me."

His arms tightened around her. "I thought about you constantly while I was away. You're the only thing that kept me sane."

"I love you," she said with an ache in her voice. "And I'm so glad you found your way back to me."

He tucked a red tendril behind her ear. "I love you more than I ever thought possible and I'm never leaving you again. Every woman I saw couldn't measure up to you."

"Really?" She lifted an eyebrow and couldn't resist adding, "Not even Yvette?"

"Not even Yvette." He grinned.

She ran her finger along his lower lip. "I need happy memories."

"God, me, too," he murmured and kissed her deeply.

He rested his face against hers. "Let's go home."

Sarah closed the door and slipped her arm through Daniel's. She'd finally found her home, her place to belong. As she already knew, it had nothing to do with a material object. It was all about a feeling—love. Her love, her home was Daniel and would be for the rest of their lives.

EPILOGUE

One year later

THE ALARM CLOCK shrilled and Sarah reached to turn it off. Her husband groaned and tightened his arm around her. She nestled into him, feeling content, happy and so very loved. Never again would she have to face heartache and sorrow alone. Never again would the past have the power to control her. Never again would she feel unloved. She had happy memories to share with a man she loved more than anything.

"Is it that time again?" Daniel asked, kissing her shoulder, her arm.

"Yes. We'd better get up and..." Sarah caught her breath as his hand cupped her rounded stomach. "Daniel," she moaned as his tongue stroked her tender breasts.

"Hmm?" He smiled into her eyes.

"You keep doing that and I'll never get up."

"Sounds like a plan." His smile broadened.

"We have a big day ahead of us."

"Yes." He rested his face on her stomach. "I just want a few minutes with my wife and child."

She ran her fingers through his hair. "You're going to be a great father." They'd agreed to start a family right away. Still, it had happened sooner than they'd anticipated, but they were ecstatic.

"I never thought this would actually happen for me. It wasn't something I could envision." He placed kisses along her stomach and she closed her eyes, reveling in his touch. "Now I plan to be the best father ever. We're going to have big Christmases with a real tree and everything. I want this child to grow up in a loving family."

She caressed his neck. "I don't think there's any doubt about that. Gran and Celia are excited and your mother has taken up knitting. Every day it's something new she's planning for the baby."

He raised his head and stared into her eyes. "She's going to be a better grandmother than she was a mother."

Sarah nodded. "Yes. She's not afraid to love anymore."

"All because of you."

"We've all been through a great deal and we've learned and grown, and all I see in our lives is happiness."

His eyes darkened. "I never knew it was possible to be this happy."

"Me, neither," she admitted. "Until I loved you."

He kissed her deeply and rolled onto her as she wrapped her arms and legs around him. The importance of this day was forgotten in their passion for each other.

Later, as they rushed to get dressed, Sarah put on the pearl-and-diamond necklace Daniel had given her on their wedding day and sat for a moment thinking back. A year had made such a difference. Daniel and his parents had forged a new relationship. Together they had decided what to do in Drew's memory. It had been Daniel's idea to build Drew's House, a counsel-

ing center for teens to help keep them off drugs. Today
was the dedication with city officials and dignitaries.

Daniel had pulled it all together in a short amount
of time. His father had sold all of his business interests
and devoted his time and money to the project. Daniel
had found an old three-story house and started reno-
vations. They'd knocked out walls and made a large
recreational room, added bathrooms and installed a
basketball court. Sarah was unaware Daniel had
known so much about construction or that his father
had known a lot more. It'd been a family effort.

Sarah and Muriel had worked on funding, accredi-
tation and getting doctors and nurses to volunteer their
time when needed. Karen was glad to be one of those
doctors. Although there was some other funding, the
majority had been done with Garrett money. Daniel
was the director and she was one of the counselors.
She would now be working with her husband.

Daniel had resigned from the police department,
though he'd agreed to stay on as an advisor to the
narcotics squads. He gave talks in schools, he gave
seminars for parents, trying to educate the children and
their parents about drugs and its effects on a family.
Most of his time would now be spent helping other
kids and she would be right beside him.

There'd been other changes, too. Brooke was back
in college and doing remarkably well. She kept up
with counseling and had started dating, which was a
big step. Sarah was very proud of her.

Russ and his wife, Cathy, had remarried and Russ
helped out at Drew's House, as did Cathy, who was a
nurse. The four of them were now close friends.

Life was full—everything Sarah had ever dreamed
it could be. They'd purchased a home for them-

selves—a rambling house on an acre with plenty of room for a family. She was six months' pregnant and soon their first child would be born. She'd always thought Serena would be the happy one, but she'd been wrong. They'd both found incredibly good men and Sarah now knew what real love was all about.

Five hours later the family gathered at their house. After a meal, Gran, Celia, Muriel and Dan played bridge. Daniel and Ethan sat on the patio. Ethan held his three-month-old son, Ethan James, in his lap. Sarah and Serena strolled arm in arm toward a gazebo Daniel had built. Jassy was already in it jumping around.

Daniel watched Sarah and Serena. "From this angle, with their backs to us, can you tell which one is your wife?" he asked Ethan.

"Even if I didn't know what my wife was wearing, yes, she's the one on the left."

"Isn't that amazing? They're identical and I always know which one is Sarah, too."

"Let's keep it that way, okay?" Ethan grinned, bouncing Jamie on his knee.

"I can't wait to be a father."

"You don't have that much longer."

"Daddy, Daddy," Jassy called, waving from the gazebo.

Ethan waved back. "Get used to hearing that a lot."

"Since we know it's going to be a boy, Sarah wants to name him Patrick Drew. That was my brother's name."

"I think that's a very good idea and what you're doing with Drew's House is something that's good, too."

Daniel rubbed his hands together. "I couldn't help Drew, but I plan to help others."

"You will. I'm glad you're still involved with narcotics," Ethan said.

Daniel nodded. "I can't believe how much my life has changed. I was feeling tired and burned out. Now I'm energized and happy."

"The right woman will do that to you."

Daniel smiled, staring at Sarah. "I definitely have found the right woman." Whatever he had to face in the years ahead, he would do so with her by his side living life to the fullest and loving her completely. The future never looked so bright.

They both had finally found the home they'd longed for—with each other.

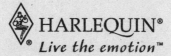